BLOOD IN THE TREES

BY

PAUL DAVIDS

ISBN-13: 978-1539420125
ISBN-10: 1539420124

Dedicated to the mum I love, the dad I miss,
and to Lisa my love to kiss.

CONTENTS

ACKNOWLEDGMENTS

Thank you to Lisa who put up with looking at a laptop where my head should have been for a while.

CHAPTER 1

Trees

It was a new start, dream job, new home, new town, new school for Ben.

It had been a long drive, it was dark and the rain had been hammering down for the last few hours. As he drove the occasional bout of lightning would sheet across the sky and light up the bleak view of the countryside in this weather. He was looking forward to getting in and climbing into bed. Mike had accepted the job as it was a dream opportunity, he had convinced Madison that the country living and new private school would be good for Ben. So with the promise from his new employers that they would organise his move and pay for Ben's private school fees and even employ a nanny to assist with Ben. It was a no-brainer that they would go. Mike was a hard man in business and wanted Ben to grow up in his footsteps: "Private School will be the making of the lad". They had only seen their new house in pictures and it was stunning but the pictures didn't do it justice! Mike saw it in the distance and his mouth opened in awe. It looked like a manor house that would hold a multitude of servants. At this point Mike decided to wake Madison up. "Mad, Mad, wake up Mad we are here." Madison stirred and Mike told her that he had just seen the house in the distance and it was amazing. The sign at the side of the road that lit up when his headlights flicked past told him that his new house was off this entrance. He turned into the drive. It was a 400 metre long gravel drive with grass verges on each side. Along the grass verge on each side were trees. They were planted in lines as if to stand to attention and give whoever entered a tree guard of honour, however, whoever had planned the planting it was doubtful they had this sight in mind, as they looked horrendous. The wind and rain was swinging them around as if they were all seizing in some group fit. Madison looked then glanced at Mike and just said, "Mmmm lovely."

Mike looked back and just gave a cheeky wink, "So the grounds need some work!" At that point there was a thunder clap, lightning lit up the sky and then a scream, and it was the loudest and most frightening scream the adults had ever heard. Mike slammed on his brakes, the vehicle was not going fast but due to the gravel, it still travelled a fare distance before stopping. The scream had not stopped, Ben had woken up in the back and was absolutely petrified. Both parents were trying to tell him that everything was okay, he had obviously just had a dream. Ben's eyes were as wide as they could get and his breathing was sharp and quick. It took a moment or two to calm him down before they could realise what was wrong. "You scared the hell out of me then Ben."

Mike started back up the drive towards the house. All the while along the drive Ben's eyes were fixed on the thing that had panicked him, the trees!

He had woken up the split second before the lightning had eliminated the sky. The first thing he saw was the sky light up and this gnarled monster trying to reach into the car and grab him. As the monster reached for him there was an enormous crack of thunder. The monster was actually one of the many awful trees lining the drive. He looked at each one as the car drove slowly towards his new home. The house was lovely and very grand but Ben would not have noticed if it was the *Disney* castle. As the car stopped and he got out he looked back up the drive and the site gave Ben a shiver. As he looked there was another blast of lightning. The drive was wide enough for two cars to pass each other by going on the grass so the actual gap between the trees was quite small, and during this weather they were all swaying and wriggling and looked as if they were grabbing each other's branches and fighting. Trying to rip each other apart with their long, gnarled but sharp looking "limbs". Ben didn't look at the house he just wanted to get in. He followed his mum into the main entrance'. Mike's employers had been true to their word, all their belongings were in the house ready. A woman seemed to float down the curved staircase and announced loudly, "Good evening Mr and Mrs Oscar, I am Bella the nanny Global Blue have employed on your behalf." As Bella glided down the steps Ben automatically took a step back. His mum had asked him why after but he didn't know! "If you would care to go into the lounge I will show young Ben to his room, I am sure he is tired and would like to sleep now." Bella pointed to the left with her left hand while smiling at Mike and Madison and in the same one fluid movement, swept Ben towards the stairs with her right. Ben was ushered upstairs, into his room and was alone within moments. It all seemed a bit of a shock but he soon took in his surroundings. It was huge, his room was bigger than he could ever have imagined. Large bed, great big solid wooden draws, cupboards and wardrobes. There was even a toilet connected to his room, his own toilet! "Wow," he said flushing it for no reason what-so-ever. He noticed the huge curtains, they were the type that looked like they weighed a ton, they were thick and embroidered with golds, browns, yellows and oranges. He thought they looked like autumn. Ben opened the curtain and peeked out, he shut them very quickly! The trees that lined the drive were not just confined to guard the drive but they were scattered around the rest of the grounds too and one was right outside his window. It took him a little while for his heart to slow to its normal rhythm. Once he was calm he decided to brush his teeth and get into bed. He brushed his teeth but instead of climbing into bed he had a thought, it's only a tree let's be sensible about this. Ben went back over to the window took a deep breath and stuck his head through the curtains. The trunk was thick but looked very twisted and sharp and it was moving erratically as if it was caught in somewhere hot and couldn't get out. All of a sudden one of the branches shot forward towards the window and in Ben's mind's eye it looked like it was making a grab for him. He jumped and fell backwards, scrabbling at the polished hard wooden floor to regain his feet. Once up again he ran and jumped straight onto his bed. Where he sat just staring at the curtains knowing it couldn't but all the same expecting the tree to come in and make another swipe at him. It was a long night but eventually he fell asleep. Not surprisingly his dreams that night were full of trees.

Ben woke up abruptly. "Come on lazy, up for breakfast and you are meant to sleep in the bed not on it!" The curtains were swished wide open by the nanny Bella. Ben took a sharp intake of breath as she opened them expecting the tree to rush in, but nothing. He sighed with relief and followed Bella down to the dining room. For the first time he took in the full majesty of his new home. It looked like something from one of those period dramas that his mum watches. Huge paintings depicting country scenes, ornate vases on little tables, large wood panelling, sweeping spiral staircase with chunky wooden banisters, pretty patterns on the ceiling, marble like floor, it was all amazing to look at. As Ben entered the dining room his parents were already sitting at the table. The table fitted the grandeur of the rest of the house and had numerous hot plates and bowls on it. "Come in Ben have a hearty breakfast and then we can explore the grounds, how did you sleep?" Ben wondered if he should tell his dad about the trees and thought well he might as well. Ben explained about the trees and how he didn't like them, he didn't go into every detail he just said he didn't like the look of them so didn't sleep very well. Mike laughed and said, "Well we are in the country now son, not everything is perfectly regular out of a factory." Madison was a little more sympathetic, "I know what you mean Ben, I don't like the look of them either but they are only trees." Ben had his fill of bacon, eggs, sausages and tomatoes and felt a lot better than he had the previous night.

CHAPTER 2

The Scene

A drizzle of water ran down the chest of the corps hanging in the tree. The rain had soaked the leaves so that every few seconds more water would fall on to the body. The body was that of a well-proportioned middle aged male. He was completely naked apart from the rope that was holding him above the ground. The floor was thick with the blood that had collected over the time the body had been hanging. The rain had stopped but the water from the tree was still dripping and it was now regularly dropping from the intestines protruding out from the victim's abdomen, it was tapping a regular beat on the patch of congealed blood on the floor. It had now made a dent in the dried blood which had started to produce a small puddle of pink water on the surface. The man's face that was looking at the body wore an immaculately trimmed beard. It was one of those beards that looked painted on as it was so perfectly formed. It was dark brown and at this precise moment sat on a face that was motionless, it was being stroked by the hand that belonged to the face. The face was that of Inspector Jeff Boston.

To those below him in rank he was known as Boss. To everyone else he was simply known as Bos. The distinction between the two names is difficult to grasp. It is also irrelevant, as it is just one of life's coincidences that Bos is naturally "in charge" of most situations.

Bos stood staring at the body, the only movement was his right shovel like hand stroking his beard. There were 5 people around him but no one moved, they were all waiting for Bos to finish with his appraisal of the situation. After a few minutes had passed one of the men in the background who was holding a medium sized silver coloured case, passed comment to a colleague. His words were quiet but obviously a little frustrated, "Are we going to get on or not?"

The male next to him was immediate with his response, "No not yet."

Another minute passed and his irritation had mounted, "But we are just standing here for nothing!"

Bos stopped stroking his chin at this time and turned to the newcomer to the crime scene investigation unit, "You can start now young man, I usually like to have a look at a scene alone before anything is done. It gives me a bit of a feel for the crime."

Steve was the new addition to the unit and was obviously a good CSI otherwise he wouldn't have got into the team, but picking up the body language of his colleagues was not something he would win awards for. If this was a talent he possessed, he would have noticed the effect his very next words had on the others around him, "But we could have got on while you were just looking." The reactions that Steve was blissfully unaware of were quite synchronised. Every other person around the crime scene shook their heads, even the corpse in the tree took part although that was merely the breeze playing with the head that was hanging limply from the horrendously stretched neck. But this did add to the seemingly coordinated effect.

Bos looked directly at him and lifted one eyebrow, "Yes but you record the scene as you see it, I am sure you will do a fantastic job, but you may not pass on to me everything that I want." As Steve was about to reply, Bos held up a finger to halt his comment. The finger slowly pointed to the tree, "What type of tree is that?"

Steve was becoming increasingly irritated now, not only had he been standing in the cold waiting for this bloke to stand and stare at a corpse but he has now been silenced by a finger. This had astonished him to start with as he didn't know why he just stopped what he was about to say, but now he was getting annoyed with himself, and the irritating self-confidence of the smart arse in front of him was getting to him. "I don't know, and what the bloody hell has that got to do with the poor bastard hanging in it!"

Bos smiled and answered softly, "The fact that he died *while* hanging in it, may have mattered to him and I presume will matter to any relatives or friends he may have had. Do you know that the type of tree is not an important fact? If you don't know for certain that it's not important it should be noted."

Steve was about to speak again but the colleague on his left grabbed his arm and said, “Come on Steve, let’s get to it,” and hastily ushered him forward towards the male hanging in the tree. The crime unit were used to dealing with gruesome situations so began immediately with the job in hand. They were all in their white paper suits and masks. Paper even covered their feet. They recorded everything they thought possible about the scene.

Bos walked away, leaving the unit to record the scene but this murder was troubling him. He had a bad feeling. He knew by the pattern of blood on the trunk of the tree that the male had been cut while hanging but the pattern worried him, however as of yet he didn’t quite know why? He had stood for a while trying to see why, perhaps he was just tired due to the call out and his recent insomnia. Bos clicked the button on his key fob and opened the door on his immaculately tidy white *Nissan Juke*. The niggle at his brain was puzzling, after 30 seconds he shook his head and started the engine. His drive home seemed to be timeless, he knew it had taken him a while but he couldn’t remember the journey, he still had the murder scene vividly in his head. Bos entered his house and poured himself a generous glass of neat vodka and sat staring through his patio doors that led out to his small but tidy rear garden.

Everything in Bos’s world was tidy, well organised and “in its place,” it was the way he had always been. He was brought up by his mother and father to know his place and the place of everything around him, and to keep it all in its place!

He sat in quiet contemplation for a few minutes

every so often lifting his huge arm to take a swig from his vodka. Until on one swig he caught sight of the picture of a beautiful looking long haired red head on the wall. The woman in the picture was provocatively but elegantly laid across a black leather sofa, her long hair falling over the edge of the arm and her head tilted looking at the camera but also laying on her left arm. Her legs were slightly apart and bent towards the back of the sofa, they were slim, long and pale and looked like they went on forever. The look the quite stunning woman was giving Bos from her elevated position in the living room was to say, "What's wrong squidge?" The lady in the picture was Helen, Bos and Helen had been married for two years and was the only person on the planet who would have dreamt of calling the huge man holding the vodka "squidge".

Bos had buried his beloved wife just four months ago after a hit and run had killed her. Bos knew she had been killed outright and he was told that she did not suffer but this was not a huge comfort as he looked longingly in the bright blue eyes of the woman he still loved. They had not caught the bastard who had killed her and were no closer now than the day she died.

Bos lifted his glass to the picture and muttered, "Sorry honey," and drank a huge gulp. He so wished she was here, he always thought better with her in his arms, and he knew she would have disapproved of the large glass of alcohol in his hand. He was so tired, he had been exhausted for the last week but didn't quite understand why.

"Okay, okay I'm going." He stood up emptied the remains of the vodka down his throat and put the glass in the dishwasher. He was determined to sleep in his bed tonight, he thought he was getting enough sleep in his chair by the patio but was always exhausted. He just didn't want to climb into the bed knowing that Helen would not be there too.

CHAPTER 3

I.D.

Bos woke up for the first time in a while in his bed. It was a huge ornate four poster that he and Helen had bought together. He had always loved the bed but now as so many other things it just reminded him of the life he had with Helen and it looked to him far too vast. What was once a comfy white paradise now reminded him of an Alaskan snow scene, cold, empty and lonely. He dragged himself out and wondered why he was still exhausted. His whole body ached, he looked in his shaving mirror and wondered who the hell was looking back at him. "Look what grief can do Helen, I look and feel about 80." He shaved, leaving his slender beard to cover his chisel sharp chin and went downstairs for breakfast. While eating his toast his mind wandered back to the crime scene he had looked across yesterday. There was still something at the back of his mind troubling him about it but he couldn't quite see why yet.

Half an hour later and he was pulling into the

station. He sat at his desk and looked through the pictures of the scene. In his many years in the force he had seen many gruesome sights, some quite considerably worse than this one. He stared at the picture that showed the man hanging in the tree. He could see the man had obviously not hung himself as there was no steps or a ladder nearby to get him to that height by himself. He was a big man and would take some lifting to get up there unconscious but his victim was alive while hung, unless he was sedated and woken while in the noose. Bos stroked his immaculate thin beard while thinking. The blood pattern told him that he was cut while alive and was moving around when it happened. Bos stood sharply and said to nobody in particular, "I need another look."

Bos arrived at the scene that was still taped off and guarded but was void of a body in the tree. He said good morning to the officer on scene guard and filled in the scene log with his details. He noticed that the body had been removed just an hour or so ago.

"Thanks, I hopefully won't be too long just want another look."

The Pc replied, "No problem Sir, I'll be here for a while."

Bos ducked under the scene tape, "Just call me Bos, most do," and walked towards the tree. The blood spatter was still on the trunk of the tree. He imagined the body as he had seen it the night before. The man's neck was stretched but not in a way that suggested he had been dropped from a height. He looked at the branch that the male was hung on, he couldn't quite see it. He looked around for something to stand on, nothing. Bos walked over to the PC,

"How do you feel about giving me a hand?"

The Pc was fairly new and wondered how on earth he could help Bos. "If I can Sir, yes."

"It's Bos, and I need to get a look of the branch our friend was hung from."

The young Pc was a little disappointed that the help he was asked for was just to be a ladder, but rallied well, "Of course S-s… Bos." The next couple of minutes were passed by a young wiry Pc trying to give a leg up on a tree to a rather large Inspector. Eventually the angles were right that got him a decent grip and he climbed up to where he knew the rope had been. Considering his size, he climbed the tree extremely adeptly. It was like watching an Orangutan climb, but upright, very large and in a tailored suit. He inspected where the rope had been, the bark was blackened and smooth. "Thank you, I am coming down now."

The young Pc was still dripping with sweat from the effort and exertion of balancing Bos in his hands like some warped Khyber toss. "Did you get what you wanted Bos?"

Bos clapped his hands together as if a builder removing brick dust. "Yes indeed I did, the trunk is blackened where the rope was." Bos smiled waiting…

"Why is that important?"

"Have you ever climbed a rope and lost your grip?" When the Pc nodded, Bos continued, "Burnt didn't it?!" Bos then went on to tell his human ladder that he has just found out that the victim had been pulled up to the top of the branch straight from the ground or at least from near the ground. "To get that burn the rope would have had to have been pulled along for a while to get that much friction damage."

It was a quick trip back to the office as the scene was still going through his mind. He had a pretty good idea of how the crime progressed, why is another matter! He ran through the events in his mind. Male stripped, tied, rope noose around neck pulled up to the height of about 30-60cm off the floor. Then when awake, his stomach was sliced open and then hauled up to the top of the tree. This was all deduced by the evidence at the scene. He opened his email and saw a new one titled "I.D. of tree case", he immediately opened it to read this new information. I.D BROARD Matthew D.O.B 25-01-1970 age 45. Bos stopped reading and looked again at the picture of the man in the tree. A shiver went down his spine, he knew him! Matthew Broard was one of his early cases. Years ago he had walked from court on an evidence technicality. He had crashed his car into a house and injured a mother and daughter. He was found to have been drunk driving but never got convicted of it. Bos remembered the frustrations he had all those years ago. "Mm no lawyer to get you out of that one then?!" He put the photo down and leant back on his chair stretching and resting his shovel hands behind his head. So why you, was it random or reason? These where the thoughts going through his mind. He needed to take a look at Matthew's home, see if that would be able to shed light on any reason someone may want to string him up.

CHAPTER 4

House

25 Hamlet Drive, an unassuming house in an otherwise ordinary road however Bos on this occasion knew different. It was the residence, or ex residence, of Matthew Broard who had recently been hung naked and his stomach opened. He was hoping that his home may shed some light on why. Walking up the crazy paved path there was no sign of anything untoward. No smashed windows, no blood on the path, no illuminated sign saying, "I am so and so and I killed him!" Unlikely yes, but would have been nice and helpful. His finger pushed the doorbell and he then sighed with distaste at the awful chimes that erupted from the property. "Jesus, should have been strung up just for that." Bos waited and then approached the doorbell for another go, halted just before pressing and moved and lifted the letter box. He hammered down on this a number of times and then lifted it again, he put his nose to it. To a bystander that must have looked quite odd but Bos

had smelt death a number of times and wanted to see if that recognisable odour was here. After a first tentative sniff, just in case! If there was a corpse that had been festering for a while the smell could really sting the nostrils and water eyes. He took in a bigger nose full, it stunk but not of death. He peered in through the gap, the place was a tip. Rubbish festooned the floor, he could see flies banqueting on the collection of fast food wrappings and empty food cans, the walls looked thick with nicotine stains. The thought had often crossed his mind through the years how strange some people's ways of lives were. How one person's disgusting situation can be another's normal. He had come to terms with this a long time ago and had now come to the conclusion that if people want to live like cockroaches who was he to argue or judge. He will just wipe his feet when he leaves instead of when he arrives. "Hello, anyone home, this is the police," this still got no response.

On walking around the rear of the property the lack of care seen though the letter box was just as evident in the garden. Weeds and rubbish were everywhere, what was once a raised shrub or flower bed was now an overgrown jungle of nettles and brambles. He rounded the corner and could see the back door, he put his sleeve over his hand and pushed down on the end of the handle. It was unlocked. Unfortunately, he knew the way the situation was he had no legal right to enter the property at this time. It took a second and he stepped back, and in a monotone voice said, "Oh no I think I can smell something it reminds me of a dead body, I can also see flies in the property." He then opened the door, again with his sleeve. The back door went straight into the kitchen but saying this place was a kitchen was like saying an old exhaust you see on the road is a car! There would be no way on this planet he would eat anything from this "kitchen" just looking at it made you feel like you could come down with food poisoning. It was a place where plates came to die, a plate grave yard. The immediate search of the downstairs revealed no answers to why anyone would want to kill the occupant apart from cruelty to crockery! The steps creaked and squealed as he walked up them and they were as disgusting as the rooms below, discarded toilet tissue, empty drinks cans, and other detritus lay on each step.

Stepping through the rubbish it looked like he was some kind of tomb raider avoiding an elaborate trap. No spears would come from the walls and no large ball would roll towards him, the major threat he was trying to avoid was a broken neck from tripping over all the crap! The bathroom was a whole new level of disgusting, he couldn't even put his head in the room without his eyes watering. "Sod that," he said out loud and walked towards another room. He entered the bedroom and his eyes scanned the place, it was the same kind of mess as the entire house but his eyes caught a picture on the wall, it was an autumn scene painted in oils. It was an impressive sight of a tunnel of trees blowing in the wind with autumn leaves falling down which had covered the floor. However, scrawled across the painting were the words *Placare Arbores!* It was written in a substance that was red and had congealed on the surface of the painting. *Blood!* He thought and then went for a closer inspection. It didn't look right, he smelt it, it didn't smell right. On the bed immediately to the right of the painting was a dirty plate, not necessarily out of the ordinary for this house but the bed was clear apart from just that and the fork next to it. The plate had been used to hold some chips as there were a few of them on the floor covered with the same sauce from the plate. The fork had sauce on it too but it was on the handle not the prongs. It was odd, he looked at the painting and then again at the fork. Whoever had written the words had used the fork, it was the same size as the markings in the red. It wasn't blood on the painting it was the sauce from the plate.

His chin was being stroked again, he was trying to remember the latin classes he attended when young. "*Placare arbores!* That's to do with trees… appease the trees." At that moment he called in a forensics team. He didn't envy that job in this house but he definitely needed this place recorded. Photos of the painting, and the fork definitely needed inspecting. A nice juicy fingerprint would be handy. Bos left by the back door, he wiped his feet when he left. He then knocked on each door in the road asking all the residents that would answer about their neighbour at 25. With each and every one the same response, no arguments, no strange visitors, in fact no visitors at all and he kept himself to himself and didn't cause any issues. No CCTV, he didn't have a vehicle, no wife, no children and no real ties that he could find and no job either. Not a lot to go on. At that point there was a familiar jingle of *'Lady in Red'* from his phone, it saddened him every time he heard it. It was his and Helen's song he just couldn't bring himself to change it. "Hello, Inspector Boston speaking," there was a pause and then, "WHAT!" Another pause, "Have you no one else to *babysit?"* He spat the word babysit with venom. He paused again, this time longer and eventually he hung up. He shut his eyes, then whispered, "Bollocks." As if he wasn't tired enough he had to have someone with him, a newly promoted Inspector who they want to shadow an experienced officer for a while.

CHAPTER 5

Bella

Ben knew his dad would be away a lot because of his new job, he didn't realise that his mum was connected in some way too. They had taken a couple of weeks off work so they could all settle into the new house. The last week of it Ben had to start his new school but all too quickly the two weeks disappeared. Not just for Ben but his mum and dad too. It was Mike's last evening off before he started his job properly and he was walking the grounds with his son. They liked just walking round the huge grounds, seeing what kind of wildlife they could spot. Ben always kept clear of the strange trees though, he had still not got over his fear of them. He even kept the curtains in his bedroom shut to stop his view of them. He thought it odd but he shivered every time he looked at one. He mentioned it to his dad as they strolled around the grounds, but he was just told that, "Nature can be strange sometimes, they do look odd but so do many things in life." Somehow this didn't ease his troubling feeling of dread whenever he thought of them.

"Do you like your new home Ben?" Mike was worried that he had made a bad choice to bring his son here.

"I don't like the trees!"

"Forget about the trees, I mean in general, are you okay about being here?"

Ben didn't want to upset his dad as he could see the concern on his face, so he told him he was fine. He didn't want to mention the fact that he disliked his new school, certainly didn't like the uniform, he didn't like the teachers or any of the other students and he didn't like the fact that he was going to see very little of his parents during the week. He just said, "It's great Dad," and picked up a small twig and started breaking it into tiny pieces. He didn't know why this ritual calmed him down, it just did. Twig after little twig would be snapped and thrown down. They arrived back at the house later than usual and their meals were waiting for them, Bella had made shepherd's pie which Mike loved. Ben didn't have much of an appetite as he knew it was back to St Bartholomew's school for boys' tomorrow, which he hated. So he ate just enough to keep his parents happy and then left the table for a bath and to get ready for bed. After his soak he climbed into his super large bed and drifted into a broken night's sleep. He dreamt of running from his school, it was one of those dreams that were frightening to go through but to try and explain when you awake would sound pathetic.

He was snapping twigs walking toward his school

gates. The gates were large black iron with Eagle shields as centre pieces on each gate. As he approached, the shields came to life and looked at him, he panicked and started to run. The Eagles didn't follow but the entire gates and walls moved forward towards him. As he ran the school followed. He was running and suddenly the twig in his hand started to scream and trees started to close in on him from each side. He snapped the twig to shut it up but this just made the scream louder, the more he panicked and snapped the louder the scream became and the closer the trees become. The noise was deafening, the trees with their clawing branches were just inches away. Suddenly Ben awoke, he sat up and screamed just as Bella was about to wake him. Bella was given the fright of her life and jumped backward in shock, she didn't look like she jumped. It looked more like as if she had just been electrocuted and had been thrown backwards. "What the hell do you think you are trying to do, kill me?" shouted Bella. She had gone bright red in the face and seemed to grow in size with her anger.

Ben was a wreck, he was sitting in a puddle and was pale and dripping with sweat. He was panting with rivulets of sweat chasing down his face, he couldn't talk. He looked down at the bed and noticed the liquid, he tried to move his arm to wipe his brow but he was very unsteady, he licked his lips as his mouth seemed so dry. He could taste the salt from the sweat but he was dehydrated and found trying to moisten his lips quite impossible. "I, I, I am sorry," he gasped through the desert that was his mouth. "I think I have had a bit of an accident." Ben was going through a multitude of emotions at that moment, fear was still there, shock was one of the crowd, relief was in the background waving at him and now embarrassment had joined the party. Embarrassment was a new comer but was starting to overtake the rest, and as Ben sat feeling colder by the second as the urine and sweat started to cool it seemed that it was now embarrassment's party all to himself!

Bella shouted again, "An accident! An accident!" As she looked at the bed sheets she added some more, "You wet the bed, how old are you, three?!"

Ben apologised and tried to explain about his dream but she just cut him off and shouted at him to just get out and get washed. Ben felt awful, he was 8 and had not wet the bed for as long as he could remember but the dream had really shaken him, picturing those trees reaching out and grabbing for him made him shiver again as he lay in the steaming bath. Once he had finished his bath his bed was clean and remade but Bella had gone. He wanted to explain that it was not a regular thing and that he had had a nightmare. Ben dressed in his uniform and went downstairs for breakfast and to explain. As he walked into the dining room Bella was at the table. "I am sorry for the bed Bella, I had a nightmare."

Bella turned sharply and grunted, "Nightmare phfff! Just eat your breakfast ready for school."

Ben sat at the table and instead of the cereals or cooked breakfast there was just a few pieces of toast in the small silver toast rack. Bella was arms folded standing at the door that lead to the kitchen. Ben decided not to ask for cereal. "Could I have some butter and jam for the toast please?"

Bella walked toward him with her arms still folded and as she stood just in front of his she bent down and whispered in a nasty voice, "Little boys who wet themselves get dry toast, they need something to soak up the extra water!" With this she turned and left.

During his day at school he had decided that he would explain his dream to Bella so she would understand. So as soon as he walked in the house he looked for her. She was in the kitchen. Ben took a deep breath and spoke, "I am sorry about the bed Bella, I had an awful dream about the trees, I hate those trees and they followed me…erm in my dream they followed me and well I was scared and erm…" as he was saying it he could tell how daft it sounded.

"What trees?" Bella spoke calmly but it was not a nice calm, it sounded like soup on the boil! The part where it hissed but no explosion of boiling bubble came up. It was the sound of someone boiling but not showing it.

Ben panicked and just said, "I will show you." As Ben walked out of the house his heart began to beat faster, from as far away as he could he pointed to the trees and told Bella, "Those trees, I hate them and in my dream they chased me."

Bella just sneered at him and asked, "Which tree?"

"All of them, they all scare me." He was expecting and hoping that things would get a little calmer between him and Bella after he explained, but he didn't notice any thaw in her attitude towards him. In fact, it seemed to have got frostier after telling her about the trees.

She crossed her arms and scowled, "You wet the

bed because of our trees?" She walked towards Ben and he again automatically stepped back, unfortunately he had backed up in the wrong direction and had pinned himself against the wall of the house. It didn't stop him trying to continue to walk, the gravel moved under his feet as he moon walked against the wall. "Now you listen boy," the emphasis she put on the word boy was as if she was swearing at him, "if you don't start making my life easier I will tell you the real story behind those trees! If you wet my beds again, make me jump or in fact add to my work in any way… I will explain why they look that way." She left this sentence hanging in the air for a moment and then just abruptly turned and stormed away. Ben was pinned to the wall, what on earth was she on about! Real story? He was scared by the look of them but what could be behind them? His mind spun with the thoughts about the trees and of Bella. He eventually peeled himself away from the wall and dejectedly walked back into the house.

CHAPTER 6

Shadow

Bos left his house, resigned to the fact that he would be meeting his new work shadow today. He had not done anything special, he had gone through the same rituals to get ready as always. He was smart, well groomed and ready for his shift as usual. He did wonder what the new man was going to be like but it never worried him as he would just work the same as ever anyway. He parked his *Duke* in the station car park and walked to the main entrance. He had just walked through the door when a male came up and grabbed his hand, "Hello sir, I am Del and it's great to meet you." Bos shook his hand bemused. Del whoever he was, just grinned while continuing to shake hands.

Bos was a patient man but there is a point where it becomes creepy. "Can I help you?" Bos asked, while trying to release the grip on the man in front of him. This was not easy as Del was the type to shake hands with one and then use his other hand to grab the shaking pair as if he was making a point that if I am friendly with one hand, that means you can trust me implicitly because I use two! Something that Bos disliked immensely, it reminded him of a car salesman or some other type of wallet predator.

"I am to be with you for a while, I think you were expecting me." It was an unsettling grin, teeth everywhere, mix that with the hand shake and he reminded Bos of a shark.

"Oh okay, follow me and I will get you up to speed on the case I am on." He emphasised the word I, in the hope that Del would read between the lines and know that it's his case and to follow, but to butt out! The unease he felt with Del did not fade while explaining the murder investigation to him. He continually butted in with obvious questions and asking if things had been done that were very standard and would be done as a matter of course. Just as Del was asking if there had been any house to house enquires completed Bos's phone rang. This was quite a relief "Good morning, Inspector Bos speaking." He waited for a while and then added, "Yes I know where that is, on my way." He put the phone down and then turned to Del, "Come on let's go, we have another body."

During the journey Bos listened to what seemed like Del's entire life story, about his dad being a coper, his mum leaving when he was young, to his life in the police up to and including this recent promotion. After a while Del miraculously seemed to pick up on the fact that Bos hadn't actually said anything! "Erm I know I have been chatting on, but I am actually quite excited about working with you for a while, sorry if that makes you uncomfortable. I just notice that you haven't said much."

"I am more of a thinker than a talker!" Del had noticed.

"Everyone knows that you are great at what you do, I was very happy to be put with you but if you prefer I will ask to be moved with someone else?"

This statement hung in the air for a while and then burst with the words from Bos, "No you are fine, I am a little off at the moment. I am always tired and it's making me a little on edge." Bos felt a little guilty as he hadn't really given Del a chance. "Well now is your chance to get on my good side, let's see what we have!" The area was again a secluded, there were a number of PC's on guard making sure the public could not come near.

"Morning Bos, the scene is just down the path, if you stick to just that path you will be fine as that path has been photographed and examined already."

The PC guarding the entrance to the small wood handed the scene log to Bos, it was completed in silence and then passed back with a, "Thanks, anything important found yet?"

"Not yet Bos no, lots of different footprints going down there so difficult to tell what's important." As the inspectors walked down the mud track Del quietly muttered "Oh shit," as they approached a small clearing. A tree just off the clearing was cordoned off. It had crime scene tape pinned around it in a five meter spacing in each direction. It was the inner cordon where the major part of the incident was presumed to take place. There was blood and a lot of it. They could see feet dangling out from the canopy but nothing else until they walked a little closer. The feet were red with blood, as they walked closer they could see the legs were too as were the branches and the tree trunk. They both stood now standing against the tape line. Looking up was not a pretty site. A male was again naked and strung up by his neck, he was high in the tree and his belly had been opened the same as the previous victim. Bos raised an eyebrow as he noticed that the tree was the same species as the first victim was killed in a large Oak. This scene was however a little different. Bos looked at the trunk and again at the body. "He was strung up alive, same as before," Bos had thought it but the words came from Del.

"Mmmm would seem so. The thing is, if you were being taken to a tree and strung up you would put up one hell of a fight wouldn't you? So why is there no sign of any struggle at all?" this again was Del's voice.

Bingo, Bos thought, *that is what has been troubling me from the first moment I set eyes on the scene at bluebell hill.* The place everywhere around it was a perfect setting, no sign that anyone had been rustling about let alone a life and death struggle. Why the hell didn't he see that? "So what does it mean then Del? Tell me?" Bos was actually impressed with his new colleague, he had been here for a moment and sized the scene up immediately.

"Well it is just conjecture but we know he was alive in the tree however he must have been incapacitated somehow, so we are either looking for one big suspect or more than one person." Del said this and then due to Bos saying nothing he added,

"Because there are no tracks to the tree, he wasn't dragged he must have been carried." Still nothing from Bos, "What do you think?" a pause. The pause seemed to last forever to Del as he watched Bos just stand there and scratch his chin hair.

"I think, you are better at this than I gave you credit for," Bos smiled at Del and winked. "I think you are right and quite frankly it is something I should have seen at the first crime scene!" They looked up again at the grizzly sight. This scene was worse, the intestines this time were hanging from his belly and then like some ghastly looking Christmas decoration, were looped over the nearby branches. It was a disturbing view, he either had time to finish or he has progressed his need or fantasy. Bos spoke to the forensic man who was working across the other side of the tree, "Bud, can you make sure someone takes a picture of where the rope is on the tree please? I want to make sure the friction burn marks are present here too." Bud didn't say a word he just stuck his thumb up in the air in acknowledgement. Bos couldn't see the victim's face and if it was like before his clothes would not be around here so he would have to wait to see if the poor sod was known.

"Makes you wonder why though doesn't it?" said Del still looking at the male dangling like some naked parachute accident. "I mean that is one hell of a ritual to go through!"

Bos started to walk away, as he turned he said, "Come on I want to show you something." On the way back to the station Bos asked Del, "So in your opinion, using the info we have from the details on the first scene and the little we have from the second, have you a profile of the type of killer we are after?"

Del explained off the cuff some ideas and opinions. "Well I think we can assume the two crimes were committed by the same person or persons. For one the similarities are striking and two I would hate to think there are more than this person or group on our patch capable of this butchery!" there was a small pause, "Also to leave little evidence behind from such an act takes planning and I presume knowledge rather than luck, so an intelligent man."

Bos glanced over across from the driver's seat, "Why a man then?" Bos was smiling as he asked this.

"It may be a bit of a leap but if a woman has a beef with men and plans to go murderous on them some of the damage is usually directed at the genitals, this was not the case on either of the victims we have. Oh and plus, not being sexist at all but it would take a lot to get bodies up those trees."

Bos looked at him again and said, "Interesting." He was actually pleased, he was dreading working with someone else but Del reminded him of himself, well himself a couple of years ago! Del was sharp. Bos was still sharp but his was one that had been kept that way by hard work, Del was still new and gleaming. Bos thought again, *am I still on my game? I should have noticed the lack of disturbance at the scene not just thought something was odd. I have been ridiculously tired recently too. I need to be on my game for this one, but at least I don't have to wipe some idiots arse along the way.*

Del's voice nudged Bos from his thoughts, "Well?"

"What sorry I was miles away?"

Del repeated the question that was missed, "I said

what was it you wanted to show me?"

"I want to show you an idea I have had since looking at the last scene." Bos knew that a way of catching what now looked like a serial killer was to find the links. It may be links that the killer left deliberately and are part of the reason behind the killings or links that the killer never even thought about and just did instinctively. "Whatever they are we need to find them as they will be the key to stopping this." Bos explained this to his new colleague as they were coming up close to the station.

"Do you think it will continue then? You think we have more to come?"

The *Nisan* pulled into the parking space and as he pulled the handbrake on, Bos looked over with a face of stone and said, "Unfortunately I would put money on it." The two men walked through the main station doors and the established inspector said, "You get the coffees and I will meet you in conference room 3 in about 20 minutes." Bos then walked off in the other direction, it was a walk that meant business. He didn't go to his desk he walked straight to the lift, he pressed the call button and waited. It only took about 20 seconds and the lift pinged to a stop and the doors smoothly opened.

Out from the lift came a large built man with receding dark hair that was thinning and greased back. "Morning Bos, fancy a game of hang man?" The man didn't say anything else he winked and continued past.

"Morning Gav," he was used to Gavin's sense of humour, sick but whatever helps you get through. Stepping into the lift he pressed the button on the top of the pad. Floor after floor tumbled past and they eventually opened into a moderately lit corridor. Immediately out of the lift door was a sign. It was a run of the mill white plastic sign and black writing. Nothing fancy, this was not a place the public saw. Admin to the left Stores to the right, to the right he could see a couple of bulbs had blown. He humph-ed in amusement as it cast a dreary atmosphere down there, about right too, no bugger goes down there unless they have to. You had to be a certain type of person to work in the police stores. Bos had thought for years the application must stipulate: must be tighter than a virgin birth, wear a permanent sneer and be fucking miserable. Bos happily turned left toward the admin offices. He opened the door to the admin room and walked in, it was an open plan room with just above waist height partitions. There were around 6 members of staff in the room but he knew who he was heading for. As he approached the computer on the far right of the room he said, "Morning Deb, how are you?" The woman at the desk had long light brown hair she looked striking. She looked the type that would stop people working just to watch her walk past. She was beautiful but it was only until you took a closer look you realised that she wore no make up at all, no false eyelashes, no false nails, no hair grips, bunches or anything. She was medium build apart from her chest which was ample and Bos presumed not fake either!

"Hi Bos, haven't seen you up here for ages hun, how are you doing?" Bos told her he had been better and said that he had just come from a bit of a grizzly murder scene. "I don't know how you cope with that hun, I wouldn't that's for sure, Sue cut her finger the other day and I nearly collapsed." With that Deb taped him playfully on the arm. Bos had known Deb for a long time now, the Sue she was referring to was her partner, they had been together longer than he had known her. So to an outside eye it may have seemed like some flirting going on but Bos knew that Deb was a one woman, woman!

"I need a favour actually Deb and I need it done as quick as possible, could you get a map of our beat areas… say 4 through to 18 and have it printed on an A3 sheet for me please?"

Deb thought for a second and asked, "Yes I think so, when do you want it for?" Bos said that ideally two minutes ago. Deb smiled and said, "Wait here for a minute and I will see what I can do." 5 minutes later she was back with a piece of paper rolled in a cardboard tube. "Here you go Bos, easy when you know how hun."

He took the roll and said, "Thanks Deb you are a star, if I thought you were into it I would give you a kiss," Bos winked as he said it.

"You devil, if you didn't have a penis perhaps I would kiss you back," she patted him on the arm again and beamed a smile that light up the room. Bos said thanks again as he walked away from her desk and once again headed for the door. He knew he could act like that with Deb as there was no sexual tension between them, he was the same when his Helen was alive. Helen knew it too she was there some of the time when they had similar conversations, he smiled and reminisced on the time at the dinner party they threw together and Deb and Sue came along. He remembered the looks on some of the other guests faces when Deb held up a Cumberland sausage from the buffet and shouted, "Here Bos this ain't yours is it, cos if you have gone through with the change I may be after you." He was in the lift again now and had a bit of a chuckle to himself. This time it was the second floor button that was pressed, he was heading off for conference room 3 to meet with Del. The door to the lift pinged open and the difference was marked, this corridor had lush carpets, bright lights and signs that were silver with police blue writing on and the constabulary crest too. This corridor was not just for the police staff but on occasion high powered local government and officials had meeting on this level. So it was essential to 'show the polish' as Bos put it. He walked down the corridor and headed for conference room three. He pushed he heavy set wooden door open, he knew it was empty as the silver plaque on the top said so, he could also see through the gleaming glass panel in the centre that Del was already in sitting at the table. Well more accurately sitting on the table. As he walked in Del was sitting side saddle on the large conference desk, he had one leg dangling and one resting on a plush blue velvet looking chair. It was a large oval dark wood table and in the centre was a black plastic monstrosity. It resembled a *Dalek's* head but was black with small ramps coming off it in about 6 directions. Bos knew what it was and had been in some meetings when they used it. It was the equipment they used to have meetings over a number of different locations. It was a disappointment as it summed up the police service as far as Bos could tell. Chairs, carpets, doors and tables all immaculate and high quality but the brass tacks of the service, the things they needed more than for effect and it was cheap shit and not up for the job! "Okay Bos, what is it you are showing me?"

Bos rolled out the map on the desk, making sure to roll it through the other way first to stop it pinging up like some comedy sketch. He pointed out that this is the map of most of their beat areas, the ones that surround our scenes. Bos looked around and picked up a dry wipe pen from the white board in the corner. "Here was where the first body was found, and here is the victims address." He wrote a one and circled it and then drew a house and wrote one inside it. "Now here is victim two," he wrote a two and circled it. "I told you I look for the patterns, the first victim was hung in an Oak tree and it was under a mile from his home address. The second has also been hung in an Oak tree and until we get some kind of I.D. we don't know where he lived but if the trees are a pattern then we need to locate all the secluded Oak tree sites we can."

Del looked at the map and then again at Bos, "Okay so if there is only a couple of secluded Oak sites we can hold up and nab him because we know the victims are still alive when they arrive on scene, but if there are hundreds we are screwed… and so are they!"

Bos knew it was a long shot but it was the only shot they had at the moment, "You call the local arborist's and I will call the Council horticulture department. When you find a secluded Oak spot mark it on the map with a green triangle." During the course of the day the map slowly but surely became infested with green triangles. There were 20-30 Oak tree sites, some obviously more secluded than others. They hadn't put the ones on the map that were in the middle of busy built up areas. The two men stood back and looked at the map.

Del shook his head, "Who would have thought there were so many bloody Oak trees about?!"

Bos had hoped that there were not as many but you have to deal with the job in front of you, "Okay we need to visit these sites and see which ones are the more likely kill sites." Bos was usually alone during his investigations and liked it that way but for some reason he was enjoying Del's company on this one, they seemed to get on well and were well suited in the way they thought. It had been quite a day, the highs and lows were quiet distinctive. It was a strange way to look at a murder scene and call it a high but as far as his work day went he would always rank that as a high compared with the rest of the day on the phone pinpointing Oak tree sites, finding so many of them was a definite low at the end of the day. "Well today has been up and down, fancy a drink?"

Del thought about the offer for about a nano second, a month ago he would never have thought he would be working with Bos and going out for a drink to wind down after a difficult day. "Sure, I will leave my car here and ask my wife to pick me up later." As usual in a town there was a pub that hosted more police than any other, it was a bit of a mystery why a certain pub would be singled out for the attention of the local constabulary. One would think it would have a calm, quiet, polite atmosphere with a lot of professional personnel chilling out over a quiet drink… one would be wrong! If you are aware of the term work hard play hard it would fit perfectly well here. It was rowdy, loud and the air was usually blue, more thick blue expletives rather than thin blue line! The thing is they felt safe to vent in here as they knew it was the pub frequented by them. It was taken years ago so no one was sure why but its name was changed in the mists of time too. The sign hanging outside was of a piece of old beaten up scroll, yellow stained in colour with the words 'labour cost 3d parts 2d.' In a large black font above it on the top of the sign was written "The Old Bill," obviously some landlord in the past had a sense of humour about being stuck with the clientele he had.

The two detectives walked in and went straight to the bar and sat. It was fairly empty at the moment but that was likely to change soon enough, a police bar didn't usually go out of business, there were a lot of sins to drown. Not necessarily committed by the drinker but certainly seen by them! The large man behind the bar walked over, compared to the building and its contents he was actually quiet clean and well turned out. "What can I get you gentlemen?"

Bos and Del both said simultaneously, "Vodka… neat." Both men looked at each other and kind of laughed, it was more just like an expulsion of air with a little grunt but meant the same from both of them: 'well bloody hell'.

"Sure thing," and the barman set off to get the drinks. He filled two glasses from the huge vodka bottle hanging upside down at the back of the bar. Bars usually have normal sized bottles in a row like this but this bar had a row of large bottles in a line, obviously a sign that the barman was fed up of replacing the empties so often. "Do you want ice?" Both men answered at the same time but this time with different responses, Bos said no and Del said yes.

Another grunt and Bos picked up his drink, raised it and said, "Different after all," and smiled.

"That will be £4.80 please."

Bos gave the barman a £20, "Take it for another round too, this isn't going to hang around long." He was right, the first drink didn't stay around for very long. "How long have you been married then Del?" Del was 38 and had been married for 12 years, he told him how he and Janice had met at school and then drifted apart only to meet again in some accidental way. On a train actually, she had missed her stop and he had got on at the stop after so they shouldn't really have bumped into each other at all.

"I don't really believe in fate but it is strange how things happen!" Del knew about Bos's wife Helen, word gets about fast and travels far and wide in the police. People get transferred here there and everywhere and the friendships forged usually stay, so the police net is tight and wide. "Are they any closer to catching who killed Helen?" Bos stopped mid gulp and turned his eyes towards Del, "It had to come up eventually Bos, I just wanted to ask straight out." Bos told him that there were no new lines of enquiry and he thinks they have basically given up unless more evidence drops in their laps.

With that sad admission Bos downed his drink. "Another?" Del held up his and shook his head as if to say no mine is still full. Bos waved his glass at the barman and pointed to it and showed the barman one finger. The man was obviously experienced enough to know what it meant. He put his glass down and sighed, "I am not coping very well to be honest, I put on a front but I am permanently knackered. I sleep but feel awful when I get up. I have been trying to throw myself into work but to be honest when I see the people strung up in the trees I wish it was the bastard that killed Helen!" He looked at Del and said, "I know, sick isn't it?" Grief plays people in different ways and Bos was empty, he felt like a part of him was gone and nothing he could do would bring it back.

"How about family, any kids?"

Bos explained to his new confidante that he hadn't had children and he hadn't any real family to speak of, "I have adoptive parents but I have never been close to them to be honest. My real parents left me when I was young apparently."

Del frowned at that part, "What do you mean apparently? Surely you know?"

Bos described how he remembers nothing about his young life but he was told by his adoptive parents that he had a critical illness when he was younger, he survived it but the fall out of the illness was a total blank from before his recovery. They had told him that his parents couldn't cope so left. They said they didn't know what illness as they were not told it when they took him in. "So all in all I have a good career but not a lot else, another drink?"

Del was in a bit of shock, the man that all held up in high regard as a superb detective was actually a bloody mess. "No I won't, sorry but I need to get back to Janice and to be honest you shouldn't have more either, we have both seen the fall out of finding solace in the bottom of a bottle. Looking in a bottle for answers is only going to find you one thing, your head stuck!" He looked at Bos and shrugged sympathetically.

Bos knew he was right and just said, "Yeah I suppose so." Del offered him a lift back to his place and called Janice to pick them up. It wasn't long before Janice arrived. She was a short plump woman with round glasses and short bobbed hair. He didn't know what he was expecting but she was not it.

Del introduced his wife, "It is lovely to meet you, Del has been going on about working with you since he found out." She smiled and Bos could then see why Del was with her, her face beamed when she smiled and made her look a completely different person. Del hurried his wife out of the door in case she said anything else too cringe-worthy. The short journey to drop Bos off at home was strangely quiet, Janice sensed some unease from her husband so said nothing and concentrated on her driving. Bos thanked them for the lift and headed for his house, he used to call it home but not anymore.

CHAPTER 7

Mind Games

Life had become uncomfortable for Ben, he was on edge all the time. It was partly to do with the trees that were always on his mind now. He was also on edge because of the nanny, Bella was awful whenever his parents were not about. At every opportunity she would stare and sneer at him. He didn't want to say anything to his parents about it, he didn't want to hear anything more about the trees. He was intrigued but in no way did he want to find out in case it made him feel worse around them than he already did. He tiptoed around the place making sure he did nothing to antagonise Bella. Unfortunately, he was a kid and it was only a matter of time before he forgot himself and acted like one! It was a Tuesday evening and he was as usual without his parents as they were working late again. He went to the kitchen for a drink, he poured himself a drink of milk and opened the biscuit tin for a snack. Chocolate biscuits were his favourite and to his enormous pleasure there were some rather lovely looking chunky chocolate ones in the tin. He took three out and placed the tin back where he got it from. He took a bite from one of them, "Oh wow they are lovely." Ben picked up his glass of milk and walked toward the dining table. It all happened in slow motion for Ben, he could see it all happening and he was trying to stop it but he was powerless. On his way through the door from the kitchen he was taking more care looking at the biscuit in his right hand than the doorway he was walking through. His left elbow caught the door frame and sent a tsunami of milk over the top of his glass. This is where things slowed, he could see the milk starting to flow over the top of his glass. He panicked and tried to put his other hand over the top of the glass to stop more of the white liquid flowing over to land on the polished floor. Unfortunately, his hand didn't land on the top of the glass but smacked into the side of it, this caused the glass to move out of his full grip and more milk came crashing over the lip of the glass. This time not in one wave but in a new and more vigorous pattern. If things were moving this slowly surely he should be able to stop them, no! The momentum of the bump into the door frame had swung him round and he had hit the glass with this momentum and it was heading out of his grasp. He made a desperate attempt to keep the glass in his hand but gravity was against him too, he was falling. One last try and his right arm flung out to try and cling on the fleeing glass, all this did was to bat it to a different trajectory. To Ben's horror it was now heading for the dresser. This was a cabinet with crockery on show. The crockery was very thin and had pale flowers around the edge and Japanese scenes painted in the middle.

He fell backwards, he was powerless to stop the glass hurtling toward it. The biscuits he had were now released and happy to escape in the other direction as Ben's hands went instinctively towards his mouth in absolute horror. The crash was deafening, the glass hit one plate directly in the centre and it smashed instantly. Ben was still watching in slow motion, the plate seemed to burst and open like an explosion. It reminded him of a firework, well he had lit this one and it was too late to stop.

A split second after the plate flew apart the glass did the same, this one was not as elegant. The milk that was left in the glass hung in the air slightly longer than the glass shards until it remembered about Newton laws and decided to stick to them! The milk splashing on the back of the dresser was the last thing he saw as a searing pain shot through his head, he had landed and smashed the left side of his head on the polished wooden floor. The pain was immediate and blinding, all thought of milk, glass, plates and furniture disappeared. He screamed in pain and curled up in the foetal position, clung on to his head with both hands and cried. Bella came into the kitchen in an absolute rage, she had heard the crash and obviously assumed the worse. As she stormed in, the worse was what she found. She did not register the body crying on the floor but looked at the gap on the dresser where there should be a plate and the milk that had covered the rest of it. She walked over to it, now for some strange reason slowly. She could now see the fragments of plate and glass over the dresser and floor. It was only then that she took any notice of the whimpering body curled up on the floor. "What have you done now boy, how the hell have you caused such devastation in my dining room?" Bella growled in disgust. Ben did not respond to this, he was vaguely aware that someone had said something but did not register what and from whom. Bella bent down and grabbed his arm. "Get up you stupid boy, look what you have done," she pulled him up and he did get to his feet. Bella was totally indignant about the lump that had grown on the side of Ben's head. It was huge and had come up straight after the impact with the floor. Ben was still in pain and could not concentrate on anything that was being asked of him, he just lifted his left hand to hold his head. "What did you do, and leave it alone and stand still," Bella shouted this and slapped his arm away from his head. Ben tried to tell her that he had only got a drink but his sentence did not come out of his mouth correctly he had bitten his tongue too but due to the pain in his head this had not registered. "Get to bed, the trees will be watching you now, you mark my words!" She let go of his arm and pushed him towards the door to leave. She turned to face the mess again, took in the sight and then stormed off into the kitchen mumbling, "Little shit!"

The rest of the night was a bit of a blur for Ben but he was woken up the next morning by Bella shouting at him, "Get up, get up, get up!" This was being repeated until she knew he was awake, "Get ready for school!" She then crossed her arms and said, "You do know that those trees will be watching now." Ben's head was aching but he did hear what she said now, he asked her what she meant. Bella told him that the grounds once housed a home for delinquent boys, "Naughty ones like you." She told him that the trees were normal then but the manager of the home used to punish the boys by tying them to the trees and caning them. This continued for years, some boys disappeared too. It was found that when the boys were too bad, the manager would cane them until they died and buried them under the trees. "So you see it's the naughty boys that twisted those trees," Ben was horrified and was frozen, "boys like you, so now if any boy misbehaves here they expect blood in return." Bella was loving the fear in Bens eyes, she continued to say that over the years many people had died in or near those trees and it was all because of naughty boys. "So the moral of this is… BE GOOD OR DIE, they know what you are like." She stared at him for a little while to take in the pure horror she had created and then turned in satisfaction to the door and sauntered out.

She had opened the curtains, Ben was petrified to walk past the window now. He scrambled out of bed and ran to the bathroom where he vomited. This spiralled his panic further, he spent 10 minutes clearing up his own sick so he didn't incur the wrath of Bella and it would be the good boy thing to do. Ben then went downstairs, he really didn't feel like eating anything, his stomach was doing somersaults and his head still ached. "Oh decided to get up now have you, lazy, another BAD trait." Bella then put a paper plate on the table with one piece of dry toast on it. "You obviously can't be trusted around proper plates." Bella put her nose in the air and walked out. Ben knew that it was supposed to be a punishment but this morning he was very glad to have just a piece of dry toast. He felt very groggy this morning, however, he was certainly not going to ask to have a day off school sick, he would rather crawl in on his hands and knees than to stay at home with Bella! Plus, he desperately wanted to be good and avoid any attention of the trees.

Chapter 8

I.D. 2

Bos awoke and felt ill, it was not a hangover as he had not drunk that much. He arose and shuffled to his bathroom. He placed his hands each side of the sink as if to hold himself up and looked up into the large mirror above it, "Ugh, god you look shit." His eyes had darkened bags under them. He had been in bed for one night but seemed to have aged a year! He stood there looking at himself for a minute. "What the hell is wrong with you?" he said out loud to himself. "You used to get up feeling as sharp as a hedgehog's arse! Jesus, now you just look like its arse!" He turned and left for the kitchen. He made himself a coffee and some toast and tried to set up in his mind what he was going to be up to today. His mind went to the matter at hand and that was to find the likely sites for any next murder. He hadn't had a lot to go on yet and was feeling just as run down as he had done in weeks, but he was determined as ever to catch this sick bastard. He finished his coffee and placed it meticulously in the correct place in the dishwasher. It always went in the same place, just like the plate for his toast went in the same place. He went to the bathroom again to try and tidy up his tired looking face. A wash and a shave and he at least looked a little better. He left for the station and was not surprised when he arrived to see Del already there waiting for him.

Del had thought of Bos as a hugely inspiring character, his work in the police was unprecedented and very impressive. However, as Bos walked in today he didn't seem the impressive man he had imagined, he even seemed to have lost some stature from yesterday. "Morning Bos." Bos said good morning and then told him that they were going to have a busy day categorising the 20-30 Oak sites they had pinpointed. The two men spent the first half hour listing the sites in the best order to visit so they were not zigzagging all over the place.

"Right we are set, we need to find where the sicko may strike next". They headed out to the car park.

"Are you okay this morning Bos, you look a little jaded?"

Bos reached the car and beeped it unlocked. "Tired as usual, don't know why though slept right through." He climbed in the car and handed the list of sites to Del, "Where is the first one?"

"That is the clearing off Ram Hill." The engine started with its usual purr and they set off for the first Oak. Bos pulled up at the top of Ram Hill and pulled on the hand brake. There was a style to climb and a sign saying public footpath. "It's a little way down here, I believe this is the only entrance so not ideal access for people to carry a body." Both men walked down the small path and Del noticed that along the left was a hedge line but it was broken in many places which showed clear views of a housing estate a couple of hundred meters across an open field, "Not ideal for privacy for the walk either." After a minute or so they arrived at a small wooded area, there was indeed an Oak tree, a couple in fact but it held no privacy at all. "Not good, you can see right through the trees to the other side, I doubt this would be a site worthy of our killer," Del said this while standing next to one of the Oaks, "I don't actually think it's big enough either." Bos was of the same mind too. He told Del that he thought the same and that they should cross this site from their list. They headed back to the car along the dirt track they had come up.

As they trudged along the path the silence was broken by the tune Lady in Red from Bos's phone. Again his mind raced towards the wife he had no more, he sighed and answered it, "Morning, Inspector Bos speaking." The silence and anticipation was almost too much for Del, he wanted to ask if it was another body but held his question back. He was biting his lip in suspense, Bos just said, "Okay thanks," and hung up. He did not stop walking but spoke to Del while leading the way back to the vehicle, "That was Bud from forensics, they have an I.D. on the last male. Bud said he has sent me an email with the detail but just wanted to let me know it is there waiting for me."

"What was the name?" Del had a warm glow in his stomach, he always got that when he knew new information was coming in a case.

"Bud said the victim's name was Terence Hill, know him?" By this time, they were close to the car.

"No, doesn't ring anything with me, are we going back to the station to have a look?" It was a definite reason to head back, they had crossed one site off the list and were now going to search up the details on the last victim. Not a huge leap forward but it was a step in the right direction at least. During the trip back Bos asked Del how Janice was with them going for a drink. "She was fine, she doesn't mind me letting off some steam every now and then, she is one in a million I don't know what I would do without her," the moment he said it he wanted to take it back. He wanted the car to eject him.

Bos could see the look on his face and took pity on him, "Don't worry, it's not your fault, embrace it, take every moment you have together and treasure it. I wish I would have embraced my time with Helen more." Del was mortified, he was sure he couldn't have caused more anguish on the man's face if he had physically smashed him in the gut. He decided though to cut his losses and add no more comments, nothing he could say would make it better, the only thing he could do was make himself or Bos feel worse. The rest of that journey was held in silence, the kind of silence you could feel, the silence that seemed to get louder! They arrived at the station after what seemed to Del a three hour journey but was really only minutes. On their way up to the office, Bos told Del again, "Look don't worry about it honestly it's not your issue to skirt around, now let's get some info on this guy." Bos opened his email and looked at the report. He looked at the PNC report and froze,

"What the fuck!" Del was having a look too but couldn't see anything out of the ordinary. "This can't be right, that is just too fucking weird."

Del looked again, "What's up, what are you looking at?"

Bos looked at Del and said, "I don't like this, I told you that I knew the first victim didn't I?" Del acknowledged this, "He was a case of mine that got off on a technicality."

Del sounded calm and quiet now "Yes, and?"

"This one is an old case too! I knew him as Terry Hill and he did go down for the offence but the sentence was unbelievably lenient. I remember being extremely pissed off in court when the sentence was given." Bos was long enough in the tooth to dislike coincidences. It is very rare that a coincidence in these cases turn out to be coincidence and he definitely didn't like where this was heading. "So we have another pattern then, not one we like but a pattern none the less!" Bos unravelled the map and drew on a house where the last victim lived. "A visit to 3 Victoria cottages is in order," said Bos, standing up he seemed to be revitalised with the knowledge that the second victim had a connection to him like the first did. He marched towards the exit with renewed vigour.

Del hurried after him as they headed towards the vehicle to make another house call. "So Bos what do you think is going on, coincidence or not?"

"Coincidence my arse! There is a reason for this, I don't know what exactly but it's a punishment of some kind." Bos looked at Del and raised just one eyebrow.

Del was intrigued, "What do you mean a

punishment? A punishment for who?"

Bos was standing against his car now and speaking to Del over the roof he explained that, "If I knew that I would be a lot closer to catching the bastard, however that being the case I think it will either be someone punishing the victims, the courts, the police or…" he paused at this and then said, "well, me!"

CHAPTER 9

3 Victoria Cottages

Number 3 Victoria cottages was under a mile away from the site of the grizzly second murder. Victoria cottages were a row of 5 small dwellings with a small wooden fence surrounding them all. The wooden fence seemed stuck to the hedge, on the property side these gardens took a lot of upkeep to maintain the look. Each garden had an arch above the wooden gates that lead to the front doors. The gardens themselves were packed with flowers and shrubs. It looked from an untrained eye as if it was left to go wild but this was certainly not the case, they took a lot of work. Bos opened the gate, it creaked and twanged, it was on a spring that automatically shut it when you went through. He waited until Del had walked through and then deliberately let it go. The spring twanged with the joy of being able to return to its normal position and the latch thudded into place making quite a loud noise. "That would be risky if you were up to no good!" Del said nodding, "And this frontage isn't exactly snooper proof, the

neighbours can see everything." Bos went to the front door, he put his hand in his sleeve and pushed it. It was shut, there was no bell so he lifted the knocker and smashed it down a couple of times. No reply. He didn't even try again, he just turned and walked out of the garden. He was in the zone now and it was as if Del wasn't there. As he left the front garden he turned left and walked to the end of the cottages and followed the hedge line around to the back. The hedge line increased in height as it ran the length of the side of the front garden so by the time it reached the start of the rear it was around two metres and still immaculately kept. The rear of the property was an alley way about four meters wide with two dirt tracks and three grass strips. On the right was a wooden fence and the left was a pure wall of hedge with just 5 wooden gates equally spaced along the length.

Bos walked towards the middle gate looking towards the floor to see if he could see anything that may point towards something being wrong or out of place. When he reached the gate he pushed it with a finger and it swung open. The rear garden was a different style to the front it was still well kept, it had a lawn to the left of the path and to the right was a pond surrounded by wild flowers and grass. As he walked down the path Bos could see the back door was open. "That doesn't look good," he said, as nothing was out of place in the garden. Bos poked his head through the door and shouted, "Hello, anyone home? Hello, it's the police, we need to see if you are okay!" He walked in. The difference between this house and the first victim's house was worlds apart. There was nothing out of place anywhere. The rooms were small but immaculately tidy. "We need to see the bedroom," this was the first time in a while that Bos had actually acknowledged that Del was there with him. They walked up the stairs, which creaked under the pressure of their footsteps. When they stepped onto the landing there were three doors, all shut. "Go on then pick a door, any door?"

Del looked and just said, "Well I go for the middle."

Bos put his hand in his sleeve again and opened the door, "Well, well give yourself a coconut, the master bedroom right away." This room was not out of the ordinary for the rest of the cottage. It was tidy with nothing out of place. Bos looked for a painting or a picture that may have some writing on it. "In the other property there was a message written on a painting, I was wondering and hoping there may be one here too." The men looked around the room but nothing stood out. "Shit, let's just try the others." Bos turned left and walked into a study type of room, small but again tidy. Del went right and entered the bathroom, there were no immediate signs of any writing and the room by and large was as tidy as the rest of the house, apart from one thing. A bar of soap lay in the sink, Del thought it odd as there was a soap dish and everything else in the house was in its place that was meant for it. He had a closer look and the bar was an oval shape but one end was flattened somehow.

"Bos have a look at this." Bos entered the bathroom which made it quite cramped. "Don't you think the soap is a little out of place, not to mention out of shape!" The large man stood still for a moment just rubbing his chin in thought. After a while Del saw his eyebrow raise, Bos leaned forward and huffed out some breath on the mirror. As he breathed out and fogged up the mirror, the words *placare arbores* appeared.

"Call scenes of crime, let's go." Del was stunned and impressed the man in front of him had gone from a policing hero to a love lost drunk and back up to bloody brilliant within days.

Del followed him out of the cottage, "How did you know that writing was there?"

Bos told him that he didn't but the first scene has writing that was done by using something in the room, "Ketchup at that time." He then explained that the only thing out of place in that entire house was the soap and it was worn down in a very odd way, "Soap would never wear away like that if used correctly, so what else would wear it down, writing with it! The mirror just seemed the obvious choice then."

Del was silent and was happy to walk along with Bos. "But why would the killer do that?" Del said.

"What do you mean?" asked Bos.

"Why would he write a message nobody may read?"

Bos had a little think about it, "That is a question we are unable to answer… yet, but it is either they wrote it to someone who knew how to read it or didn't care if anyone read it." The two inspectors climbed back into the vehicle, "Right, back to the search for the next possible site I think, what is the next one on the list?"

Del took the list from the glove box, looked at it and said, "Homestead Farm wood." On the way to the next Oak site, Del watched Bos and was disturbed to see the change in him. It was as if the last hour was adrenalin fuelled and now it had run out, he was back to the man of yesterday. He seemed to visibly deflate, it was like watching a camp bed when you take out the stopper. The area under his eyes looked darker again. "You having trouble sleeping?" Del asked him. Bos told him that sleeping wasn't the problem, he went out like a light each night. It was the case that he woke up knackered still, it had been going on for a couple of weeks now and was becoming intolerable. "Perhaps you should see your doctor." Bos avoided the Doctors whenever he could. Once he cut his hand while attempting some DIY; it was deep and ordinarily would have had stiches. He just said to Helen that it was amazing what insulating tape can do and used just that!

"Yes perhaps," he said pulling into Homestead Farm Lane. The farm was deep down the Lane and beyond the farm the Lane turned into a track that led into Homestead Farm wood. The wood was large and the entrance was narrow but passable. They parked near the entrance to the wood and took to foot. After the initial 5-6 meters of narrow undergrowth it cleared slightly and a path went off to the left and to the right. They both went left and followed the track round, about 20 meters in and there stood a very large Oak in a clearing off to the right. "Now that is a beauty!" Del was liking this site, "Yes, nice and secluded but has access, large tree able to sustain the weight of a man, I think we have a candidate here."

Bos then asked Del to mark the list he had with a tick for this site, "I reckon this one gets a 10 out of 10 for possible site don't you?" During the rest of the shift they spent their time visiting one site after another and ranking them out of 10 for possible hanging sites. They sat in the station at the end of the day with a finished list. They had six 10 out of 10, a couple of 9's, some 8's, a few 7's then the rest 6's and under. In all there were 22 sites.

"What do you think, concentrate on the 10, 9, and 8's?" said Del cautiously.

"Sod that, I want to catch this son of a bitch. There were only days between the first two bodies so let's get a copper out on each site." Del wondered if the top brass would go for that but Bos did have the knack of getting things done. "I reckon I can get the boss to give us 22 coppers for about 4 days, anything more than that he will start to whine about purse strings."

CHAPTER 10

Blood

Ben was permanently worried, he didn't want to be a bad boy, he didn't want the trees watching him. Any time he even looked like he was going to speak out of turn, step where he shouldn't, drop a crumb or anything Bella would look at him! She would look and wait until he noticed and mouth, "They are watching boy." A nice weekend came and his mum and dad had surprised him by arranging for a friend from his old school to stay the night. Charley was dropped off at 11:00 on the Saturday and was not going until Sunday about 18:00. When the car pulled up Ben shot out the front door and ran to see his friend. "Charley," he shouted and hugged him.

Charley was a little taken back but rallied well, "Alright Ben, how's it going, I can't believe this is your house its huge!"

"You should see my room," and Ben dragged him towards the house.

"See you Sunday then Charley," shouted his dad

smiling at Mike.

Ben flung open his bedroom door and said, "Look at this," while running in to his room, he spun round with his arms wide showing off his vast room.

"Wow, and look at the bed!" Charley ran to the bed and dived on to it. Ben joined his friend and they both jumped happily up and down on the bed. The two boys laughed and played in the room, Ben was so happy to see an old friend he had totally forgot about Bella and the trees. They ran downstairs for a drink and Charley asked to see the garden.

"We have loads of land, I will take you for a walk later, there is a lake on our ground too we can skim stones." A drink and a few biscuits later and the boys were running out the front door to wander the grounds, have fun and generally be loud and excitable. It was a wondrous day for Ben, at about 17:15 they headed back to the house. Hunger had overcome the fun and had started banging on their bellies. Ben showed Charley how to use the foot scraper that was built into the wall and they went into the house.

Madison had made dinner and was just about to dish it up, "You must have smelt this, go wash your hands boys." They all sat at the table and Ben told his mum and dad excitedly what he and his friend had been up to. The stew disappeared very quickly from Ben and Charley's plates, they were obviously hungrier than they realised. They both had second helpings. Mike and Madison sat blooming with pleasure at seeing Ben so happy. Ben was just telling them about how they had made spears from branches and he had beaten Charley with the distance his spear went.

"So are you going out again for a little while?" asked Mike with a smile so wide it could quite easily have fitted a banana in it.

"I think that is an excellent idea, but only after dessert." Ben asked his mum what it was and when she said trifle he shouted, "Yes!" Once the boys had eaten trifle they were not in the mood to go back out, they were very full. "I know let's watch some videos instead," the video library that Ben had was epic. Mike and Madison seemed to buy him videos to try and make up for the fact that they were away so much. The two boys chatted to each other, watched films and ate sweets all night and fell asleep in the early hours on the quilt that they had pulled off of the bed. It was a magical time for Ben as he had been so lonely since moving here. The next day went in an absolute blur of fun and play and before long Charley's dad was in the drive waiting to collect him. After waving him off Ben came dejectedly back into the house and sat in the lounge. Madison was in there too, "Did you enjoy your weekend with Charley?" Ben said it was fantastic but he was sad it was over and he had to leave. Madison asked if he wanted a hot chocolate to cheer him up and went off to make it.

"I suppose you think I don't know what you got up too with your friend?" Bella had come in and stood quietly behind the sofa that Ben was on. She has whispered her remark but put a nasty spin on the word friend. Ben spun round in shock and was brought crashing down to reality by seeing Bella's horrible twisted grin. "I notice the quilt is off your bed, on the floor and has chocolate stains all over it." Ben was just about to say something but she butted in, "I hear you have been throwing stones in the lake too," she tutted a few times, "the trees are not going to forgive you easily for that you know!" Ben's face dropped in horror. "And as for making spears from branches, how do you think they will take that? They don't like people mutilating other trees." Yet again Bella was enjoying her cruelty, "I do hope your little friend doesn't come back, I hate to think what they will do to him if they are not made to feel better."

Ben was appalled, "B-b-but Charley is my friend."

Bella just looked at him said, "Your choice," and walked away.

It was a couple of minutes later when Madison came out of the kitchen with two mugs of hot chocolate but Ben was not there. She went to the lounge door and shouted, "Ben your hot chocolate is ready if you still want it," blissfully unaware of the turmoil her son was going through. Ben had ran upstairs and was pacing his room, he didn't want anything bad to happen because of him.

After a couple of minutes though he left to find Bella. He found her polishing a vase in the conservatory. "Bella?" She looked round in disgust and then turned back to continue to clean. "What did you mean when you said if they are not made to feel better?"

Bella sighed in response, "I mean they get upset and angry when people are naughty, when they get angry horrible things happen, people have died or got injured here for no reason, they do it, they do it to stop the bad people." Bella walked towards him, she flung out her right arm with the yellow cloth she had been using towards the trees outside the conservatory. "Some people are too stupid to see it, I know what they do… are you too stupid... are you going to be the reason other people are hurt or killed?" She left a pause before and after the 'are you stupid?' comment for effect.

It seemed to have the impact she wanted because Ben then asked what she was wanting to hear, "How can I stop it, how can I make them feel better?"

Bella turned sharply away and continued to polish and without looking at him she said, "That's easy… blood… blood calms them down, if you don't give them blood they WILL take it!" She emphasised the word WILL by raising her voice and by turning to face Ben as she said it.

Ben was again shocked and horrified at the woman's words, "But how do I do that I can't get blood," Ben's voice had become slightly higher but quieter.

"That is the kind of stupidity that gets people killed, come with me I will show you how to make them happy." Bella took Ben outside and walked him to one of the more secluded trees. He really didn't like to be near them but he was determined now to see how he was going to stop people dying. Bella looked at him and then at the tree, she told Ben that he should watch her. Bella stroked the tree and said, "We are sorry to make you angry, here is a gift to appease you," with that she took out a penknife from her pocket and in a fluid movement opened it and sliced the palm of her hand. She placed her bleeding hand on the trunk of the tree, "I appease you with my blood so you needn't take another's." She stroked the tree with her hand and then faced Ben, "That is how easy it is, but a word of warning boy the worse you are the more it takes to stop them." She wiped her hand on her trousers and just walked away leaving Ben to absorb what he had just seen. He was in a complete panic now, he didn't want anybody hurt because of him but he didn't want to cut himself either. He stared at the brownish red stain that was in a line down the bark where Bella had just stroked the tree, he was sure he couldn't do that. He very slowly and dejectedly walked back to the house and went straight to his room to try and calm himself down. He lay on his bed thinking and worrying about his friends and his family.

The time seemed to fly past and twenty minutes later Bella came into his room, she was carrying a mug. "Here is your hot chocolate." Ben was shocked he never expected anything nice from her, he sat up and said thank you. "Don't thank me, it's cold! Your mum has made you a drink and you have just left it to waste," she placed it on his side table and walked out. A few steps before she left the room she turned to face Ben again, "The trees HATE waste!" she gave him a sad look and shook her head then left. Ben grabbed the mug and drank the drink, it was disgusting with a thick film of congealed milk on the top. He gagged but continued and finished the contents. He was not going to be bad and upset them! Now Bella had made them feel better he was not going to upset them again, he did not want to have to cut himself. He lay back on his bed, he didn't feel very well now. The mix of hearing about the trees, seeing what Bella did, thinking about having to do it himself and then drinking the awful drink had set his stomach into doing cartwheels. He had heard of the term butterflies in the stomach but these were no kind of butterflies he had seen, these must have steel wings as they were bashing his belly about something horrendous. His Mum at that moment decided to call him for dinner. He really didn't feel like eating however he decided he wanted to waste food even less in case he angered them!

CHAPTER 11

Prison

Bos's health had continued to deteriorate, he was starting to look pale and the bags under his eyes were definitely more prominent. He was also getting it in the neck about budget constraints. Five days he had staff watching all 22 sites and not a sniff of any activity, nothing that could be classed as even suspect let alone someone stringing up and then carving up a person. He was going to have to cut back on the areas being watched, top brass had said one more day and then cut it back to 5 staff. Bos was sure that the murderer would not stop voluntarily. He has either been stopped by health or hindrance. Him being ill is a long shot and nothing they can do about that. The staff have not been visible enough to stop him attempting his crimes, they were there to stop him once in the act. So has he been hindered in another way, perhaps he has been arrested for something else!
"We are going to have to reduce the number of staff after tomorrow, top brass wants us down to just 5 bodies."

Del was expecting that, "Okay but we have six 10/10 sites we have to pick one of them to downgrade." They rolled out the map and went through the list. It was a difficult decision to make but in the end they reduced their Marsh lane site as it was the closest to the main road.

"Now we have that part covered, I don't think this bastard has finished killing so if he has halted it is for a reason," Bos explained the possibility of arrest. Del and Bos scoured the databases for details of arrests in all the station in their area and a little further too. It became apparent after a few hours that only 3 men had been arrested during the last five days who have been remanded in custody for that time. They presumed that if he was arrested, processed and released he would then continue to kill so the way to make him stop would be to remove him from the streets entirely, hence the remand idea. Bos called the arresting officer for each offender to gather info on their crimes. They were going to visit the men to feel out the idea of a connection. All three males were being held at Longbridge correctional facility 60 miles away on the outskirts of their police district. Martin GRIGGS, John ROLLINS and Jeff HOLLIS where the men they were going to speak to. Griggs was in for suspected rape, Rollins has stabbed an office clerk and Hollis for robbery, he had a history of breaching bale conditions. All three were of interest due to being on remand for the last five days but due to the knife being used, Rollins was the one Bos wanted to speak to most.

Longbridge was a low medium security facility. The perimeter fence was a standard red brick wall but there was nothing standard about its height, it was prominent from a distance. Outside to the brick wall a metal fence jutted out, this contained car parking facilities for around 200 visitor vehicles. At the front of this car park was a security point. The security building was white, there was a white pole barrier and under the barrier were two metal posts that lifted and dropped by the say so of the guard in the hut. Running the length of the barrier was also a strip of spikes pointing up in both directions, these raised and lowered for entry and exit also. Bos pulled up to the security box. "Afternoon, I am Inspector Boston I believe I am expected, I am here to speak to a couple of your guests." He lifted his I.D. and showed the guard.

"Hello Inspector if I give you this card it will let you into the staff car park on the right, it will give you access to the car park but you will still need to enter via the intercom." The guard was well dressed and smart and unlike some others Bos had met, he looked like he was actually doing the job he was meant to instead of watching the TV or listening to the radio. Bos took the visiting staff pass and thanked him for his help. The spikes lowered with little noise and then the poles stared to sink into the ground, the poles gave a clunk and the barrier lifted. Bos drove to the staff car park and beeped the pass across the scanner, the large gate swung open. There were a lot of cars but space for a lot more. The place was built with a larger capacity in mind, unusual but nice to see. The inspectors left the car park via a smaller gate and went to the intercom next to the main door and pressed the button. "Hello please state your name and reason for visiting," the voice that came out of the speaker was a female voice, softly spoken and quite calming.

"I am Inspector Boston, I am with my colleague Inspector Martin and we are here to speak to three of your inmates." There was a couple of seconds wait and then the door buzzed open. They entered through the door and it was a pleasant surprise that the inside was actually quite nice. It was a bit like a private doctor's surgery rather than the expected clinical type of warehouse look. They went to the reception desk to speak to the woman.

As they approached the woman looked, smiled and said, "Hello Inspectors, I will buzz you through the corridor if you go and wait in room 7 I will have your guests escorted up one at a time for you."

Both men looked shocked at how smooth this was going, "Thank you for that Miss, what should we do when finished?"

She smiled again at Bos and said, "No problem the guard will let me know when you have finished, just come to the window and buzz and I will let you back through here," she pointed to a meter square window across the room. They walked towards the door and just steps away it buzzed open.

"You have got to be shitting me, things can't be this smooth can they?!" Bos looked at Del with his left eyebrow so high on his head it was looking that at any moment it may fly off! "I have to admit I am waiting for someone to tell us we are in the wrong place." They were not in the wrong place and after 5 minutes waiting in room number 7, the door opened and a man entered with a guard walking behind him. The prisoner sat at the desk in front of the two Inspectors.

"Inspectors this is prisoner 2564748 Martin Griggs," the guard read this from a printed piece of paper that was attached to his sleeve. Bos said thank you to the guard who never acknowledged it, he just put his hands on his utility belt just near to his CS spray and watched the prisoner.

"Mr Griggs, I am Inspector Boston and I am here just to ask you a few things but first of all I want to check that you have said that you are willing to talk to me without a solicitor here with you, is that correct?"

Griggs looked up at Bos and said, "Yes, they said this ain't about the rape so I am alright with it, I ain't done nothing so its fine."

Bos continued then, "Okay thank you, this by the way is Inspector Martin he is working with me at the moment. Can you tell me where you were and what you were doing on the day and night of the 15th and 18th of this month?" Bos had his note book out and was ready to record what was said.

"Bloody hell you don't want a lot do you, Christ that was weeks ago." Bos told him that it was Friday today and the 18th was last Sunday and the 15th was the Thursday before it. "Well I ain't got a clue about the Sunday but the Thursday I know alright, at twelve o'clock I was waiting in the bloody hospital, I was getting my cast off. Four bloody hours I was waiting in that shit hole."

Bos stopped writing, "Cast! what cast?"

"My arm, I fractured my arm and I had the cast off that day, last Thursday." Griggs pointed to his heavily tattooed right arm, "See that, that is where the bone poked out," he pointed to a tattoo of a woman holding a snake and pointed to her breasts. "Look, fucking ruined her tits it did."

Bos looked across to Del and puffed his cheeks while exhaling, if this was true this is definitely not our man. "Okay thank you Mr Griggs, one last thing, what was the name of the hospital you had your cast removed in please?" It was a forlorn hope but perhaps he was lying.

"Yes sure, St Mary's in Gummerton, bloody useless place." Bos thanked the prisoner for his assistance and asked the guard for their next visitor. The guard escorted Griggs from the room and when the door was shut the words bollocks came straight out of Bos's mouth.

"If that checks out we are a suspect short then."

Bos said yes but he always pinned more hopes on Rollins than the other two, "So let's just see what the next one brings shall we?" The efficiency of the prison continued and before too long the door opened again and the same guard entered behind another male.

"Prisoner 2569437 Jeffrey Hollis." Bos again thanked the guard. This prisoner was below average height, skinny with short spikey bright ginger hair which clashed horribly with the pink prisoner overalls.

Bos came out with the same sentence he did with Griggs and this time Hollis said, "No don't need a solicitor, I won't answer anything I don't want to anyway." He was asked what he was doing on the 15th and 18th just like Griggs was but this time the answer was nowhere near as helpful, "Huh how the fuck should I know?" Del pointed out that if it helps it was last Sunday and the Thursday before that. "Again, how the fuck should I know, I am fuckin hammered most of the time, that week was a bit of a fuckin blur. Me and me bitch hit the town big time that fuckin week."

Bos's eyebrow was starting to climb again! "When you say hit the town big time, was it alcohol or narcotics and can you tell me some of the premises you frequented?" Jeff's reaction to that sentence was an absolute picture, not any type of Da Vinci or Rembrandt more like Pollock or Picasso. His features twisted with the attempt to decipher it.

Del piped in to try and stop his little brain exploding, "Was you on the booze, pills or powder and where did you go?"

"Oh fuck right, yeah all of the above but dunno where, just where the fuckin shit takes us innit?" Bos's eyebrow was now doing some kind of can-can on his forehead. It was up and down more often than a rabbit's arse.

"Okay Guard thank you for bringing us this gentleman, can we have our next one please?" The Guard left with the prisoner and the door shut behind them. Bos put his head on the desk, "Jesus if that man is our killer I'm a nun, bloody hell he has less brain cells than legs, surely it would be kinder to put him down, we do it for dumb animals that are suffering!"

Del smiled, "Trouble is I think he is happy with his life, it's the rest of us that suffer for it." Bos was dejected but still held out hope for his next visitor. True to form a couple of minutes later the guard returned with the last hope for Bos.

"Prisoner 2568453 John Rollins."

The same scenario happened as the twice before, "No I do not need a solicitor, I am fine answering your questions officers." Bos said thank you and asked him about the 15th and 18th. John Rollins was a large man, he looked fat but he was like one of those men you see on the world's strongest men competitions, look fat but can lift a bloody train! He had short dark brown hair and a voice that did not fit his looks. He had a calm well-spoken voice, "I am afraid officer that I cannot quite recall my activities from those dates, may I ask why?"

Bos at this point was interested in John Rollins, even more that he was before. "Yes you may ask, however it is unfortunate that we are not at liberty to divulge such information at present, but any help you can pass to us that could pinpoint your location on those particular dates would be very much appreciated."

Mr Rollins looked at Bos and smiled, "Well officer I would very much like to assist you in your enquiries however my location on those nights are going to have to stay pure speculation as I do not recall my whereabouts, I do apologise sir." John Rollins then stood up, "Is there anything else I can help you lovely gentlemen with, if not I shall return to my small but quaint abode and await my release which is hopefully going to be imminent? Oh and best of luck with your killer search." Before either Inspector could answer he stood and walked to the door where the guard was still watching him and stood with his back to the officers, waiting to be escorted out.

The guard looked at Bos, "Are you finished with

the prisoner?" Bos didn't say anything he just winked at the guard and nodded his head. "Thank you, I will let reception know to expect you now," with that he turned, opened the door and prisoner John Rollins walked out without any further acknowledgement of the officers he left behind.

The two inspector looked at each other and Bos smiled and said "Let's go." The reception lady was waiting to see them and as soon as they buzzed she let them through. On their way out Bos stopped at her desk, "Thank you for your help today Miss and I must congratulate you on a fantastically well organised facility." The lady beamed and thanked him. They only spoke again once securely back in the vehicle. "Two of those were a waste of time but the third! If we have no more murders while he is locked up I think we have our man, now just to prove it." Bos started the car and drove out of the staff car park.

"He definitely seems to fit the bill, cocky bastard too," Del was intrigued by Rollins but was not entirely sure he was a rip your intestines out and hang them in a tree type of guy, he felt he was more the piss me off and you will drop where you stand type of gentleman! The pass was handed back to the guard in the box and the men left to head back to their station.

CHAPTER 12

Offering

It was a couple of day after Bella had cut herself at the tree and Ben had been feeling very ill and on edge trying not to put a foot wrong anywhere. He had become very withdrawn and would spend as much time as possible in his room. Bella was still watching him at any and every opportunity. It was Wednesday and he had come home from school and went directly upstairs to his room again. After a couple of minutes Bella came in, as soon as Ben saw her he went rigid with fear as to what was coming. He was sitting on his bed, she walked towards him with purpose and menace in her eyes. His mind was racing, he had not done anything to annoy the trees, *I haven't, I haven't, I know I haven't,* he thought. *Have I?* Bella reached him and bent down towards him, she stunk of bleach and gin. "Are you trying to anger them? You are, aren't you? Boys who spend every minute of the day in their rooms are obviously either lazy or dirty!" she left this statement hanging in the air for a second and then added, "They hate lazy and dirty people, let's hope no one gets hurt because of you," she spat the word you and then stormed off. Ben was now in a state of panic he didn't know what to do for the best, tears of fear and frustration were racing down his cheeks. If he behaved as normal, he did things to upset them and now if he hid away they didn't like it. At that moment he heard a crash and a scream from downstairs. He ran out of his room and down the curved stairs. As he entered the kitchen he saw glass strewn across the floor, Bella was next to it and she was holding her right hand with her left. Her hand was covered in what looked like blood, the blood was on the floor beneath her hand too. "YOU," she shouted, "you did this." Bella looked as angry as he had ever seen her. She lifted her hand towards him, "Blood, I told you they want blood."

Ben was staring with his mouth open, tears were still running down his face but at that moment he was totally unaware of them. "I am sorry, I didn't mean to," he sobbed between the sentence.

"I told you what they want, now make up for what you did before anyone else gets hurt," she was still shouting and she again lifted her hand in the air to show him her bloodied hand. Ben could not stand it anymore he turned and ran out of the kitchen and out of the house. When he left Bella smiled and went to the sink and rinsed off the blood on her hands, there was no huge cut, no slice in the skin not even a graze. She picked up the liver she removed from the packaging and placed it on some cellophane, she wrapped it in it and placed it in the fridge. She then picked up the plastic packaging it came in and laughed to herself, "Stupid little boy, amazing how much blood you get from a liver," and she threw it in the bin. She then started humming a happy tune while she collected the dustpan and brush from the cupboard and cleaned up the glass from the floor.

Ben on the other hand was not in a good frame of mind. He had run to the tree that Bella had cut herself near. He was leaning against the tree sobbing, "I am not lazy," he stammered, "I am not dirty." He continued to sob and he continued to repeat the same thing again and again. He became very weary and tired after a few minutes of this and collapsed in a heap leaning against the tree. He had stopped crying but was still making the odd sob noise every couple of seconds. He was thinking of blood, his blood and how he was to cut himself to get it. He didn't want people hurt because of him. *I could get a knife from the kitchen, I would have to do it on a week day when mum is not cooking.* "Huh," Ben took a sharp intake of breath, "cooking, that would work." He stood up and ran back to the house. He ran into the kitchen and shouted, "Bella." Bella was just sinking another Gin at that moment and wasn't expecting him back and recovered so quickly. She hid her right hand that was obviously blood and wound free.

"What do you want boy? You scared the life out of me… AGAIN!" She shouted to try and take any thought of her previous injury away from Ben's mind, "You do not want to keep doing that… DO YOU?" She glanced out of the window in a motion at looking towards the trees.

"I am sorry but I have an idea, I thought if I get some meat from the fridge I could use that to put blood on the tree," Ben grinned with satisfaction.

Bella was actually quite impressed that he had thought of doing something very similar to what she had done. However, she certainly wasn't going to show him that. "How stupid are you, over the year with all these people getting hurt and dying, do you think we haven't tried that?" She tapped the side of her head, "Unlike you boy, the trees know what is going on and are not stupid, every time someone tries that they get angry and someone DIES!" she shouted the word dies. "Now if you are happy for people to get hurt or die because of you, just you carry on. But heed this, to appease the trees you need blood, fresh blood, anything else WILL NOT DO!" She was enjoying this again now, "Whoever gets hurt or killed now, the blood is on your hands not mine! I have lost enough," and she stormed out of the kitchen, with her glass of gin in her hand. Ben was now in turmoil once again. He thought he had the perfect solution but he could now only see one way to keep people safe.

He slowly and dejectedly walked back upstairs to his room, still sobbing occasionally. An hour went past and Ben was still wrestling with the idea of going to the tree and giving it an offering of his blood, "I need to please the trees," he stood up determined to do what he had to do. He went to the kitchen and searched the cutlery draw for a knife he thought would be best. He picked up a number of differing sized and shaped ones, some smooth, some serrated, but settled on a small basic but sharp fruit knife.

"What are you doing in here?" Ben heard Bella shout from the doorway and nearly dropped the knife as he spun round in surprise.

"I am doing what you said, I am going to please the trees."

Bella sighed, "Its appease the trees you fool, they need to be appeased, and it's about time. Do it and do it right before someone else gets hurt." Ben walked out and straight past Bella adamant in his mind that he was going to do what needed doing. He marched towards the same tree as before, his steps became slower and slower the closer he came to the tree. He reached it and outstretched his left hand, he held the knife in his sweating right hand and laid the blade across his palm. He was shaking, sweat was coming hard down his face, the effort of attempting to pull the blade to slice his own flesh was immense. His hands were shaking but try as hard as he could he could not bring himself to make the decisive motion. Ben just stood there locked in the trauma of trying to protect others by hurting himself. Again and again he tried, "Right this time 4, 3, 2, 1…" Nothing, "Okay 1, 2, 3, go." It was becoming dark and Ben had been outside standing at the tree for over an hour. His shoulders gave a huge sag and he took the blade off his palm. It had made a red line on his hand but no more than that, he walked slowly back to the house with his head as low as it could possibly be held. "I am so weak," he walked upstairs, he put the knife on his side table and climbed into bed. He was fully clothed but mentally exhausted. He slept all night but his dreams, not surprisingly, were of trees growing in blood.

CHAPTER 13

Toothcomb

Both Inspectors returned to their home station in good cheer. "Right I want to go through everything we have with a fine toothcomb to try and link John Rollins with these murders." Bos was visibly tired and looked drained but was also looking determined. Del said okay and that he thinks they should lay out in timeline style the evidence from the CSI files and any info from neighbours and witnesses. Bos checked the booking files and conference room 5 was empty, he booked it out and they started collecting everything they had on the hangings. Bos walked in the room with the first box of evidence and placed it on the table, he grabbed a white board pen and drew a line on the polished top. He then waited for thirty seconds and wiped it with his sleeve. "That's good enough for me," he walked to the right of the large table and wrote Friday 23rd April on the end of the table right in the centre. "Okay that's today and we work back from there."

"Yep okay you're the Boss er Bos," Del put the box he was carrying down and watched as Bos wrote the days and dates along the table. The dates continued to the left until the last one was the Sunday the 10th.

"This is gonna take a while," Bos said, puffing his cheeks and rubbing his chin. They started with the photographs of the first scene and placed them on the table above and below the Thursday 15th. Next were the photos from scene two, they were placed on Sunday 18th. Each piece of information gleaned was put on a post-it-note and placed along the timeline. It was slow going, they waded through file after file, house to house enquires. Statements from people, who thought they saw something. Statements from people who heard something. Even a statement from a man convinced he saw an alien land in his garden and do it. Considering he said the alien looked like Michael Jackson and had ordered him not to tell anyone, it was not considered entirely credible. Bos looked at Del, "Have you read this one? Now I could believe Jackson could have been an alien but there is no way he could have lifted our victims!" Bos put that statement away without adding a post-it-note to the timeline. After a couple of hours, the two men stepped back and looked at their work. It was a piece of art. Pictures and post-its were covering the large wooden table and each one had a line drawn on the table connecting it to a date on the timeline.

"Now that is a thing of beauty," said Del admiring the work.

"Indeed it is, I do notice one thing straight away though!" Bos turned to face Del, raised his usual eyebrow and said, "Do you think that fucking table is Oak?" Del looked back at the table and commented that it would be poetic if they put together a clue that could catch the Butcher by using an Oak table. It was starting to get late in the day and Bos was again feeling the day dragging him down as if he hadn't slept in weeks. "I need some coffee if I am going to look at this lot with my eyes open." Del said that he would get them and walked out of the room. When he came back with two coffees, Bos was still staring at the timeline. "What the hell are we missing here, is there anything else we can glean from this?" He then said thanks and took the hot coffee from Del. The men bandied a few comments like do we really think there is more than one person doing this, if so why haven't they left more evidence? They looked again at the medical and scenes of crime reports. "Due to the blood pattern we know the blood was pumping when the body was cut, this means whoever did it would be at the very least spattered with blood," Bos wrote this on the large white board in the room.

Dell added in: "The vics where hoisted up due to the lack of any stand to jump off and the position the rope was tied off, this would take quite some strength." The men continued to add lines on the board. From post mortem they knew the mouths were taped but removed later. Lack of evidence so intelligent and planned. Both male and no genital mutilation, suggesting a male perpetrator. Both victims were known by Inspector Bos as having a criminal past and a past linked with his career, so a possible punishment motive. Due to the time of death established the crimes were committed during the night. Since John Rollins had been in custody, no more victims had come to light, Rollins had a history of violence and with knives. Bos took another long swig of his coffee and then rubbed his eyes. His eyes were red and the skin around them was looking darker than they should be.

"Jesus I wish I didn't feel so crap, I can't think straight," Bos slumped down in one of the plush chairs but still looked at the table.

Del said, "The damage to the body has progressed and due to lack of evidence I suspect it is not because he was disturbed half way through," and wrote it on the board. No other links between the victims as far as we can find, was also added. Del looked at one of the pictures of the second crime scene and frowned, he picked it off the table and took a closer look. Bos was rubbing his eyes again at this moment so didn't notice but Del was now holding the one picture in his left hand and looking through the others one by one. "Gotcha, Bos what the hell is this?" Bos stirred himself from trying to clear his fuzzy head and looked up. He was shown the two pictures, they showed an area just off to the side of where the body was strung up. Both pictures had the area in the background and both were from different angles. "Look at that area there," Del pointed to a patch of grass, it had been flattened by something. It wasn't hugely noticeable but was oddly different to the rest of the foliage.

Bos looked at them, "It looks like something has been laid on the ground for a while!" He went to the pictures from the first site and started looking through them. He snatched one up and said, "Fuck me it's here too!" They looked at the pictures from both sites and the marks looked to be the same size and shape. "It's a rectangle in shape, how big do you think that is?" Bos said, as he was holding the picture from the first scene about a foot away from his face and tilting his head from one way to the other. Del said that he thought it looked about 2 meters in length and about 30 cm wide. Bos walked over to the post mortem report from the first site, "Okay Mr Broard how tall were you?" 180cm had been written, "That's about 6 foot, what about Mr Hill?" Del looked through the report on the second victim and read that he was around 166cm. "So that is about 5 foot 6ish, not a lot in it but that shape looks too long to be either of their bodies." Bos sighed and said, "That's all we need, something else we don't know about, we seem to be making more questions than we answer." He returned the picture to their places on the table. "I will see you tomorrow Del, I'm going home to see if I can get some rest." He walked away but this time not rubbing his eyes but his temples. His hands were huge and he rubbed both temples with the one hand quite easily. Del was left in the conference room holding the pictures of the first scene. He stood for a moment a little perturbed by what had just happened, he started to leave and then remembered he still had the crime scene pictures in his hand. He turned and replaced them and then left the room too. He shut the door and gently pushed across the sign to read in use, he humphed as if to say, "Well bloody hell," and slowly just walked away and left to go home too.

CHAPTER 14

A Rest

Bos left the station feeling like absolute crap, he wasn't quite sure why he had just walked out at that stage but he was definitely getting fed up with feeling so tired permanently. Now he just wanted to go to the house, curl up and sleep for a week. Then perhaps he would feel like himself again. He desperately wanted to catch the killer but felt like he was treading through treacle all the time at the moment. His journey out of the station was uneventful. Numerous people had actually spoken to him but this went largely unnoticed by Bos at this time. He approached his car and found it remarkably difficult to remove his keys out of his pocket, not to mention the altogether more targeted action of actually placing the key in the ignition. He climbed into his car and headed for home. His eyes felt so heavy, they were closing and he didn't want them to. He put the radio on and opened his window, it didn't help, the radio seemed to be in a different place. He could hear the music and the DJ but they were somehow distant. The air blowing in from the window didn't have the desired effect either, instead of keeping his eyes open he had to keep shutting them because the breeze seemed to be sucking all the moisture from them. He blinked them shut to stop them being so dry and the effort he had to use to open them again was astonishing. They closed again and he relaxed for a second. It was bliss for a short while as his eyes were telling him that they needed to stay shut, it was the best thing for him. He became light and relaxed for a short but all too brief moment. However, he was now being shaken awake. It was not shaken as if a kindly person was waking you up with breakfast in bed, this was a, "Wake up, wake up your house is on fire and you are burning," type of violence. However, it was not any person doing the shaking it was the car bouncing and bumping over the grass verges on the left. He was being thrown around like a rag doll in a running child's pocket.

Bos still only registered what was happening slowly, his hands were by his side and the steering wheel was going from one direction to another in turn with the oscillations in the grass bank. As the situation started to dawn on him he grabbed the wheel and pressed the breaks. The buffeting didn't stop immediately but did slow. He managed to stop the vehicle seemingly without any major damage to it, him or anyone else, although his neck was feeling a little achy after his head being flopped around while in his sleeping state. He puffed out his cheek and let out a huge sigh. "Fuck," was about all he could muster at that moment, his heart was thumping a beat that felt like it was about to leave his chest and bang itself on the steering wheel. He breathed in and out slowly trying to reduce his heart beat from a drum roll towards some kind of a healthier pace. It slowly became apparent that Madonna was singing on the radio, *"Like a virgin, touched for the very first time,"* came singing in his ears, after the belting heart beat that had been deafening his ears previously had abated. "You really are taking the piss, virgin, Jesus, I was very nearly fucked then!" and he lent forward and turned the radio off. He got out of the car on rather unsteady adrenalin filled legs and checked it for any terminal damage. There were a few dents and the odd clump of soil attached but other than that it seemed okay. No leaks from underneath that he could see, "Good girl, no leaks." He stood up from looking underneath the vehicle and then added, "Don't know about you but I very nearly took one!" Bos climbed back into the vehicle and strangely enough felt a little bit more awake. He started her up again and slowly pulled off the verge back onto the road.

The rest of the journey back to his house was thankfully less traumatic. He walked into his house, he walked past the picture of Helen on the wall and said, "Nearly joined you then babe." He walked straight past and went to the bedroom. He was so tired he pushed his boots off without undoing them and shuffled into the bathroom. He picked up his toothbrush and squirted a generous amount of paste over the bristles. Over the bristles was precisely what he did, he missed them and the paste went spiralling into the sink below. He squirted some more and this time a little more accurately so at least some of it hit its target. He brushed his teeth but may as well not have bothered, he was not a man in any state to do anything remotely coordinated. It looked more like a toilet brush being jiggled round a u-bend than anything resembling teeth brushing. If he was in any kind of normal frame of mind this may have been ironic enough for him to comment because he felt like shit. He finished smacking his teeth about and filled the sink with warm water. He washed his face with as much effort that he could drag out of himself, smashed himself in the face a couple of time with a towel. He then dragged himself like some sort of 1950 mummy over to his bed and just fell on to the top of the quilt. After a couple of moments, he mumbled, "No no not allowed." He fumbled around like a baby Joey trying to find its mummies pouch and eventually wriggled himself into bed and passed very quickly into a hopefully peaceful and fully rejuvenating sleep.

CHAPTER 15

Number Three

It was Saturday 24th April and it was only his second day back on shift and Bos woke up feeling worse than he had at the start of yesterday. That did not bode well for the end of the day. He dragged his feet off the bed and sat up, his arms ached, his head hurt and his eyes felt like bowling balls sat in buckets of jelly. He decided that if he had time today he would order a new mattress, perhaps he had reached the age he needed a firmer one, perhaps that had something to do with his aches and pains! Anything was worth a try. He wandered into the bathroom and stood at the toilet, he couldn't even be bothered to hold himself he just dangled and peed in the hope he hit the target. He walked to the mirror, *"Errghh,"* he made a disgusted sound after catching the first look of his reflection. He looked awful, his eyes were sunken with bags under them the same as yesterday but a little more so. His lips were dry and cracked, he stuck out his tongue and wished he hadn't, he really didn't want to stick that thing back in his mouth! He shut his eyes and turned away, "Coffee," he shuffled away from the bathroom and made his way to his kitchen. It was still tidy just not immaculate as weeks ago. There was a plate in the sink, that was something that would have been unthinkable a little while ago but now he thought he would deal with it later when he feels better. He made himself an instant coffee and shuffled out of the kitchen, past the sink with the plate in. He walked out of the kitchen and caught site of the lovely Helen on the wall. "I know, I know, I will get it later honestly. If you could see me now honey you really would be telling me off." He slumped in the chair he often slept in following the weeks after Helens death, he looked out of the window into the garden area and sighed, "Oh honey I do wish you were here." He laid his head back on the chair, "Fucking hit and run bastard," he shut his eyes and before long had nodded off.

He had a disturbing dream, he was chasing a car on foot, in the grill of the car was a rag doll. Only Bos knew the rag doll was Helen, he was chasing to try and stop her getting hurt but just could catch up. He ran and ran as fast as he could but he was getting nowhere. The car spun out and Helen came flying off the car's grill and landed on the floor. He was stood over her and could hear an ambulance coming. He instinctively knew it was an ambulance, the siren got louder and louder. It was an odd ambulance siren, it was ringing like a bell. Bos woke up at that moment and the bell from the ambulance turned out to be his home phone, he was sweating from his dream but went and answered the phone. It was Del, he had been waiting at the station and Bos had not arrived yet so wanted to call to see if he was okay. "Yes, er yes, car trouble just fixing it and I will be with you soon."

The next sentence hit Bos like a bucket of cold water, "We have another body." Bos had woken up abruptly with that and shot off to get ready. He was ready, clean, dressed and in the car within thirty minutes of the call. He was curious heading to the station, he wanted to find out as quickly as possible if John Rollins was still spending time at her Majesties pleasure. He arrived at the station and hurried to meet up with Del.

"Right sorry about that, what do we have?"

Del looked at Bos, "Bos you look like shit, how was your night then?" Bos told him that it was the same as usual but he wanted to know what was going on here. "Well I hope you are ready for this because you are not going to like it." Del then explained that they have had a call and a dog walker had found a body hanging in a tree. "It's at Oak ridge Bos!" Del cringed when he said it.

Bos was motionless, "I feel a fucking email waiting to be sent, but I will wait until I can write it calmly." Oak ridge was the 10/10 site that had staff removed due to cost implications. "Pound signs have cost us this nicking and cost some poor bastard their life," Bos wasn't shouting or throwing things about like others Del had seen in the past, he just looked extremely pissed off but determined. "Have you put a call in to see if Rollins has been released?" Bos asked.

"Yes I did, that's the other thing, he is still locked up."

"Fuck, come on let's go see what we are dealing with." Bos and Del left the station in sombre moods and didn't say too much on the journey to Oak ridge. The reason they had reduced this site from a 10 to a 9 was not that it was not a perfect site to use it was the fact that one site HAD to be reduced. The only reason for this one was that it was closer to the main road than any of the others, in all other respects this was an ideal place for the killer to use. They parked in the layby on the main road and walked up the track to Oak ridge. Oak ridge was a small wood, the name suggests it would contain a lot of Oaks but it was named a long while ago when this was the case. Now it contained just the one. It was a large one and had been there for a very long time, its trunk was one and a half metre wide. Even though it had been standing for a great many years it probably hadn't seen what it had witnessed last night before. Scenes of crime personnel were already there with their white suits, the scene had been taped off already. Bos went to the PC with a clip board and asked if he had the log, the PC handed the log and looked a little groggy, "Is this the first bloodied site you have seen?"

The PC nodded and said, "Well I have seen blood before but this is more gruesome than I was expecting to be honest." Bos handed him back the clipboard and told him that hopefully they will catch the bastard so it will be the last around here. The people in the white suits stopped their work and watched Bos. Bos looked over and noticed that the officer who got frustrated at the first scene was standing and waiting. "Morning young man, how are you this morning? Is it okay with you if my colleague and I walk down this route to the scene?" Bos moved his hand to point in a direct line straight to the tree. "Have you recorded anything yet?"

The male stuttered a little but rallied well, "Er, er yes that is fine, I have taken pictures of the path but there are no markings, similar to the first one."

Bos looked over to the tree and then quickly scanned the area. "Would you be so kind as to make sure you record that patch of grass over there please, and let me know if you find anything odd about it." Bos then walked directly to the tree. It was a disturbing site once more. Around five feet off the floor were the feet of a male, he was naked just like the first two victims. He was not tied up, he was purely being held by one single rope by his neck, his neck was consistent with a prolonged hanging, his face was too. His neck was stretched and his face was darkened by the blood that had filled it, the rope had stopped the blood from exiting the head and leaving via the other wounds. It was not a face he recognised but then again he didn't look human at the moment, he looked more like one of those Ribena characters on the TV. Bos shook that image from his head and continued to look around the scene. Blood was everywhere, the tree had the same pattern as the first two. This said that again the victim was opened up while alive, the blood had obviously pumped out and the victim writhed around while bleeding. The intestines were out again and strung up across nearby branches. There was a difference here though, the opening to remove the intestines was straight across as was the others. This victim had however been opened from the middle of that incision up to meet the chest plate. "This is getting worse each time, he has now opened his entire body up," hanging from the gaping wound were a number of organs, it reminded Bos of a piñata he had seen once. The adult had filled it with sticky sweets and had left it in a damp room. When it was smacked and burst open the sweets did not tumble out but sort of clung to each other. It looked like they wanted to stay in it. The victim would have probably felt the same, he would have preferred his organs on the inside! There was a lot of blood on the floor. Just above the floor was a crevice, Bos caught site of a glint of colour from it and bent down further to look. Inside he could see a sticky red lump. "What the fuck is our bloke up to now?!" Bos stood up and looked around. He saw who he was after, "Bud when you are done can you make sure you pay special attention to the gap under this tree?" Bud did his usual and just stuck his thumb in the air as acknowledgement. Bos then turned his attention back to the other young man, "Have you found anything over there?"

The male came over with a small clear plastic bag. "I have actually and it is a little odd, I have found fibres from a carpet in amongst the grass that you pointed out. It was difficult to find and hard to see the flattened part of grass but it is definitely there and nowhere else." He held up the bag with a few small pieces of material in.

Bos lifted his large hand and started scratching his chin, "Mmm okay thank you, what is your name by the way? Can't keep calling you young man." The new forensics man told Bos that he was Steve. Steve turned away and walked back to what he was doing. "Carpet in the middle of a crime scene!" Bos wasn't saying that to anyone in particular but thinking out loud. Bos decided to go to a local café for some food and have a think. "Have you had anything to eat yet, how about going to the café for a bite of breakfast and a think?"

Del wasn't a greasy café type of person and had had his cornflakes this morning, "Okay I will have a coffee but no food." The Road Side Diner was a café for truckers and taxi drivers but Bos had been known to pop in on the odd hungover days and he liked it. If asked he would not be able to say why, it was run by a man who looked more Michelin man than cooked Michelin stars. If he was asked if he had ever heard of cleanliness Brian behind the counter would be asking where in Scotland it was.

They walked in and Bos sat straight down and shouted across the room to the man behind the counter, "Full breakfast and two coffees please Brian."

Brian said, "Right you are Bos."

Bos asked Del what he thought about the carpet fibres. "It's an odd one isn't it, mixed with the 2m length flattening I presume the only explanation is a carpet being laid down there but why a carpet is beyond me!" Del shrugged his shoulders and then was about to put his hands on the table but thought better of it and just put them on his lap. Bos was thinking the same thing, he didn't know why a carpet would be placed next to each kill site. "What about a prayer matt?" said Del, "I mean it seems very ritualistic, the killings, perhaps it has religious connotations." Bos said that is it was a good thought but prayer mats are not usually 2m long. They spoke about if they thought the carpet was there for the killings or for something before it.

"I think the carpet was there for the killing, whatever the carpet is for it was not there for a long time otherwise the grass would have started to yellow and it would not recover at that speed. After a little while you can hardly tell the ground had been flattened at all." Del just *mmm-ed* in acknowledgement. Brian brought over the coffees and told Bos that his breakfast would be ready very soon. The two men took their mugs and held them and pondered for a little while. Brian was true to his word and it wasn't long before he was back with the food for Bos. When Brian did a full breakfast he meant it, bacon, eggs, tomatoes, sausages, fried bread, beans, mushrooms, black pudding, pigs in blankets, toast and hash browns. The plate was bursting and Bos then added the cherry on the top, well tomato on top, what looked like a bottle of it, ketchup.

"Bloody hell Bos, we just left a site like that!"

Bos ignored that and tucked in. "I feel like crap, I am ridiculously tired still, I ache and my eyes feel like they have had a blow dry. I am hoping this will get me going a bit." As soon as those words had stopped a sausage filled the void the words left! "Kill or cure hay!" Del watched as Bos ploughed through the assault on his arteries.

Just as Bos was about to put another forkful in his mouth, Del grabbed his arm and stopped him shouted, "Fuck, fuck, look what you are eating."

Bos move his fork away from his mouth and twisted it round for a 360 degree view, "Yes it's a sausage in bacon, so, you gone all vegan on me?"

Del took the fork off him and grabbed the knife

too. "Look," said Del, "remind you of anything?" He put the pig in blanket on the table and unrolled the bacon, he then put the bacon to one side "How about pig in carpet?! We wondered how the person got there without a struggle, Jesus you can't struggle wrapped in a carpet." Bos was impressed, he said nice one, and picked up the pig and ate it. Del cringed and said, "I have seen some horrible things today Bos but that was fucking disgusting."

CHAPTER 16

A Replacement

Ben awoke on the Thursday morning and got straight out of bed, he had been through another night of frightening dreams. He had to get ready for school but he would please those tree later, he had to. He collected his usual plain bread sandwiches from the lovely Bella before he left to catch the bus to school. She told him again that he was a horrible boy and didn't deserve anything else, "You need to do your duty and keep your family safe, you will regret it if you don't boy. Mark my words." He walked away without saying anything, which led to Bella adding, "Ignorance, they hate that too." Ben thought that he could have said something but she would have said something horrible to that too, like talking back to elders and betters or something. He trudged off slowly to the bus with what seemed like the weight of the world on his shoulders. The day at school was rather uneventful, he disliked school but at the moment school was a happy release from the horrors at home. Before too long the bell for the end of the day had sounded and he was once again heading home. *At least the weekend is nearly here and I can see mum and dad.* He hadn't decided if he was going to go straight up to his room or try and go to the tree right away. He decided as he walked towards the front door that he would go to his room first. He got changed and sat on his bed. Bella came rushing up the stairs, "Come with me boy, I can help you." Ben doubted very much that she would help him but went with her. She walked down and out of the house and headed for the rear of the house. After a minute or so she reached a little shed that Ben knew housed the gardening tools. Bella creaked open the dirty looking door and went in, it was dark and smelt of damp but she soon came out holding a spade. "Come with me," she was off again at quick pace towards one of the horrible type of trees. "Look, look there," she pointed at a rabbit near to the tree. The rabbit was still but had its eyes open. "This can help us all boy, that rabbit is sick and in pain, the trees need appeasing and you need to protect your family," she went on to say that she has never known it before but perhaps it could work. "Kill the rabbit," she handed him the spade, "Kill it and wipe its blood on the tree." She pushed him towards the rabbit that still didn't move.

"I can't do that," Ben shouted in horror.

"You must, go on, go on boy. Do you want me to get hurt again? Or your mum or dad what if they are hurt next?" Bella was starting to get louder and more agitated. Her eyes were wide and she had started to dribble and spit. "You need to stupid selfish boy," she pushed him closer towards the rabbit.

He started to panic, "What is wrong with it?"

"It is dying, it is in pain you need to help it, do it DO IT." After this outburst Bella went quiet, she held the spade in Bens hand and said, "Look you just need to lay the spade on the rabbit here," she moved the blade of the spade over the top of the rabbit's neck, "and you put the handle here." She placed the handle of the spade under Ben's belt and she let go. "AND THEN YOU JUST DO IIITT!" she shouted. She pushed Ben from behind and he fell forward. The creature made no sound apart from the crunch as the blade of the spade parted the rabbits head from its torso. Ben felt the force on the handle change as it parted the rabbit and sunk into the soil. Bella screeched with pleasure and shouted, "Now spread it on the tree." Ben was frozen, he had just killed a rabbit, he had never hurt anything before let alone kill something but now he had chopped an animal's head off. Ben was sick, he bent over and vomited in disgust at what had just happened. "You fool, come on you killed it. You need to appease the trees now otherwise you killed it for nothing!" Bella bent down and picked up the rabbit's head by its ears, she thrust it toward ben and he pushed it away. The poor animal was being flung around like some sick hammer throw and blood was still draining from its head. She grabbed his hand and placed the head in it, not getting him to hold its ears she placed the rabbits severed neck right in the palm of Ben's hand. He was revolted, it felt like warm jelly, he threw it and it bounced off the tree leaving a spatter mark on its trunk. "Yes now wipe your hand on the tree." She didn't have to tell him that part twice, he ran to the tree and rubbed his hand with the blood on down the trunk. He did this about three times and then ran.

"You did it, you did it. Killer!" Bella shouted this to him as he ran towards the house, she was absolutely ecstatic. Her plan had come off perfectly. The rabbit was not sick at all, she had caught it in a trap and then sedated it and tied it to the floor just in case it tried to move. She will take great delight in telling him that at a later date. That will be a fun day. Bella looked around to see where the head had landed and picked it up. She then grabbed the torso and yanked it up from the floor. All four legs were tied to a stake in the ground. As she pulled it there was a slight crack and one of the legs had broken. She looked at the body and found the leg that had snapped, she held it in her other hand and pulled violently. The leg detached and Bella giggled, "Oh lucky rabbits foot," and put it in her pocket. She picked up the spade too and left to put the spade away and cook the rabbit. "A sedative won't do him any harm, stupid boy."

Ben had run upstairs to his room and was franticly washing his hands. He was sobbing while he was doing it. "I killed it, I killed it," he repeated this while washing. He washed and washed but all he could see was his hand covered in the blood of the rabbit he had just decapitated. Tears were rolling down his face, he could still feel the sensation of the spade slicing through the poor animal. He could still feel the warmth of its blood on his hand. He glanced down and on his shoes he could see blood, he bent down and took them off and put them in the sink. He washed the blood off his shoes too, he didn't want any trace of the thing he had just done. He could wash the blood from his hand, from his trainers and from his cloths. The rain will wash the blood from the tree, but how is he ever going to be able to erase the awful memory of seeing its head part and roll away and knowing that he did it?

CHAPTER 17

Writing on the Wall

Bos finished off his breakfast with the last slurp of coffee. "Feel any better?" Del was looking across the table amazed that anyone could eat that much crap, let alone feel better after it.

Bos said a bit and then picked up his phone and dialled. "Hello Nick can you talk?" Del heard a muffled reply but could not make out what was said. "A few questions for you," again some more muffled words, "Are you still in traffic? Do you have a lantern with you? And are you near Oak Ridge?" There was a bit more spoken and then Bos said, "Great could I meet you at the ridge in about ten minutes, there is a crime scene there that I want your help with." He then said thanks and hung up. Del didn't say anything, he just tilted his head in a request to be told. "I have just asked an old colleague of mine if he would meet us at the crime scene. I am thinking if this victim is anything like our others he is going to have a criminal past. If he has, he will be on our database. I am going to get Nick to run our vics prints through lantern and see if it is a hit." Lantern was the mobile fingerprinting machine that some traffic cars carried around with them. It could take a print and check the database for a match within moments. Bos stood up and walked over to the counter, "Thanks Brian, tasty as ever."

"No problem Bos, always good to feed the boys in blue, never know when you will need their help, 4 pound please."

Del looked across, "Is that the weight of fat in it or the cost?" Bos smiled and told Brian to ignore his pasty vegan friend and gave him a fiver and said not to worry about the change.

"Thanks Bos, vegan hay, bloody hell if I had known I would have put a nice fluffy cushion down for the delicate little flower. Never know when these vegans will keel over from malnourishment."

Del shook his head, "I am not a bloody vegan, I just don't like the look of that fucking health hazard!" It was all said in good humour and they were all smiling, Bos added that it would put meat on his bones, as they walked out Del opened the door and it creaked loudly. "Did you hear that creak, it wasn't the door you know that was your arteries groaning!" Bos walked through the door and Del followed and gave a friendly salute type wave to Brian as he did so. They waited in the car in the layby near Oak Ridge and soon enough a traffic patrol car pulled up. It parked up behind the *Nissan* and Nick stepped out of the driver's side. Nick was one of those policeman you look at and think, if all coppers looked like that we would have virtually no crime. He was big, not fat just big. It was amazing that he fitted in the patrol car, he was 6 foot 7 and looked just as wide.

"Hello Bos, haven't seen you in a while. What is going on that you need the help of a humble traffic cop?" His voice was straight out of a film trailer, if it was any deeper you would need deep sea diving gear just to listen to it.

Bos went over and shook his hand, "Good to see you again, how is Terry?"

Nick told him that his wife and kids were fine, "Kids are getting big now."

Bos laughed, looked him up and down and said, "I bet they bloody are." Nick stuttered a bit and told Bos that he was sorry to hear about Helen and that she was a lovely lady. Del saw Bos's face drop, he looked bad enough before but what colour was in it seemed of fade away.

"Thanks, it's not been a good time, I, well you know!" his voice became quieter and quieter as the sentence progressed.

Del spoke up, "Nice to meet you Nick, have you got lantern with you?"

Nick turned, said he had and collected it from the car, "What's up then?" Bos had recovered quickly and spoke to Nick briefly about the case and the situation about wanting a quick I.D. The three men walked towards the area where the body was hanging. The body was still hanging and from a distance with his intestines coming out in different directions and looping around the branches he looked a bit like a spider sitting waiting for a snake to land. "Jesus someone did a real number on him didn't they?!" said

Nick, as a traffic officer he had seen his fair share of bloodied and twisted scenes but none of his were deliberate mutilation. This on the other hand was done with gruesome precision.

They walked to the PC holding the scene log. "Nick you log in and get his print, we don't need to go near again." Nick told Bos that it was fine and it wouldn't take long. Nick signed the form and ducked under the tape, a feat in itself, the size of the man. He walked over to the pendulum gently swaying in the tree, he took out his lantern machine and fiddled with it for a while. Bos saw him hold the man's index finger on his right hand and look at it. He let it go and came walking back, "Has anyone got a wipe or something? he has blood all over his hands and I want a clean print."

The PC with the clip board pulled out a small pack of wet wipes from his pocket and saw the looks the other men gave him, "Never know what you could come across as a PC, best be prepared!" Bos looked impressed and nodded agreeably. Nick took one wipe said thanks and walked back to the body. He wiped the one fingertip and pressed it on the screen.

While they waited Bud came over, "Bos,I have had a look at your hole." Bos raised an eyebrow. "Don't be daft, look," said Bud holding up an evidence bag. Inside it was a heart, "This I believe was removed from our victim and squashed into the hole under the tree, it has all been documented and will be in the report, just thought I would tell you as you are here." Bud turned and walked away.

Bos shouted his thanks to the retreating Bud. "What the fuck is our bloke up to?" Moments later

Nick was walking back. "Well?" Bos was impatient to find out if they had a hit.

"You were right he is known and known well."

Bos nodded with pleasure, "Okay spill the beans, who is he then?"

Nick said the name and all three men said, "What?"

"Yes you heard me right, that thing swinging up there is Tony Malino, the best known fucking dealer we couldn't catch," said Nick looking back to the corpse.

"Someone caught him," Del knew of him too, most police staff did.

Bos was in thought, "This is the third victim who is known to me, this one muddies the water slightly as he is known to everybody, but still a little perturbing. Has it got an address for us?" Nick went over the radio and asked for an up to date address check on our system and on the voters' register. Both came back with the same address, 29 Stevenage Road. Bos shook Nicks hand and thanked him for the help. They all walked back to the end of the track and Nick went to his patrol vehicle and the other two went to the *Nissan.*

"Right let's see what is waiting for us at 29 Stevenage Road." They arrived at number 29 and it was a nice road with some lovely houses, 29 was one of them.

"See what crime can do! And they say it never pays," Del shook his head when saying it but Bos turned to face him.

"Well yes but would you want to swap with Tony Malino now? He didn't look well to me, lost a lot of weight I thought particularly around the middle! Come on," Bos walked towards the front of the house smiling and Del followed a little shocked but amused. The house was beautiful. It had a huge lawn immaculately kept, perfectly manicured shrubs lining the white concrete looking walls. The windows were large and circular, it reminded Bos of a Mediterranean style property. The front door was a large double solid wood, dark wood with patterns engraved in it. The patterns were not glued on, they were carved into the wood. This was expensive, the doorbell was a posh one too, it was a chrome ball, under it had a small sign saying pull for assistance. Del nudged Bos before he gave it a pull, "Whats up?" Del pointed to the pretty house frame that was hanging on the wall next to the door. It was a white house shape with hand painted flowers all around it. In a square in the middle was written in fancy swirling writing 'Home is where the heart is.'

Del said, "Shall I write that it's under a fucking tree!"

Bos smiled and said, "Possibly not," he pulled on the bell and waited. It wasn't long before a female opened the door. She had dark brown hair that had been scrapped back into a tight ponytail, she was plastered in makeup, so much she looked a little orange and she had a young child on her right hip.

"Yeah what?" a voice like that really didn't belong to a house like this.

"Sorry to bother you madam but could we speak to Mr Malino please?" Bos was politeness personified.

"No, well you could but the son of a bitch ain't come home yet, out all fucking night again… out with another slag of his I reckon, dirty bastard." The voice could grate cheese thought Del.

"We are both police Inspectors, are you his next of kin?" Bos asked.

"Next to his what? Kin! What's a fuckin Kin?" The woman was pure class, she was frowning as if he had asked her the meaning of life, and chewing gum with a mouth so wide it reminded Bos of watching a washing machine with one garment in it.

"Are you a relative of Mr Malino?" Bos spoke this time quite slowly, he thought that if he spoke too quickly surely her little brain would explode with the attempt to decipher his words!

"Relative, no fuck off, I'm his wife."

"Wife?" asked Bos.

"Yeah I am Latisha and this is his son little Milo." Bos could feel Del's look and took a glance over to him. *I wish I had a camera for that,* he thought. Del was not moving a muscle but his mouth was open and he had the best look of shock, horror and amusement Bos had ever seen.

Bos said "Erm Milo? Milo Malino?"

This question went straight over her head and she just answered with, "Yeah ain't he lovely bless him."

"Could we come in and have a chat with you please? We have some rather distressing news," Bos now wanted to get in, look about and then get out before he wanted to strangle her. Del on the other hand was transfixed, he was amazed that anyone with that fewer brain cell could actually walk at all, let alone walk, talk and breathe at the same time. She ushered them into the lounge area, the house was perfect it was like something out of L.A. "Please sit down Mrs Malino, I have some bad news for you about Tony," Bos motioned with his hand for her to sit down.

"What's he fucking done, if he has been nicked I'll kill him," she continued to chew her gum as if her life depended on it.

"I am sorry to have to tell you this but he is dead, we believe he was murdered last night." Latisha didn't say anything, she did thankfully stop chewing. "Do you know where your husband was last night?" Bos waited for a response and meanwhile wrote on his hand, *call for a liaison officer* and showed it to Del. Del excused himself from the conversation and walked a few paces away and called headquarters. Bos continued to try and get some information from Latisha but she had shut down. He got that he was at the lockup and that she was okay if they looked around but that was all. Once Del was off the phone, Bos told him to look about the place while he stayed with Mrs Malino, "Just have a look about, you know what we are after." Del did know, he was after any kind of message written by the killer. He looked around the house and found absolutely nothing out of place, it was immaculate. He thought quite cynically that, *the cleaner does a good job, no way does Mrs Malino do this, I would be surprised if she could tie her own shoes.* Del walked into the lounge and noticed that a female PC was sitting next to the wife now, he looked around and caught site of Bos standing near the front door. As Del looked over, Bos gave him a jog of the head to say come on let's go. They walked out and walked back to the car.

"Well that was a joy, pity I am married I could go for an intelligent woman like that!"

Bos agreed and said at least she has money and seemed happy enough. "Did you find anything?"

Del shook his head, "No not a thing, I looked everywhere but Bos that place was polished from top to bottom, no one has been in there."

The engine started and then pulled away, "Right one more place to look then, she gave me his spare keys and said I can look around the lockup." Bos had a huge grin on his face. He suspected for years that his lock up garage was where he dealt his drugs but they could never find enough evidence for a search warrant. Now he didn't need one, he had permission. The garage was a lockup in a low run down place in the city under an underpass. It was an industrial estate that had seen better days. Mr Malino's was the same as the myriad of others. His unit was in the middle of a row of around seven. They had heavy duty metal shutters from top to bottom and a small door in the bottom left that could open to let people in. Bos parked in front of the large shutters. "These are not easy to break into." Bos and Del left the car and walked the few metres to the small door. "This does not look good," the door was not locked, it was not even shut. It just opened with a push. There was no way that Tony would leave this unlocked let alone open. Bos took a step in through the door, it was dark, only a strip along the side was lit up with the small amount of light coming in through the open door. It was not exactly bright around this place so there was even less that wanted to stray into this dusty lockup. "I need a torch before I go snooping around in here," Bos took the step back out and went to the car. He had a torch with him but only one. "I only have the one so I will let you wait at the door," Bos smiled and winked at Del when he said that. Del tutted with his head and rolled his eyes. The first step was taken again, he flicked his torch on that lit up a single thin stream of light. It was still dark everywhere apart from the one strip of light.

"What the bloody hell kind of torch do you call that?! Jesus Christ you look like a fucking FBI agent in a film, if I had known you was a wannabe FBI agent I would have called you mouldy," Del was standing at the door taking the piss while Bos eyed up the lockup. It was a standard garage set up with a car lift and work benches but as his torch passed across he noticed that there were no tools anywhere.

"What kind of garage has no tools in it?!" He continued round the edge of the room and still the place was empty of anything. His torch suddenly highlighted an office in the far right corner. He aimed his beam at the door, it was shut at least. Bos stepped over to it and opened it, he highlighted the office with his light. It was a 6 foot by 8 foot room, it had a shelf with cupboards underneath running the length of the right wall. It had small scales on the shelf and behind them was a large safe sat in plain view. He opened one of the draws and inside were boxes and boxes on clear plastic bags. He opened the cupboard and whispered, "Holy shit, I knew it." Inside were around 5 large sealed bags and one open one. They were around the size of a bag of flour, they also contained some white powder but you wouldn't want this in your cakes. He continued and in another draw he found 10-20 of the clear plastic bags, this time containing some of the powder from the large ones. On each bag was written 'C ten grams.' It was written in a black marker pen.

Bos turned to walk out and caught a glimpse of some writing on the left wall. He was so excited by the other find, he had almost forgot what he was actually looking for. He read what was on the wall, "Placare arbores. The blood of the innocent will be shed no more. They are watching the many, while I watch you. P.S. don't feel bad for missing me at the ridge Bos man." It was signed Justice. "Holy fuck," he walked out stunned and went to meet Del who was patiently waiting at the door. "Call for crime scene investigators," Bos walked straight past Del and went and sat down in the car.

Del came and sat too. "What the hell was in there? You look a bit shocked."

Bos looked over at his colleague, he felt very tired again all of a sudden, "We are being watched, this bastard knows what we are doing." Bos then told Del what was written on the wall in the office.

"What the hell does that mean they are watching the many while I watch you?" Bos shook his head, he had been thinking the same thing. He hadn't a clue what that part meant but he definitely didn't like the part about them missing him and him knowing it. Bos was feeling poorly again now, the day was not over and he was knackered. He rubbed his eyes and felt his head, it had started to pound. This was not normal, was the case getting to him or was it something more sinister? He needed to see a doctor. Bos heard a sound but didn't react, he was miles away. "Well?" Del had asked a question but Bos was just sitting rubbing his temples.

"Sorry what?"

Del asked him again, "I said did you find any carpet that may have been used?"

Bos snapped out of his own thoughts, "Oh er... no, I couldn't really search properly with just the torch." He rested his head on the steering wheel to try and stop his head thumping. It didn't work! He got out of the car and just started walking around, he thought if he focused on the job in hand perhaps that will ease it. "Right who the hell could be watching us? Who knew about us leaving the ridge unguarded?" His head felt like it was in a vice but he tried to push through it.

"Us, high brass, the PC's on patrol at the sites and let's face it they wouldn't keep it to themselves unless asked so everyone in our nick and their families," Del continued, "and well anybody they may tell, so anybody really!"

Bos looked over and said that from now on they need to put the word out that it is a need to know operation. "If someone wants to try and keep an eye on what we are doing let's make it as difficult as possible so they may slip up."

As the two were running through their conversation, the CSI unit arrived, "Morning Bos, what have we got here?" It was Bud who said this as he climbed out of the white scenes of crime van.

Bos told him what they had, he explained about the house search having shed no light so they had permission from the wife to come and look through his work unit. "Inside I found very little activity of any mechanic work having taken place, however there is a vast amount of what I presume to be cocaine in the office in the corner. Also in the office is a note written on the wall from the oak tree killer, it is written directly to me!" Bud was on his own here at the moment as the rest were still at the scene of the murder. "Bud you need to have someone else with you there is no way you should be going in there on your own!"

Bud looked at the men with slight confusion, "Why the killer ain't still in there is he?" he smiled.

Bos told him about the drugs and the safe, "I am just presuming that with the quantity of drugs in there that safe is likely to have a fair bit of cash in it." Bud understood then and said he would wait and call up for another pair of hands. Bos went back to the car and started its engine. Once Del had got in too, he reversed to leave, "We are going back to the station to update our timeline." While back at the station the inspectors added post it notes on the 24th for the new site on the ridge and notes for the lockup and home address. They also added notes about the carpet and the notion of wrapping the body to keep them still.

Del looked at the last entry about the carpet, "I wonder if it is a carpet from each site or he has his own! It seems a regular size in all scenes so I presume it's his own, what do you think?" Del turned to Bos, "Fuck me you look like shit Bos."

"Yeah thanks for that, good, I would hate to feel

like this but look like my usually lovely self." He rubbed his eyes and tried to focus but he was finding that quite difficult.

"Well we have put in a good few hours today, why don't you go home and get some sleep?"

Bos thought about it and he wouldn't normally even contemplate going at this stage but at this point he was starting to feel if he didn't lay down he would fall. "I think I will actually do that, my head feels like I have been hung in a tree, before I go I need to make one call." Bos picked up the phone and dialled an internal number. He waited a while and then spoke, "Hello sir, Bos here I need the 22 men back," he waited a while, "I know the cost sir but this bastard is watching us and I don't want another corpse in a tree, this son of a bitch is hanging people up like baubles on a fucking Christmas tree and we are just pussy footing around letting him. I want to stop this fuck before he tries it again and he will try again I guarantee it," again it went quiet for a while then Bos just put the phone down. "We had better catch this sick bastard soon, I have just had permission for the 22 men to be reposted to all sites."

Del was impressed "For how long?" Bos told him that he hadn't got a clue but it won't take long before the big nobs start to feel a twinge in their wallets. He left but only after he asked if Del could make the call to recall the men and to make it secret squirrel time. He walked slowly out of the station and got into his car, he didn't want to leave so late that he was in danger of crashing his car again.

CHAPTER 18

The Kill

Norman Dale was not very nice, in fact he was a real nasty piece of work. He ran a dog fighting arena. He fronted this business as being a dog breeder. From outward appearances everything was as it should be, nice house, good kennel facilities and good healthy animals. But that was the front, in the rear was the arena and that was a different atmosphere altogether. It was dark, damp, dirty underfoot and stunk of sweat, urine and faeces. This was where he made his money. He was a small man but had a patience to match and he had a cruel streak that could have gone round a dozen men and would still have made them all bastards. In fact, you couldn't really say he had a cruel streak, he was cruel to the core. He enjoyed watching the hell that is dog fighting and he would do anything to make it more of a spectacle. If he thought a match was unequal he would think nothing of ripping out a few claws before the match, he would think nothing of smashing a few teeth to even them up a bit. If he thought that wouldn't even things up, he would throw two in to one. If he thought that a fight was dragging on and was making the crowd go quiet, he had been known to replace both dog and shoot them on the spot in the ring. He ran it with people who bought their own dogs to fight but also ran fights for 'amusement' at the breaks between what he classed as the professional fights. For these he would use his dogs that didn't sell, the runts, the lame and the old, he would even nick dogs from people. If he saw a dog that would be entertaining, he would go all out to get it. He had been arrested in the past but that was when he just ran the fights. Now he uses his breeding facility as a front, the law agencies could never seem to nab him.

Norman or Norm to his friends, most others referred to him as the dog man, was just cleaning the arena before he went in for the night. It was 01:30, a long night. He had just thrown the body of a ravaged boxer dog into one of the large wheelie bins, it was bleeding profusely from all manner of wounds. It had collapsed and given up after a good effort. At the end of that fight it was taken out and thrown to one side. He had put up a decent fight considering he had his teeth smashed out before being put in with the poodle, particularly as the poodle had metal claws strapped to the bottom of his legs so it could inflict serious damage. He threw it unceremoniously in the skip without even checking to see if it was still alive, it had served its purpose and entertained the crowd for a while. He collected his takings and was counting it as he left the arena. *Not a great night but had worse*, he thought to himself, *nearly four grand.* He had spent about an hour clearing up and it was only now that he had unlocked the takings tin and counted it.

He walked towards the door at the far end of the arena that led to his home. It was a large place and since his girlfriend left he had it all to himself. She had got fed up with the prostitutes he ordered on a regular basis and had left. He walked into his house and an arm came from behind him and he had a cloth smashed into his face, it covered his nose and mouth and reached his eyes too. Struggle as he might, he couldn't get out of the vice like grip. He tried to shout but the cloth was pressed too hard. He started to feel light and see the blackness, he had been knocked out by the chemical on the cloth. The attacker laid him gently on the ground. The assailant walked away for a moment and then returned carrying a large purple and blue plaid rug. He was wearing a white paper suit. He placed the rug to Norman's side and unravelled it. He then got a plastic sheet and covered the rug with the plastic. The large man picked Norman up as if he was a twig on the floor and placed him on the rug so his mouth and nose were just above the edge and he rolled him. He rolled him tight until the entire rug was wrapped around the hapless fellow inside. He nonchalantly walked away and came back with some cable ties. He placed five ties at equal distances over the rug and pulled them all tight. Norman was not going anywhere, he then placed some tape over his mouth and again just casually walked away. The man went into the arena and walked over to the chalk board that was near the main ring, he was wearing cream coloured disposable gloves and he picked up the gloves and wrote, *'Bos man you will not stop me, you cannot stop me. Placare arbores. I like Oak but that is not the only tree. Sorry to pull my rug from under your feet,'* he threw the chalk down and walked back into the main house.

He shut the door and went back to the rolled up Norman. In one easy motion he picked the carpet up with the body in and threw it over his wide shoulders. He walked with the same easy pace out of Norman's place to his car that was waiting, he clicked open the boot and placed the carpet in.

The vehicle drove to a quiet local wood not far from the scene of horrific dog fighting. He parked close by and exited his car. He walked calmly to the rear of the car and picked up the carpet with Norman rolled in it. He took it over to near a large chestnut tree and laid it down on the grass close to it. In the car was rope, this was collected and hooked around the shoulder of the large man. He climbed nimbly up the tree and got high very quickly. The rope was taken off and looped over a thick high branch and both ends were dropped down to the floor. The man climbed effortlessly down in a fluid motion, he expertly looped a noose on one end of the rope. The rope was adeptly placed around the neck of the man in the carpet, it was loose enough so as not to strangle him but tight enough so it wouldn't come off. The cable ties were cut and placed carefully in his pocket. The next act took an enormous amount of strength but it was made to look effortless. The carpet was picked up and put on one shoulder, the great man took the other end of the rope and pulled until the slack was no more. The carpet was lowered and the rope pulled until the body exited the carpet. The body was lowered until its feet hit the floor. Norman just swung there, his breathing becoming difficult as the rope held him up by the neck. The carpet was placed back on the grass and the end of the rope tied to another tree to keep the body hanging at the right height. He walked back to Norman and took a small fruit knife out of his pocket. He sliced through all the clothes that Norman had on him, every so often he would slap Norman gently on the face.

Once he was naked and his clothes were in a pile on the carpet, Norman woke up. This was the time where Norman could hold his own weight so he stood to take the pressure off his neck. His hands went to his neck to release the rope. The knife reached his throat before his hands. "Remove the rope and I remove your Adam's apple and hang it in the tree." Norman stopped immediately and mumbled something under his taped mouth. His tape was removed in one clean swipe of the captor's large hand.

"W-what the fuck do you want?"

"I want to stop the blood, I want to stop the hurt, I need to appease the trees."

Norman was swaying "What the fuck are you talking about you mad bastard?"

The large man came up close to him, "You are scum, you need to bleed so others can feel free." Just as Norman was about to speak again tape was put over his mouth. Norman had fear in his eyes. The killer went to the end of the rope that was tied to the tree and undid it. He walked slowly to Norman all the while keeping the rope taught. Norman was trying to back away now but the more effort he put into trying to walk backwards, the more pressure was put on the rope to stop him. He was starting to panic now and was finding it a struggle to breath. He came in close and in a quick motion he slacked the rope and twisted the knot so it was at Norman's chin and then *bang* he lifted it as fast as he had slackened it. He could breathe properly but his head was pushed right back by the rope leading off the knot. Norman was pulled up three foot off the floor and started to writhe in panic to try and escape. The killer took his fruit knife and cut across Norman's abdomen. He didn't see the cut coming but felt the white hot pain as his skin was sliced through. He was pulled up as he writhed in agony and panic. He knew it hurt but did not know the full extent of his injury. Higher he was pulled and the juddering of the rope was pulling at his belly. Norman couldn't have realised that the pulling pressure on his stomach was his intestines tumbling out and bouncing like some awful bungee rope for an action man. If Norman had witnessed this, his end would have come a lot quicker than it did. He had started to feel light, not because of his insides tumbling but due to the loss of blood. All his effort so far was to release the rope from around his neck. All pain had stopped, he was just feeling a little cold around his midriff. He put his hands down to his stomach. It reminded him of collecting the dogs after a particularly gruesome fight. His stomach was wet and didn't seem to be the smooth six pack it should be, it now felt like it was all happening to someone else. He slowly lost consciousness and died.

He was lowered and his stomach was opened up to his chest. The intestines were taken slowly and hung around and looped on branches nearby. His chest was opened and his heart cut out. The heart was placed on the floor near a slit in the base of the tree. Then the knife was placed near Norman's nose and thrust into his face under his eye. His eyes were plucked out of his skull and were both impaled on to small branches close to the trunk. The murderer then went back to what used to look like Norman Dale and sliced his ears off as easy as removing the rind off some old cheese. These were skewered on to other protruding branches. Norman had his tape removed from his mouth and was then raised high in the tree like some kind of pirate flag. "Placare arbores. You are the blood for the tree, may you release the pain and the injustice, Take the blood and free me." The killer turned, dropped something on the floor and strolled over to the grass and collected the clothes that had been worn by Norman Dale. He also grabbed the carpet and plastic Norman had been wrapped in and continued to walk slowly towards his parked vehicle. He placed the items in the boot and then climbed into the front of the car. He opened his window, threw something, and then casually drove away.

CHAPTER 19

Another Morning

Bos opened his eyes, "Oh for fuck sake," he had slept right through but felt no better at all. He tried to lift his head from the pillow but it felt like it weighed far too much. He lifted his right arm that ached like a bitch and felt his eyes. He somehow expected them to be sticking out because they felt three times the size as usual. He groaned and sat up, "This is no good." Bos felt like he needed a good night's sleep, every sound seemed amplified in his head. He struggled to the bathroom and hesitated to look. Did he really want to see what it was he looked like? Outwardly, he looked similar to what he had done the last few days, like crap but he hadn't got any worse, he felt it, he felt like he had aged about 25 years. He stood there staring into the eyes of a man he didn't recognise as the man from last year. Last year things were perfect, he had the job, the home, the car and most importantly the woman of his dreams. Now he had a car that reminded him of the woman he doesn't have anymore, a house that used to be his home and a job that he used to be in full and emphatic control of but he felt slipping away with every passing day and every passing kill of the oak killer. He walked still naked across the bathroom towards the shower. He stood in the shower to try to feel human enough to move elsewhere.

After 5 minutes of alternating the shower from hot to cold, Bos gave up. He walked solemnly out of the shower; he put his dressing gown on over his dripping body and went to make a coffee. His wet feet left a damp footpath out of the bathroom towards the stairs and down. They diminished the closer he got to his destination. He flicked the kettle on and waited. He bent down and leant his head on the dark marble top, it felt cool on his head. The feeling was strange, he liked the cool feel but the hard surface put him on edge. He stood up once again and let out a sigh from the depths of his soul. His kettle was one of the ones that was clear glass and it lit up light blue when it was on. He watched as the bubbles started to vigorously rise and start to fight each other to the top until it finally clicked off. He grabbed a cup and made the strongest coffee he thought his stomach and mouth could cope with and sat in his usual chair facing the garden window. He sipped his drink while staring out into the greenery outside. It tasted disgusting and he cringed with every assault on his taste buds. It was doing the job he wanted it to do, waking him up. But not in the way he wanted, it was more of a punch in the guts and a smack in the mouth rather than the soft warm sun shining on your face through the window in the morning.

Once he had struggled to the bottom of the cup, he stood up and walked back to the bathroom. He looked at the hollow cheeked man staring back at him from the mirror. "Fuck me, you look like something from a zombie apocalypse," he stuck out his tongue, it was shaking, dehydrated and dark with a coffee streak down it. He scraped his tongue with his teeth and immediately wished he hadn't. As his tongue disappeared back behind the teeth they were scraping away and bringing up a wave of gunk and shit off the surface. He looked in disgust and spat it in the sink. He quickly grabbed his toothbrush and cleaned his teeth and he made sure he gave his tongue a good scrub too. He shaved and tidied up his beard so the edges looked as sharp as they could. He got dressed and made some toast and another cup of coffee but this time one that didn't try and dissolve the spoon. He still felt like crap but at least like human crap now! He picked up his phone and dialled. It was the doctor's surgery he called and he made an appointment, it wasn't until the 27th which was a couple of days away but that was the best they could do.

He left his house for the station. On arrival, he went straight to the conference room that they had commandeered.

"Morning B…" Del stopped mid-sentence as he turned to face Bos. "Holy crap what happened to you?"

Bos shook his head, "Life I reckon, I would like to say I feel better than I look but that would be a total lie. Because if I looked how I felt there would just be a steaming turd stood here!"

Del smiled, "Well at least you still have your sense of humour."

Bos did wonder for how long though. "Any developments overnight do we know?"

Del said that he hasn't had word of anything and as they had men stationed at all the Oak sites he doubted that anything would come of it, "If you say that the message said he is watching you, do you think it means you specifically or the investigation as a whole?"

Bos slumped in one of the blue velvet covered chairs, "That my friend is a question I have been running through my mind since I read it. I haven't seen anyone suspicious hanging about so I presume it is the investigation they are watching. And I hate to think it but it has crossed my mind that if they are able to keep such a close eye…" Bos paused at that part, "Is it a copper watching us?" This statement hung in the air stinking up the room for a while.

"Well we will know soon enough, I put the word about last night that this is a secret squirrel investigation now. Any information pertaining to it is only to be given out on a need to know basis."

Bos looked at Del and nodded in satisfaction, "Good, if we have rust amongst us coppers we need to dig it out." Both men looked seriously at each other and the phone in the room rang. Del looked at Bos and gestured whether he wanted him to answer it. Bos extended his arm out as if to say, go for it.

"Hello Conference room three Inspector Martin speaking," Del waited for a little while, "Yes he is right here with me," another gap came while the other person obviously spoke. "Yes okay, but it can't be our man, any work from our men out at the trees?" Again quiet and then Del said, "Okay we will take a look." Del hung up the phone in a slow thoughtful motion.

Bos wasn't sure he liked the sound of this, "What's going on?" Del told him about the call. There had been another body found hanging in a tree. "What, where?"

"That is the thing I don't understand, it is not any of our sites and none of our men have seen anything. I am wondering if it is a suicide rather that our man, I have said we will take a look in case."

Bos was a little relieved, he didn't want to spend the manpower he had and miss the bastard again anyway. "Oh right, sad but I have to say I am glad, if we had missed him and let another person hang we, well I, am going to look a right fucking dick!" Del told him that dispatch had sent a CSI out in any case so they would meet them there. It was odd but it did make Bos feel a little better thinking that he hadn't got another Oak site murder. The drive to the West Hill wood site was light hearted and it continued as they pulled up at the top of the Hill and drove down the West lane. They parked up behind a squad car and walked through an open gate towards the small group of trees that made up West Hill wood. The jovial atmosphere disappeared in an instant the second they turned a corner and came face to face with the horror of another killing by the Oak site murderer. "Fuck, shit, fuck, fuck," the air continued to turn blue as Bos vented his frustration at seeing the gruesome mess in front of them. "What the fuck is going on here, patterns, it's all about patterns and now this son of a bitch has just thrown it away, this isn't a fucking Oak tree, this is a chestnut," as he spoke he walked slowly closer to the scene.

Del looked in horror as the investigation fell apart, “He has broken the pattern but escalated the violence to another new level.” They walked closer and they could see the cut with the intestines pulled out, they were hung in the tree as normal. As with the previous site there was a large incision up to the chest and presumably with the heart removed. But this time the victim’s eyes had been cut out and stuck to the tree and his ears had gone too. A closer look and they could be seen sticking out quite ridiculously at the side. It reminded the PC on guard of his boy playing with *Mr Potato Head.* Unfortunately, he happened to say this as Bos walked past.

The inspector flew across the path to him and grabbed him by the collar, “Do you think this is some fucking joke officer? DO YOU, this is a fucking serious murder scene you piece of shit.”

With that outburst Del ran over and dragged Bos away, “Jesus Bos calm down, the officer was just joking, remember we all deal with this shit in different ways, humour is some peoples way…yours usually!”

Bos calmed slightly, “Er yeah sorry, don’t know what came over me there, this has screwed me right up.” Bos looked over to the officer who was obviously stunned to see and hear a senior officer deal with something like that in such a way. “Sorry son but I like *Mr Potato Head* so don’t diss him,” he winked and walked away back towards the body. He looked closer, “Oh shit, we don’t need fingerprints this time, I know that piece of crap in the tree. I have to say no one is more deserving.” He glanced over to Del and then said, “That is Norman Dale, dog man

Dale. I can tell by the god awful tattoo on his right arm." On the top of Norman's right arm was a tattoo of a British Bull dog wearing a union jack coat and smoking a cigar. It was standing on the bloodied body of a smaller dog. The caption under it said 'to the death'. Del pointed out that it meant this was yet another criminal that Bos knew. "Yes and I like it less now than I ever did before because there are fewer bloody patterns to catch this son of a bitch with now." The crime scene investigators hadn't really started properly yet.

Del looked at the floor and something caught his eye, ";Look at the blood." Bos looked and commented that there was loads of it, which bit did he want him to concentrate his mind on? Del bent down and pointed, directly under the body in the puddle of goo was a small clump of hair. It was just where it would be if Norman had have grabbed some of his murderer's hair and then dropped it as he died.

"Look at his hand, is there any strands of hair in it?" Del looked but couldn't see any. They really needed a break on this now and were hoping upon all hope that the dog man would hand it to them, literally. Bos walked away and looked for the tell tail sign of the flattened grass, he soon found it and it was around the same size as usual. "Come on let's leave this to the CSI blokes and make a call to the dog man kennel." Bos walked away in a determined march back through the gate and over to the car. He shouted behind him, "I have a good feeling about this one now."

Del caught up and asked about the dog man, "How do you know him then, have you nicked him?"

Bos said that he hadn't nicked him, people were trying to pin him down for years now, "He has a tendency," he stopped then and added, "had a tendency to frighten people. I have known for ages that he was a dirty bastard, now we are going to see how dirty." Bos pulled himself into the driver's seat and waited for Del to get in.

"Do you know where he lived then?"

The answer was emphatic, "Hell yes, fucking lovely pad he had." The car pulled away and went back down West Hill towards the built up town area. Norman's place was an urban paradise. In the heart of the hustle and bustle of town but the property was big enough to command peace and quiet for its occupants. For an urban property it was huge. Bos and Del both approached the house after parking in the permit holders only parking bay. There was no front garden but straight off the pavement were black iron railings, behind these dropped into an area were light presumably entered a room below ground. In the middle of the railings was a gap of about five to six foot, this gap contained a few lovely polished marble steps. There were around five steps leading to the front door. In front of the door were two white roman type columns holding up a triangular shaped ornate porch roof. The front door was white UPVC with a stained glass effect window in it. The front door was not locked, in fact, it was open a few centimetres. "Here we go!" said Bos as he pushed open the door.

The entrance was grand, it had a marble type floor on the entrance hall. Directly in front as you came in was a lovely double curve staircase. The banister rail was dark mahogany wood, Bos glanced at the stairs and got some strange flash of Deja vu. He soon shook that off as the look of the house was strange. The bottom floor had rooms coming off around the outside of the large entrance hall and the stairs were the centrepiece of the place. Aesthetically the house was a mess, it screamed for help, it was as if a number of different architects and decorators had worked on the place but not told each other what their ideas were. The pillars at the entrance looked like some Roman villa but the staircase looked like some grand manor house. Some of the furniture in the entrance hall looked as if it came straight out of the 1920s but then at the other end was a god awful unit that was plastic and from the era of the miniskirts and beehive haircuts. The cut and shut style of the house continued right the way through. If you were any kind of arty type your teeth would have been on edge walking through it. If you were an expert, it may have been likely to have your brain explode trying to cope with the hapless mix of styles and time periods. Del was neither an arty man or an expert but even he couldn't walk through without a looking as if he had just tasted something nasty, "Who the fuck was this bloke, was he some kind of style collector?"

Bos laughed, "No he was just a cock with money." Bos said that they should start right away searching the place for any message from the… Bos paused at that part because he was going to say the Oak tree killer but the last site had put some doubt on that title. "What do we call the son of a bitch now? The whole thing has obviously got sod all to do with Oak trees now!"

"I reckon it will have to just be the Butcher, he does like to hang his meat up and carve it."

Bos liked that idea, "That sounds about right, okay if the Butcher was here he would have left a note, let's find it." He walked to the first room on the left and started to search in a clockwise direction around the bottom floor. He hoped that there was going to be a message of some kind because if he had changed his tree pattern, will he change other aspects of his crimes? Each room seemed to have a mess of styles too, it wasn't a case of the house being separated into styles for each room, every room was a mess in itself. The first room had a hard wood French dresser in it but also had a wicker table with some metal frame chairs. It hurt just to view it, the style and fashion history tour continued throughout the house. Room after room and each one had no message from the hang man. Just a message from the owner to say, "Leave your taste at the door."

The entire house was searched with no result, they could find no message or no note in fact nothing that would show that anything untoward had happened. "That was definitely the dog man in that tree, there has to be a message here somewhere," Bos was becoming frustrated.

"Are you sure that body was dog man?" Del said this as he was at a gold embossed oval mirror that at the top of the curved stairs.

Bos answered very abruptly and loudly, "Sure, no, fucking positive yes." Del was quite shocked by this reaction, he had not expected that response. It was not a part of his character that he had seen before and was not one he had heard from anyone talking about

Bos. In all conversations and interaction with and about him, all he had heard on Bos was he is calm, positive, instinctive in his actions, a fantastic copper, and a fantastic gentleman. The answer he had just heard from Bos was definitely instinctive but not calm and did not sound like it came from a gentleman. It was short, sharp, loud and a little arrogant. Del understood the pressure Bos was under, his case and ideas on it were falling apart piece by piece. He didn't look at Bos but instead took in his response by looking out of an awful looking stained glass window. Four of the small panes of glass were plain and he could look through them. He gazed out and noticed the garden area was split into two. A large plain lawn then some kennels in the middle and to the right a yard area. On the left was a pure rectangle of green. This struck Del as odd, the attempt in the house at being grand and ostentatious didn't fit with the garden. He moved in closer to the glass to concentrate on the lawn. Something else struck him, the fence around the border. The fence looked around a meter in height on the left but the drop on the other side seemed considerably higher. On the right the kennels didn't look tall enough but the drop to the yard was high.

"Bos, have a look at this."

Bos walked across the landing towards him, "What's up, have you found something?"

"Not sure, look out there, what do you see?"

Bos looked out and after a couple of seconds he responded, "That is not right, that is not the garden of the man who decorated this place."

Del said, "That is exactly what I thought, look at the fence that isn't right." Both nodded and without saying another word just turned and headed down the stairs. The back door was not in any room, it was directly behind the stairs. It was a solid looking door with dead lock bolts all over it, however none of them were locked. Bos opened the door, there was a hall that went to the right and another door directly in front of him. This door had locks and bars on. They both opened the door and took in the view, it was not as the upstairs wanted to paint. It was not a plush green lawn, it was a dark rancid arena of death. It had sawdust on the floor and across the other end of the area it had a circle pen made of a Perspex type material. The pen had benches surrounding it in a semi-circle. Behind the part of the circle that had no benches were a dozen or so crates, some large and some smaller in stacks of two. The left of the arena housed four large wheelie bins. Del walked over to the bins and opened the first one, the stench hit him like a hammer to the nose. It was half full of sawdust that had been cleaned off the floor. The debris contained the faeces, urine and blood from the fighting dogs while fighting or waiting to fight. He closed the lid as quick as he could and walked to the next one, this one stunk too but it was the stink of normal rubbish. Cans, paper, wrappers and betting slips filled the bin to around a third. Del walked to the third and opened it, "Oh fuck, Jesus Christ!" The bin was full and also stunk but this one stunk of death. This bin contained the carcases of the losing dogs, it made his stomach churn, the wounds on the animals he could see were horrific, he closed this lid as quickly as he could. He opened the last lid and looked over the edge, this one was three quarters full and also contained the remains of the fighting dogs, it reeked too. He was about to shut the lid when he looked at the upper most animal. It looked as if it was moving, he lent closer to make sure. He had seen corpses move before but usually only because of the insect larvae under the skin.

As he lent in the dog opened its eyes, it was motionless for a second, Del turned to face Bos and shouted at him, "Come here," as he shouted the dog raised his lips, showed his gums and teeth, what was left of them anyway. It was not a pretty sight. It sprang up and leapt straight at Del's throat. He was quick enough to dodge to his left and the dog flew past his face. It landed on the sawdust and let out a grown, a sigh and was then motionless. As he watched and his heart was playing a beat in his throat, he could see the sawdust around the poor dog start to turn red. Del went over and carefully prodded the animal with his foot. It was dead now, he turned the dog over and its injuries were awful. As he had been thrown in the bin he had landed in such a way that his wound had somehow stayed shut. The force of the jump and subsequent landing had opened it to its full extent and had sapped the last bit of life out of the tortured animal.

"Yes very good, I would have preferred a rabbit out of a hat but yes you certainly have a talent there!" Bos had started to walk towards Del but after he had seen the flying and subsequent dying of the dog and obviously commented, he turned back to what he was doing. He was looking at the Perspex arena to see if the Butcher had written a note in something like blood or faeces on the outside of it. On his way back he glanced sideways and saw a large blackboard sign with writing on it. His heart lurched and he headed over to it. He took one glance and knew it was what they were after. "Del, over here," when Del came over they read it *'Bos man you will not stop me you cannot stop me. Placare arbores. I like Oak but that is not the only tree. Sorry to pull my rug from under your feet.'* Bos looked shocked and horrified. "What the fuck?" he backed up and sat on one of the benches.

"This is dangerous, speaking to you by name, he knows we were looking at the Oak sites and he is confident enough to mention the rug he uses," Del thought that he is either in total control or the complete opposite and can't help himself, whatever one it is this isn't going to stop without more blood being shed.

"Well at least we know why he stopped the murders in the Oak trees, he knew we were waiting." Just as Bos said this his phone rang with the normal tune of Lady in Red. "Hello inspector Boston speaking," he waited and then said, "Excellent, can a CSI unit be sent to our location ASAP please? The butcher has been here and left a message for us. We will head back to the station as soon as they relieve us here so will check that out when we get back." He hung up and looked at Del with a smile. "We have an I.D. on the hair that was found underneath dog man and it is not our victim's." Del asked who it was from but they hadn't divulged that info over the phone, it was waiting at the station for their return. They both sat on the bench and looked at the message written in chalk. "So the messages have no significance as far as the material he writes them in, it just seems he will use anything at hand," Bos said this while characteristically rubbing his chin.

"I think your right but the messages have become more relevant and detailed, I mean this one is basically sticking two fingers up." Silence fell again. The place was awful, damp, dark and extremely grim.

Bos stood up, "I think he is taking the piss and laughing at us, we will have the last laugh when we cuff the piece of shit and see him in court." Bos walked slowly away, "Come on let's wait in the main house, this place is depressing." Both men walked to the exit and returned to the front of the main house. It took over an hour for the forensic team to arrive and the atmosphere during that time was subdued to say the least. Not a lot was said but both minds were buzzing with thoughts on trees, bodies, mutilations, criminals and interpretations on what may come next from the Butcher. Their thoughts were finally interrupted by the white van from the CSI unit arriving. Bos walked outside to meet them, "Afternoon Steve, what we have is a definite site that the Butcher has been in. As yet we do not know if this was where Mr Dale was picked up from, however the Butcher has left a chalk written message addressed directly to me on the blackboard in the dog fighting arena. The arena is at the back of the house via a door directly opposite the rear door behind the large staircase in the entrance hall."

Steve took this info in, "Okay Bos, I am on my own at the moment but will take care to find anything that may be evidence for you," he said this while he was putting on his white paper CSI suit.

"Thank you, please give me a direct ring if you find anything specific," Bos and Del then walked directly to their vehicle and pulled away without hesitation and thought of further conversation, they were both eager to get back to the station and find out who the hair clump found under Norman, dog man belonged to.

CHAPTER 20

Evidence

The inspectors pulled up to the station and marched with complete confidence and determination directly to Bos's desk. There was a buff brown file sat in the middle of his immaculately tidy work area. It had on it the title: 'PRELIMINARY CRIME SCENE REPORT, WEST HILL WOOD, OIC INSPECTOR JEFFREY BOSTON,' it also had the day's date with the signature and printed name of the head CSI on scene… Bud Dolby. Bos picked it up. "Come on," he walked off and made his way directly to conference room three with Del marching quickly behind. The heavy door was pushed open unceremoniously and the two men walked in. Bos sat down in one of the blue velvet chairs and tool a deep breath. He opened the folder and the first dozen pages were pictures of the scene. It really was an awful set of photographs. He took in the damage that had been inflicted on Norman Dale but thinking back at the arena set up, Bos found it difficult to have too many sympathies for him, the amount of misery he had caused to hundreds of creatures. He had a bit of the hell back on him, "You reap what you sow Mr Dale."

Del didn't quite catch that, "What was that?"

Bos told him that he was just thinking out loud and that Norman had tasted a bit of the medicine he had been dishing out to dogs for years. He was still looking through the file and was now scanning the later pages for the information that he was specifically after. "Gotcha," Bos then read some info from the page, "The clump of hair belonged to Bernie Harris." A large grin came over Bos's face then. "You won't believe this, they also found a cigarette butt at the scene, it was found near where the carpet indentation was."

Del raised both eyebrows and said, "Well tell me then you bastard."

Bos laughed out loud and said, "DNA from the cigarette matches that from the hair, he had hair ripped out by Norman and then made his first real balls up by dropping his fag butt."

"Where does he live?" asked Del eagerly.

"76 Tulip Close, gotcha you wanker." He knew Bernie, only by name but knew he was some small time money launderer. Bos scanned the rest of the documents. It said that more carpet strands were found and they looked similar to those from previous crime scenes but await further investigative tests. The rest was expected from the other scenes and from their own interpretations of the site. Heart removed and placed under tree, eyes removed and placed on tree branches and ears removed and pinned on tree too. Nothing else was new or substantiated until the final report would be made. They had rushed through the DNA on the hair and cigarette and came through with the match. "That is enough to pay him a visit, but I am not going this early. We are going to wait until the full scene report is through but we will have a set of eyes on our man until we have categorical proof of his DNA and see what else comes up."

CHAPTER 21

The Accident

It was two weeks after the rabbit decapitation and Ben could still see the head rolling away from his spade blade, it was as vivid now as the day it happened. Bella hadn't been her normal awful self to him but did always grin when she walked past. It was Saturday afternoon and Ben was going out with his mum and dad, they were going to the zoo. They were leaving at 09:00 and the zoo was around an hour away. Ben was on his way out of the house to meet them in the car just as he was about to exit, Bella was waiting by the door. As he walked past she leaned over to him and said, "Be careful with the animals, don't kill them all! And remember they are watching." Ben walked past her and continued to the car. They arrived at the zoo on schedule at 10:00, it had been a long time since Ben had been to the zoo so he was very excited. The queue was very long but there were a lot of tills open so it was quite a quick process. In around 15 minutes they were going through the turnstiles and entering the zoo. The first thing to do was the same as most visits after a journey in the car and that was to go to the toilets, luckily as with most centres these days the toilets were close to the entrance, strangely enough just before a totem pole hut that sold drinks and ice creams. So once the kids have emptied their bladders they were straight on at you to spend money to fill them up again. After coming out of the toilets they all went to the totem and got fizzy drinks and chocolate ice creams. The zoo guides had a variety of masks inside and Ben picked a monkey, Mike was a giraffe and Madison was a panda. On a visit like this looking stupid was not something they particularly cared about.

Mike got the map out and asked Ben if he wanted to follow the guide path or wander around and find things themselves. Ben thought that he didn't want to miss anything so it would be best to follow the zoo trail. "Okay Ben if that's the case we have the butterflies first," Mike pointed to the floor and showed Ben the new zoo trail foot prints. It was a yellow set of animal prints that went to all the enclosures, so if you followed it you would get to see all the animals and attractions in the zoo and not miss a thing. Ben thought it was a fantastic idea, he remembered years ago going around and around trying to find the lions but not being able to locate them. As a fun idea they thought at that time it would be a fun idea to throw away the guide and gamble at what they found, it didn't go well. After that experience it was never done again, they took pot luck occasionally but always kept the map handy. But now you didn't need to keep looking at the map you could just follow the trail. Ben wasn't too keen on the idea of seeing a load of butterflies but went along with it as it was what the trail said. The butterfly enclosure was a large greenhouse and the footprints lead towards some huge plastic flaps. They walked through them and two metres in front of them were another set of plastic flaps. Ben walked through these, Mike and Madison always pushed Ben to go first, it was there way of imposing the full effect of whatever was to come.

As he entered he gasped, "Oh wow," he walked slowly forward and his mum and dad followed him. It was amazing. It was a flying rainbow; the room was beautiful. Butterflies were everywhere, they flew over you, past you, around you and some even landed on you. There was a speaker announcing that people should be calm and not try and remove the butterflies, they will naturally fly off by themselves. Walking through the building there were plaques with photos and descriptions of the creatures with information on them. Ben was looking around in amazement, he looked close at some that had landed and there were different types everywhere. Some were small and others were large, some had quite plain colours but others were vibrant. He continued to walk through and a large multi-coloured butterfly landed on the top of his arm. He froze and stared at it, it was lovely, it sat there occasionally twitching its wings but not flying away. Ben's grin under his mask was enormous, he didn't want to move, he wanted his new found friend to stay with him.

"Come on Ben, keep moving we will need to see others, this is still only the first enclosure," it was Madison that said this in a calm soft encouraging voice.

Ben started to walk again and became closer to the exit, "Mum what if he doesn't fly away, I don't want to hurt him." Madison told him to do as the message had said and just keep walking towards the exit and he should leave himself. A little way before the exit and there was an air fan blowing towards the oncoming people. As soon as the air hit the insects they took off. It wasn't an aggressive wind and it was a breeze obviously developed to make them take flight. Just after they flew away Ben walked through the exit flaps and then walked again through another second set. "Mum that was brilliant did you see the size of some of them and the one that landed on me was a wonderful blue colour."

She smiled broadly under the panda mask and said, "Yes I did Ben they were lovely." Next along the path was the reptile enclosure, it was a similar size building to the butterflies but this was a wooden construction. The footprints were leading to a small wooden door, Ben opened it and it made a kind of suction noise. The side of the door had a rubber seal around it. Again there was another small door in front him, he opened that too. Bang the heat hit him in the face like a slap. It was like being in front of an oven when the door is opened. He continued through and was thrilled to see the lizards and snakes. A member of staff was in there too and had a large snake that you could hold. You were only able to hold a part of the snake because it was far too heavy to hold entirely on your own. The staff would help you and your parents could photograph you. The end of the room didn't lead to outside but into a large open room with a number of staff and glass tanks around the edge. This room was hot too but not as hot as the previous one.

This one held the spiders and a range of other creepy crawly things. You could hold these as well but Ben was not keen on this idea, he watched his dad hold the big tarantula and huge leggy bug thing. It was awful to watch, it made Ben shiver just to watch let alone holding them himself. "Cool dad, weren't you scared?" shouted Ben excitedly as they exited the room by the small wooden door.

Mike laughed, "No Ben, they wouldn't put anything on us that would hurt us." Mike ruffled Ben hair and said that they should carry on the trail. They followed the yellow footprints and the next stop was the birds of prey. The prints led to an open wooden stand, it looked like half a mini stadium. It went to around 10 layers in height and the benches were split into three sections with concrete steps at the edge of each section. Ben climbed up to the middle of the first section and sat, Mike was on his left and Madison was on his right sitting on the edge next to one of the concrete staircases. It was about 20 minutes away from the next show. As they sat and looked forward they could see an open circle of grass with a couple of low tree stumps and a few taller bare trees with platforms attached. There were a number of metal perches arranged in places too. Ben was very excited and looking forward to the bird show, he loved birds of prey. They chatted about what they had seen already and Ben said that he thought the butterflies had been his surprising favourites so far as he just wasn't expecting so many. An announcement came that the next show was to be with a large eagle and everyone had to make sure to stay seated during the show. A couple of minutes later a lady came out into the grass area with a large leather glove on. She spoke to the crowd about the type of bird they were going to see and its natural habitat but this was all just background noise to Ben as he was eager to look around to see if he could spot the great bird. The lady picked what looked like a piece of meat out of a little pouch she had on her belt and held it in her protected hand and then said over the microphone, "I would like to welcome Shena," as this was said the great bird came into view flying majestically across the grass from the right. It swooped from a height, dipped low and then gained height to land on the lady's hand where the meat was. Its next flight was going to go to the right of the stand. The announcer said that the bird will fly very close to the tops of the audience so please stay still. The lady let the bird go and you could see the power as it took off. It flapped a few times and then came straight for the crowd, there were some sharp intakes of breath as it lifted above them and landed at the back of the stand. Ben was amazed, it was breath taking, the size and power were awesome but its elegance and beauty were equal. Its next flight was to go from the rear to the front right and it did this manoeuvre perfectly. It was now going to head for the centre rear perch that was behind Ben. Ben was watching the bird but out of the corner of his eye, he saw movement, he glanced across and saw a wasp. Ben hated wasps ever since he saw his mum get stung a few years before. He jumped sideways and shouted, "Wasp," he knocked his mum who jumped in panic. This all happened in an instant and just as Shena was headed for the rear perch.

Mike could only watch in horror as his wife and son jumped up and panicked in direct line of the large bird. In she came and hit Madison full on. The scream was piercing as the eagle's beak sliced into Madison's right cheek, the bird scrambled but recovered and flew onwards. The handler had collected another piece of meat and was calling Shena. But Madison was in a spiral spin out of control down the concrete steps. There was a crunch of bone as her right arm snapped with the force of hitting the first step full on. Next was a sickening thud as her head smacked down. Mike could watch only helplessly as his wife cartwheeled down the steps, her left leg took the next hit and also broke like a twig. No other bones were heard to snap but the cries of the audience were enough to drown out the sound of any further breaks. Ben had seen his mum's head hit and heard her leg snap and was instantly sick where he stood. Madison ended in a twisted wreck at the bottom of the steps, she lay there motionless. Mike couldn't move, he was frozen. The bird was rushed away and staff were on scene very quickly. Two members of staff were directing the crowd towards the exits away from the blood, Madison's femur had snapped and was protruding out of her skin at an awful angle and her head was bleeding profusely. Ben had staff with him and Mike was a mess. He was being told that an ambulance was on its way and will not be long. He was told that first aid trained staff were seeing to his wife now and he should stay where he is until the ambulance staff take them all to the hospital. The next hour was a blur for Ben, he sat in the stand white as a sheet watching numerous health staff working on his mum trying to stabilize her enough to take her to the hospital. The medical staff wanted to take her by air but due to the area being a zoo it was just not possible to land anywhere near without causing major panic for most of the animals. Ben was eventually led by his arm to the ambulance and was in the rear of it with his mum and dad being rushed with blue lights and sirens to the nearest accident and emergency hospital.

CHAPTER 22

Post-accident

Madison was lying in a hospital bed. She had countless scrapes and cuts on her face, including a deep stitched line where the eagle had struck her. Her face was so swollen and bruised it was impossible to tell it was her at first glance. She had fractured her right arm and had sustained multiple fractures to her left leg. This unfortunately was not the worst of it. She had fractured her skull too and this was the injury that had sent her into a coma. Mike was by her side in the hospital and was at his wits end, he was perched on the end of a chair bending over the edge of the bed. He had hold of her left hand and was stroking it. He was talking to her while tears trickled down his worried face and landed on the floor below him. "Ben is at home waiting for you babe, you scared the hell out of us all in the crowd. The zoo said you are not meant to try and kiss their birds," he was talking total crap but he didn't know what else to do. The doctors had said it was impossible to tell when she would wake up but they were hoping that she would wake up when the swelling in her skull had reduced. They had told Mike that talking to coma patients sometimes helps. It had been four days since the accident and Madison was in casts and stable. Mike had not left her side since she was admitted and his thoughts were totally on his wife. He was blissfully unaware of the turmoil Ben was going through at home.

Ben was sat in the kitchen, Bella had told him to sit there, "I need to talk to you, you killed the rabbit okay but I fear it was not enough. I told you they wanted blood, fresh blood."

Ben spoke and said, "The rabbit was fresh."

Bella looked at him sadly, "Yes it was but I only suggested it in the hope that it would work, the trees have taken out their anger on your mum and drawn blood from her. I told you there would be bloodshed if they were not appeased." She was shaking her head and looking very forlorn, "They have put your mum in a coma because of your actions, I fear they will not let her wake until you do something better."

Ben was in a state of total confusion, he loved his mum and wanted her better but was scared to cut himself and didn't want to hurt anything else, "But I can't kill anything."

"Why?" asked Bella holding up her hands.

"Because it's wrong," Ben went high pitched on the last word, he knew it was wrong and still had images of the rabbit's death.

"What happens then, you have already killed once, if it is so wrong you are already going to hell. If you are already going, why not do it again to save you mum?" Bella turned away and started walking out of the kitchen, she stopped just before she left the room and faced him again, "But of course if you want your mum to die, that's fine," then she left.

Ben sat rocking in his chair, he wouldn't know what to do without his mum. He needed his mum. He stood up and walked after Bella. "Bella, I want my mum to wake up," he shouted this as he came out of the kitchen but Bella wasn't far away, she had only walked out of his sight.

"Okay, that's good but will you do what is needed?"

"Yes I will try," said Ben trying to be stern.

Bella walked to the back door and said "Good, follow me." As Ben followed he became very anxious as to what was coming. He didn't want to have to kill another rabbit, the thought of seeing another head roll away was sickening. Bella walked around the side of the house and stopped next to a small cage. Ben walked a little slower as he approached. He got nearer and could hear a creature. He could hear a meow coming from the cage. Bella looked at him, "You want to save your mum, then deal with this cat."

Ben looked at the cat, "How did you get it?"

"Never mind that, I got it for you just in case you were big enough to do what is needed."

Ben took a step back, "But it's a cat."

Bella raised her voice for the first time during this encounter, "Yes it's a cat and it is here to save your mum, your mum remember! She is the one in a coma because of you." She bent down and picked up something black and took a step closer to Ben. She reached out her hand, "Take this." Ben looked and his mouth dropped open, she had handed him a gun. It was sleek and black, he took it from her and it felt heavy. "Go on then, shoot it." The young boy walked closer to the basket, he could see the cat through the bars. He lifted the gun slowly up and holding it with both hands pointed it at the cat. He aligned the sights to aim for its head, *I can do this,* he thought, *I can do this for mum.* Ben shut his eyes and pulled the trigger slowly, more pressure and more and then suddenly a bang. It wasn't the loud explosion he was expecting, it was a kind of crack. He then heard screams, it was like nothing he had heard before, it was awful. He opened his eyes and the cat in the cage was alive but it was writhing around in agony, it had a wound on its head. Bella had not given him a gun she had given him some kind of air pistol. She shouted at him, "Can you do nothing right, you haven't killed it, you have put it in pain." She ran to Ben and gave him a long kitchen knife, "Here, finish the poor creature off, put it out of its misery."

Ben was appalled, the sound was terrible, "But, but…"

"No buts boy, you caused the misery you fix it, NOW," she shouted. "Come on now, do it."

It took a huge effort for Ben to move close to the cage, the sound was deafening him. He looked at the cat, "I am sorry, so sorry."

"Do it, do it, do it now." Ben was in a state he could not think straight, the sound of the animal, the sound of Bella screaming, the idea of his mum, the trees, all these thoughts spun in his head, louder and louder.

All of a sudden, he shouted, "Shut up," and he thrust the knife towards the cat, he stabbed the cat in the shoulder and now it was louder than ever. He thrust it again and this time hit its neck. He was dimly aware of some shrieks behind him but the gurgle from the animal in front was what concentrated his mind, it was still screeching like before but dulled with gurgles of blood. He drew the knife back once more and this time brought it down, it sliced through the back of the cat's neck and silenced it. The mist that had come over Ben drifted away and his normal senses returned.

He heard Bella shouting again, "Quick get the body, get the body boy." Ben focused for the first time properly on the cage. Blood was what he saw, with a half decapitated feline laying in an ever-increasing puddle of it. He vomited. He tuned into Bella again and this time actually took in what she was screaming. He dropped the knife and lifted the latch on the crate and picked the cat up by its tail, the head flopped around and the blood was still pumping from its fatal wound. "Go on, to the tree boy." Ben ran towards the nearest awful tree he could see and threw the cat at it. It was sickening to view the feline spin in the air spurting blood in an arc as it flew towards the tree. It hit the tree the bottom end of the spine first, after the impact the head end followed through. The head then flopped up, smacked the bark, and left a spatter of blood up the tree. The cat then ricocheted off and tumbled to the floor. Bella had caught up and was still shouting, "That's not enough blood, pick it up and spread the blood, quickly." Ben's heart was thumping in his throat at this point and this was probably the only thing stopping him throwing up again. He went forwards and picked up the cat and rubbed it on the tree. "No, no not like that, squeeze the blood on your hands and put it on the tree." Ben was going on autopilot now and just following the words that were being spoken. He held the cat in his right hand and put his left straight onto the neck wound, the blood was still warm. He placed his hand on to the tree and left a bark embossed handprint, then again and again until the squawking of Bella had abated. He turned to face her and wiped the sweat that had been starting to drip down his face. He had put streaks of blood on himself without realising. "Good, excellent now we shall wait and see if that is enough." She turned and left, leaving Ben just standing next to the tree with the dead cat dangling out from his right hand. Ben dropped the cat right there and walked senselessly back to the house. He went to his bedroom and sat on the floor, what had he just done?! He looked at his hands and they were covered in blood. Ben's entire body was shaking and he felt ill. He couldn't remember everything what had just happened but remembered picking up the cat. He remembered throwing it and spreading the blood.

Ben walked to the bathroom and started washing his hands. He was now wondering how long it would be until the tree let his mum wake up. It took quite a while before his hands were clean enough in his mind to be able to leave the sink. "I need to ask Bella," Ben left his room and searched for the Nanny, she was found in her usual place, inside a bottle of gin in the kitchen. "Bella, how long do you think it will be before the trees wake mum up?"

The cruel woman turned towards him and stared

with glazed eyes, "Don't be stupid, how am I meant to know? This is all just a gamble anyway! A small cat may not be enough of a sacrifice for them," she took another swig of gin. "They might think it a bit of an insult to try and appease them with a cat."

Ben was shocked by this, "But you said that's what I had to do."

"NO," shouted Bella, "I said we could try that because you are too weak to offer your own blood." Ben visibly slumped. This was obviously a reaction that the cruel woman jumped upon. "You are pathetic, I try and help you and you try and blame me, ALL of this is down to you. You behave in such a way as to get them angry and you refuse to do what is expected. If your mum does not wake up I will try and help but don't blame me for your lack of character," she smacked the gin bottle on to the kitchen top and stood up, all be it a little unsteady but she then stormed out with as much hump as she could muster. Ben was devastated, he had killed a cat and still didn't know if it was going to save his mum.

CHAPTER 23

Bernie

Bos had managed to get home at the end of his shift in one piece but was not sure how much longer he could cope with whatever was wrong with him. He had again woken up in the morning feeling like crap as if he had not slept a wink, it was draining him of his ability to think straight. This morning he had slept through his alarm and was now rushing around trying to get ready. It was hard to get ready when you were in a rush but his fatigue was making it ten times worse. He arrived at the station at 10:16, he had meant to be in at 08:30. "Morning Bos," said Del as he watched Bos enter.

"What the hell is that supposed to mean!" Bos glared at him, if looks could kill Del would be flat on his back!

"Erm it meant good morning, but obviously I was mistaken," Del frowned, "I don't want to add to your mood but your look matches your attitude this morning, you look like fucking shit." Del walked off to the conference room they had set up as their investigation base. He was becoming increasingly worried about the man who he was shadowing. He had gone from the perfect investigator to a frail shell in a very short time. His cool unflappable presence had ebbed away and it seemed like his fuse was not just short but none existent at times. Del sat in the conference room and waited. He was sipping his coffee as Bos walked in, he too had a coffee in his hand now.

"Look sorry about that, I don't know what the hell is going on at the moment. I am sure someone is stuffing my head with cotton wool during the night." Del raised his coffee cup and said not to worry. He was though, he was not only worried about his colleague's physical health but his concern over his mental health was growing too.

"I have been looking at the map this morning and I have noticed something," Del stood up and walked to the map of the area. "The last vic's house was 17 North Street and he was strung up at West Hill wood, yes?"

Bos agreed, "Yes so what have we got then?"

"Well according to the other report our victims are killed after 01:00 or 02:00 in the morning. If you follow a direct route to West Hill wood from North Street there are only two ways he could go and fortunately enough one of those is shut from midnight to 06:00 for all of April."

Bos smiled, "So we know the route he took?"

"Yes but that's not all, the road we now know he must have gone down would be Parsons Road! That has a CCTV camera."

Bos smiled, "We are going to get a view of this shit head at last, have you asked for the CCTV?"

Del said that he had already put that request form in this morning and spoke to the staff in person, "They will send the disk direct to us with pictures of any and all vehicles that passed during the night of our murder."

Bos then asked if they had any more info from the third crime scene and was told nothing yet. "Okay what about our man watching Bernie Harris, what were his movements?"

Del said that they have had an update on that one but unfortunately, Bernie was at his home all night and never appeared again until he left this morning. "He left about 07:00 and went straight to his shop, he runs a dry cleaners in the town. On a plus note we don't have another body in a tree yet." They both knew that unless they caught this bastard it was unlikely that he would stop.

"Did you look at the routes from the other murders too?" asked Bos, looking at the map stroking his chin. Del said that he had but the others had numerous ways to travel and no CCTV near them either. "Do we know what car Bernie drives?"

Del answered this one too, "Yes it's a blue BMW M6 convertible. Its index is Bern 007." The two men were obviously waiting and hoping to see this vehicle pop up on the images from the CCTV.

Bos's phone rang: "Hello inspector Boston," there was a pause, "okay and that is a positive now is it?" another pause, "right that's good enough for me, thanks." He put the phone down and told Del that they are going to pay a visit to a dry cleaner. "The DNA from the hair and cigarette is a definite match and they are both Bernie's, let's have a chat with him." They both marched purposefully out of the station and headed for Bos's car. It was a nice day and Bos could feel the sun on his face waking him up a bit. They climbed into the car, Bos radioed for a squad car to meet them there and then headed off.

"How you going to play this then Bos?"

"I am going to nick the bastard straight off and surprise the shit; we have the crime scene photos waiting for us when we get back so it's all go." They pulled up a little way away from Bernie's shop, parked and waited for the squad car to arrive. After a few minutes, a squad car pulled up and a couple of uniformed officers climbed out.

"Morning Bos, Jesus what happened to you?" the officer said this as he walked towards Bos, they had known each other for a few years, the other officer was quite new.

"Yeah alright Dibs, I died yesterday but I am fine now."

PC Mark Dibbley, looked again and said, "Are you sure you are not still dead? I have seen healthier looking corpses." The two men shook hands. "This is my shift partner now," Dibs lifted his hands to introduce the female next to him. "This is PC Jardine, Amie Jardine," he then looked at her, "Amie, this is Inspector Boston."

Pc Jardine stepped forward and shook Bos by the hand, "Morning sir good to meet you."

Bos smiled and said, "It is lovely to meet you, I hope you are protecting my friend here, and call me Bos, everyone does. This here is Inspector Martin, he is helping me with my murder case."

Dibs laughed, "Ha see, your murder case, told you, you were dead! I hope you catch his killer sir" Del said that he would certainly try.

Bos smiled again, "We are nicking the bastard in this house as his DNA was found at the scene, two separate hits in the one scene; all we need is you to convey him for us please?"

PC Jardine looked over with shock, "Is it the Butcher?"

"Well from the evidence I would definitely say so." PC Jardine looked very happy to be involved with such a high profile case even if it was just to be a taxi to the station. "Once I go in and nick him I will bring him out and put him in your car, I will meet you at the custody area, okay?" Dibs said okay and walked back to his car with Amie. The inspectors went to the front door of shop and walked in. It was not huge and looked like a typical dry cleaners. It had a counter with a till on, behind it were countless rails with clothing hanging in clear bags with tags on. The customer's side of the premises was well lit and pleasant but the other side seemed very dark and unwelcoming. A light bell sounded as they entered. They walked the few steps to the counter and waited. It didn't take long before a female came from behind a rail. She was middle aged, her hair looked as if it was having a fight with her skull and was trying to escape. She smiled at them and they instantly wished she hadn't, her teeth were not the most attractive thing they had seen. In fact, they were so bad it made you want to look at her hair again.

"Good morning gentlemen, what can I do you for?" Del thought that there wouldn't be enough money in the world and Bos cringed on the inside, he hated that phrase and hated the way that when people use it they think it makes them sound charming and light hearted. When really it just makes them sound prats.

"Good morning we need to speak to Mr Harris please?" said Bos trying not to look at her teeth or hair, but finding it difficult to find anything on her face that would be polite and pleasant enough to rest his eye on.

"Oh sorry luv, he is in the back cooking the books," she laughed at her own hilarity.

"You need to take us to him now, I am inspector Jeff Boston and this is Inspector Del Martin," he took out his warrant card and showed her, she looked at it and then up again at Bos. "Now," said Bos firmly.

The female lifted the counter and waved for them to follow her, "Come on then, I always do what I am told when there are handcuffs about," she winked at Bos and very nearly met with the contents of his stomach. A shiver went through him as he thought about it.

"Fucking nightmare," said Bos under his breath.

She had obviously traded in her hearing for any looks because she turned and said, "Sorry what was that luv?"

Bos said, "I just have a thing about night wear that's all."

"Oh that's good then I don't wear any," she grinned and continued to walk.

Del tapped him on the back, "Stop trying to charm the ladies Bos, we have work to do," he winked in a parody of the woman.

The reply from Bos was short but with a smile, "Fuck off." They walked through the shop to a small room at the back. Grace knocked on the door and walked in, Bernie was sitting in the corner of the small room with a cigarette hanging out of his mouth. He was sitting on a swivel chair with his feet up on the desk next to him. The desk was an absolute tip with a couple of cups that looked like they were a part of a medical experiment. The large built man was leaning back with a magazine in one hand and his dick in the other.

As Grace walked in she let out a gleeful cry, "Ooh sorry Bernie luv, I didn't realise it was that kind of do not disturb. If I'd have known you were struggling I would have given you a hand," she laughed and walked away winking again at Bos. Bernie calmly took his feet off the desk, got the chair upright, put his mag down on the desk and stood up. As he stood he bent over slightly and tucked himself away, he didn't seem embarrassed at all.

"What can I do for you gentleman?"

"Well excuse me if I don't shake hands, I am Inspector Boston and this is Inspector Martin. Before I explain what we are here to discuss I will give you a couple of minutes to go and wash your hands," Bos stood to one side letting Bernie out of the office to visit a sink. Once he had gone Bos looked at Del,

"What a place, and these people are cleaning things!" It didn't take long before the large man returned. "Right now to our business here, Bernie Harris I am arresting you on suspicion of murder, you do not have to say anything, but it may harm your defence if you do not mention when questioned something that you rely on in court. Anything you do say may be used as evidence."

Bos stepped towards Bernie and took his arm, Bernie was stunned, "What? What the fuck are you on about?" Bos led him out of the back room and out through the premises. He wasn't resisting, he was numb with shock. "But I haven't killed anyone."

Bos handed him over to Dibs, "He has had his rights given to him and was placed under arrest at 11:24 please convey this gentleman for us as we discussed."

Dibs took Bernie from Bos and said, "Certainly Bos," he had his cuffs ready and Amie was in the rear of the car waiting. "Right sir I am placing these cuffs on you and you will be in the rear of the car." He cuffed him at the front and ushered him into the vehicle, he fastened his seat belt for him and then lent a little closer, "Give my colleague any hassle at all and I will rear stack you and you will be on the ground in the foot well for the rest of the journey," he shut the door. Dibs walked to the front and climbed in to the driver's seat. "All set?" he looked in the rear view mirror at Amie and she nodded.

The only words that Bernie said on the way there was, "What's happening, what murder?"

Amie said, "I am sure that will all be discussed

soon."

The journey to the station for the PC's was calm and serious but the journey for the inspectors was very light humoured. "Can you believe the balls of that bloke?" was one of the many one liners that came out on the drive back. "He was cocky," was one and "He was giving you the eye."

Bos had his favourite from Del and it was the first thing he said when they got back in the car, "Well Bos you did say he was a wanker." The puns had stopped by the time they pulled up at the station. They both got out and headed for the custody area. Bos used his tag to get into the secure door and went towards the Sgt on duty.

"Morning Sgt has Dibs arrived with my prisoner yet?" The Sgt on duty told Bos that he had and had just taken him for a wiz before they book him in.

CHAPTER 24

Interview

The room was small and had what looked like carpet covering the wall. This was to help with sound acoustics but made the place feel a little like a medical type facility! There was a black strip around the entire perimeter of the room. This was an alarm, if this was to be pressed staff from around the custody area and probably beyond would head directly for the room with the intent to stop any hassle, usually with force in the forefront of their minds, because if that alarm sounded it meant a colleague was in trouble. There was a wooden desk and on top of the desk was a tape recorder. Bos had three tapes with him, he unwrapped them from their cellophane and wrote something on them all and put them in the three decks of the recorder. He then pressed record. "For the record of the tape, present in the room is Inspector Boston, Inspector Martin, Mr Harris and his solicitor Jordan Mitchell, this is an interview in respect of the murder of Norman Dale, the date is 26th April and it is 11:06 am." Bos was looking directly at Bernie when speaking into the tape watching how he would react.

Jordan Mitchell was the next person to speak, "I would like you to know right now that my client is innocent of any charges you may be thinking about. I have advised my client to take up his right of silence as you have no evidence to suggest his guilt."

Bos sat and smiled at her, "Okay Miss Mitchell, I understand how difficult it will be to gather evidence on an innocent man and trying to convict an innocent person is the last thing I will ever want to do." There was an A4 envelope on the table it was opened and a picture taken out. Bos put the photograph in front of Bernie. "With that in mind I want you to look at a couple of pictures for me, this Mr Harris is a photograph of a pool of blood that had collected underneath Norman Dale," he put his hand on top of the picture and leaned in, "Mr Dale was the man that had his belly sliced open and his intestines hung over a tree." Bos then lifted his hand up and pointed at a part of the picture. "This part on the photo is a clump of hair, as you can see by the picture, the hair is in a large puddle of blood."

Bernie looked at the picture and then pushed it back to Bos, "Why are you showing me these, it's got nothing to do with me?" Miss Mitchell faced Bernie and reminded him of her advice.

The picture was pushed back towards Bernie, "Ah, now that is where you are wrong you see, now that clump of hair is sat right in the blood so that means it was dropped or shed onto it after our victim's death."

"So, still has nothing to do with me." Miss Mitchell

again told her client to use his right of silence.

"Mr Harris can you explain to me why the DNA test on the hair comes back categorically as your hair?" Bos then fell silent and waited.

The solicitor looked at the photo, at the Inspector and then leant over to Bernie, "Remember, no comment."

Bernie looked at Bos and said, "No comment about my hair."

Miss Mitchell looked exasperated, "No comment means be quiet Mr Harris!"

Bos was pleased with his prisoner's reaction and even happier with the reaction of his solicitor, "Okay Mr Harris you don't want to comment about your hair being found in the victim's blood, but could you humour me by giving me an example of any way an innocent man's hair could be found in a puddle of fresh blood?" this time Bernie kept quiet. "See the problem I have is if you are an innocent man how could your hair be in the puddle. If you were at the scene before the murder your hair would be under the blood, if you were there a while after your hair would be laying on top of the congealed blood. However, Mr Harris your hair was in the blood, how?" Bos sat back in his chair and waited, seconds went past he continued in silence.

After about 30 seconds that seemed like an age for Bernie, he snapped, "Don't just fucking sit there say something."

"That unfortunately is what I am waiting for you to do, you need to tell me about the hair," he waited again.

"For fuck sake I don't know, I didn't kill the bloke. I have never done anything like that, I launder dodgy money and that's all."

Miss Mitchell shut her eyes, *why her,* "Mr Harris, I am here to try and help you so do as I suggest and shut up!" Bos was enjoying himself now, he was feeling a little less crap than he had done for a while and it was good to see a solicitor and murderer squirm.

"Miss Mitchell, I know you are here to try and protect your client but surely if your client can shed any light on his innocence then that would be to his advantage. Telling him to shut up may have been useful if we had no proof against him but we have a clear DNA trace on him being at the scene. I need him or you to give me anything even a small reason to dismiss or rethink this damming evidence."

"I never did it, someone must have put it there."

Bos sat back again, "Okay thank you for that Mr Harris, that I suppose is a possibility, who do you think would want to frame you for murder?" Bernie this time didn't actually say anything he just shrugged. "You have been in here for a little while now, do you smoke?" Bernie nodded. "For the record Mr Harris nodded, what brand of cigarettes do you smoke?"

Bernie became irritated again, "Look what the fuck has that got to do with anything, are you going to give me a break for a smoke or what?"

The solicitor lent towards Bos, "Inspector Boston stop trying to play games with my client, if you are going to give him a break do it and stop asking irrelevant questions."

"Don't get me wrong, I was not offering him a break, I wanted information. Mr Harris, I will ask you again what cigarettes do you smoke?"

Bernie sighed, "I smoke *Marlboro Light* so fucking what?"

Bos opened the envelope and pushed another picture across the table, "This is another picture Mr Harris, this is not one containing blood. As you can see it is a cigarette butt laying on a patch of grass, the grass is just a few metres away from where Mr Dale was hanging. Being a smoker of that brand you will notice that the writing on it suggests it is a *Marlboro.* Can you explain that?"

Now Bernie lost control, "Look you fucking idiot do know how many people smoke in this country? There is nothing to explain."

Bos leaned in again with a very stern face, "Oh there is definitely something for you to explain, if you are an innocent man how can you have your hair in a puddle of our victim's blood and a cigarette with your DNA on it be found on the grass just off from the body? If you are an innocent man you need to help me explain these finds and convince me of your innocence." Just as he said this there was a knock at the door.

A female put her head around the door, "Excuse me sir?" she was a blond middle aged female and she waited for a response from Bos before she said anything else.

"For the tape Sgt Wood has opened the interview room door and asked to speak to me, interview terminated at 11:23." Bos stood up and without another glance at Bernie or his solicitor walked out. The attractive looking Sgt was a little way away with a disk in her had. Bos and Del walked over, "Hi Sgt, have you got something for us?"

She handed him a DVD, "You said you wanted this ASAP, it is the CCTV coverage you asked for."

Bos said excellent and went to his computer. He logged in and placed the disk into the drive. He looked at the files and there was just one on it. "Wow that is better than I had ever hoped, I was expecting to have to eliminate a dozen or so vehicles but if there was only one that has to be our killer, what are the odds it's a blue BMW M6 convertible?" He double clicked the file and watched, it was a dark street but lit up by a couple of street lights. Three seconds later a vehicle drove past, "What the fuck!" He pressed the rewind button and as the car came back into view he paused it. He shouted out loud, "Son of a fucking bitch you bastard." Bos punched a fan off of his desk and walked away and shouted again, "Fuck, fuck." He disappeared out of the room. Del looked at the screen, the vehicle was not a *BMW M6,* it wasn't a *BMW,* It wasn't even blue. It was a white *Nissan Juke,* it was the same type of car that Bos drove!

"Jesus Christ, this bloke is a twisted fucker," Del stood staring at the screed for a minute or two and Bos walked back in.

"Right let's see what this bastard is up to, can we enhance the picture on that footage?" Both men looked closer at the image, it wasn't up to much. They searched the index of the programme, they zoomed in a little and the image wasn't too bad. However, when they moved in too far the image turned too pixelated to make out any detail. From the angle they had and the footage they had, the index plate was no way visible. "Okay if there is no way we can see the index is there any other identification marks visible?" Bos was extremely focused now after his outburst before. "I don't like the bastard taking the piss out of me and using the same type of vehicle as mine, lets nail this Harris shit." Del fiddled some more with the tools on the video programme, he hit the sepia button and looked closer.

"Bos look at that area, I didn't notice it in the other colours or tones but what does that part look like to you?"

Bos looked too, "It looks like a dent, got the bastard, put a search out for white *Jukes* with dents on the rear passenger door." The mark was only slight but was visible in the sepia shade.

Del looked at Bos, "Bos we know this bloke is a bastard who has it in for you, have you checked your car?"

Bos shot him a glance, "What are you trying to say, are you saying that is my car?"

"No I didn't mean that, I just thought…"

Bos jumped in again, "I don't often lend my car to bloody serial killers for fuck sake, when I do I make sure they clean it after." Bos stormed out of the room and into the car park. He reached his car and froze, his car had a small dent in the rear passenger door. He was static and couldn't move, he just stared at it.

After four or five minutes Del walked out, "Look I didn't mean anything by it, I just thought if this bastard has it in for you we need to be sure." Bos looked at him and moved to his left. He was standing so Del wouldn't have seen the mark but as he moved he pointed to it, "Holy shit." Bos was looking jaded again now but his face was twitching with anger, he again stormed past Del but this time went into the station.

He went directly to the cell where Bernie was being held, he marched straight in and started shouting, "What the fuck is your game you devious fucking shit? Why are you doing this? Go on tell me you fucking piece of crap." He walked towards Bernie as he backed up against the cell wall to keep as much distance away from them as he could.

As Bos nearly reached him, the custody Sgt came in, "Inspector Bos, leave this man's cell immediately." Bos turned and faced the Sgt and the colour drained from his face, and he seemed to age 10 years. His stature sagged and he walked solemnly out of the cell and went back to his computer.

He slumped down in his chair, "What the hell is wrong with me, I am losing it, this shit has got to me," he said this to Del when he was back in the room.

"Bos I think you need to go home and rest, I will send in the paperwork to bail Bernie and have a couple of officers keep an eye on him."

Bos nodded silently, "Can you give me a lift please and get scenes of crime to pick my car up?"

Del said sure and held his hand up to usher the aging inspector out of the room. "I will give you a lift home and then set those things up."

CHAPTER 25

Downhill

Whenever Ben was not at school he was waiting by the phone for information on his Mum. Each day that went past made him more anxious. Bella was not being horrible to him but each time she saw him she would ask if he had heard any news. When Ben would say no she would take a large intake of breath through her teeth as if it was bad news. This would make Ben feel worse and long even more for contact from his dad with good news. Mike would ring and speak regularly but he was very guarded at giving Ben any news on his mum's recovery as he didn't want to paint an overly pessimistic view or for that matter give him any false hope. On the fifth night of her being in the coma, his Dad rang again. The phone rang and Ben immediately picked it up, "Hello."

"Hi Ben, it's Dad how are you feeling?" Ben found it odd that his dad would always start with that even though it was obvious how he would be feeling.

"I am fine I am just worried about Mum, is she

any better?" There was a sort of pleading in his voice, he didn't tell his dad but he didn't want the cat to have died for nothing.

"I'm sorry Ben but there is no change at all, I will let you know when anything does change." The conversation turned to small talk about school but Ben was not really interested then, he just wanted his mum better. The phone conversation lasted about 20 minutes and they then said goodbye.

As soon as the call had ended Bella came around the corner and said, "Well, any news?" Ben told her that there was no news at all and his mum was still in a coma. "I don't like to think about it but it looks like the cat was not enough!"

Ben was looking horrified, "What, do you mean I have to do it again?"

Bella nodded in saddened agreement, "Yes I am afraid so, if the cat was not enough the trees may decide that you have offended them too much and want to get rid of your mum."

Ben took a sharp intake of breath "Do you mean kill her?" The nanny said that it was exactly what she meant and that Ben should do all he could to persuade them otherwise. "But what can I do now?" Ben had become high pitched and his eyes had started to well up with the thought of his mum dying.

Bella looked on with amusement, "I really don't know," she said sadly, "we sacrificed the cat but that was obviously not enough we need a bigger offering to prove you are sorry." Bella smiled pathetically and added, "I will have a think and see how I can help you," she then walked away. She was delighted with the way things had gone, the timing of Madison's fall was impeccable, she could not have planned that better herself if she had of tried. Walking away from Ben she was already thinking about what she could get him to do next. *Shall I get a bigger creature or some of the same but more of them?* She was so enjoying watching the boy squirm and wriggle under her direction. Ben on the other hand was worried sick. He walked back to his room and sat on his bed thinking. *If she gets me a dog I am not sure I will be able to do it, but I need my mum. If she gets me a goat I can do it, they are ugly.* A menagerie of animals marched through his mind's eye. He was starting to make a mental list of animals he would kill and those he wouldn't want to. He was trying to put the images of the decapitated rabbit and the bloodied cat out of his mind and was trying to just focus on the result of a healthy mum. He decided to make a list, he grabbed a pad and a pen from his desk. He wrote at the top 'animals to kill'. He then started a list, he started it with rabbit and cat and ticked them because he had already done them. He then continued with dog, chicken, goat, mouse, fish and the list went on and on to more obscure creatures and ones that he would not get near let alone be able to sacrifice them to the trees. He had ticked the chicken, goat, mouse and fish and then realised that if he was to think about saving his mum he would be ticking all of them. He had even placed panda on the list and ticked it. It was comforting him but the realisation dawned on him what it was he was contemplating. He tore the list off the pad and threw it in the bin. He was shocked how easy it was for him to think about killing animals now, it was just a matter of positioning your mind in the right place. If he stood in the place to say 'I am killing an animal' he was not comfortable, however if he looked form the direction of 'I am saving my mum', well that was a different matter. From that direction he could stop at none on the list! Ben decided to have a shower before bed. He looked through his clothes draws and picked out some pyjamas to wear. It never dawned on Ben but the PJs had rabbits on them, they did all have their heads firmly attached to their bodies though. He undressed and went into the shower. Bella came in his room when he was in there and inspected his room like she usually did. Unfortunately, there was nothing out of place for her to complain about, however she did notice the paper in the bin. Bella bent down and picked it out, she unwrinkled it and looked. Her face lit up and her grin spread across her face. She scanned it and noticed the amount of ticks, "Impressive," she said and then screwed it up again and put it back in the bin. She walked out contemplating with renewed vigour what atrocities she had in store for Ben to commit. She was now just waiting for her opportunity.

The next day she got it!

It was six o'clock and the phone rang again. "Hello Dad," Ben answered it within seconds again.

"Hi Ben, how are you today?"

Ben answered with the same response as usual, "I am fine Dad, how is Mum?"

Mike stuttered with that one, "Erm, well I erm have some news about that." Ben listened quietly as his Dad explained that the hospital had said that Madison's breathing had stopped so they have now had to put her on a machine to help her to breath.

Ben didn't know what to say, "But what does that mean?"

Mike was speaking quietly and trying not to make things sound too pessimistic, "Ben, they think she has some kind of virus that has affected her badly. They don't know what is going to happen now but they say the next 24 or 48 hours are crucial. I am sorry son; I have to go I will speak to you again tomorrow." Ben was motionless for a little while until he saw Bella come round the corner. Ben placed the phone down and was crying, his tears stung his eyes and traced a track down his cheeks, they flowed freely and soon found their way off his face to the floor.

She saw his plight and her heart leapt, "What has happened?"

He looked at her blinking the tears that were welling up, "It's mum, she has gone downhill and we don't know what is going to happen." The next sentence that passed his lips shocked even Bella, he clenched his teeth sniffed and then said, "What should I kill?"

This was her opportunity to push him and prime him for some bigger and better entertainment. "Well I am not sure, the rabbit didn't work and the cat didn't seem to appease them, I do not want you to do something awful but I fear for your mum I really do. I don't know what to do." She shook her head sadly, "I will have a think about it." Bella turned and started to walk away.

"No," said Ban sternly, "we haven't got time to think about things, I don't want mum to die, we need to do something!" This was music to Bella's ears, it sounded like harp music to her, it pricked her emotions and tugged at her insides.

She was sure he may see the light that had lit up in her belly if she opened her mouth but spoke again anyway, "Okay come with me, we will do our best." She headed down the stairs and out of the house. Bella had not actually prepared anything yet, she was not expecting him to turn so fast and so readily. She was going to have to improvise. Ben followed her to the garden shed and she scanned the place quickly and took hold of some rope from a hook on the wall. "This will be good for us to use," she then looked again and her eyes lit up when she saw it, she leant across a table and picked up the sickle that was on the tool rack. "Right come on, let's try this and hope it does the trick." She marched with purpose from the shed, she was truly excited now. Bella knew exactly what her plan was now, they walked out across the house's land to the left and came to the boundary fence after about five minutes. "Come on follow me," Bella had picked up her pace and Ben was struggling to keep up but he hurried forward and caught up after he had climbed over the fence.

"How far are we going?" Ben puffed in his effort to keep up and to speak.

"Not far, it's only a field away." About 10 minutes later they arrived at a wire fence, it was a barbed fence and every now and then you could see some fluff on the barbs. Bella grabbed hold of the wire second from the top and put her foot on the wire bellow it. She opened a gap and told Ben to go through it. Ben bent down and made his way through the gap, once he was through he stood up. Ben was amazed at what he witnessed next. Bella was a fairly large woman but he looked in awe and astonishment as he saw her grab a post and then just effortlessly leap over the fence.

He was extremely impressed, "Wow, how did you do that?"

Bella looked over to him and said, "There is more to me than meets the eye boy, never judge a book by its cover. Things are not always what they first seem." She winked at him and pointed directly across the middle of the field. As they were walking Ben could see the piles of mess in the field and it dawned on him what they were after. He realised also that the list of animals he had written had not had this one on them, how could he have missed out that animal. How could he miss out a sheep? A little while longer and Bella pointed to their right, "There they are." She changed direction and headed directly towards the cloud shapes in the distance. Surprisingly it didn't take them long to put a rope around one of the creatures, Bella had seemed to be able to calm them quickly and just put the rope around one of their necks. Bella was a strong lady but once the sheep had been roped it followed quite contently. After a little while they got to the fence, Bella tied the end of the rope to the post and went over to the animal and picked it straight up. She went to the fence and dropped it over. To Ben's amazement the sheep was not hurt, it landed happily and walked away. It walked until the rope was taught and then just stopped and started chewing the grass. Bella grabbed the wire as she did before and stretched it for Ben to pass through. They were now just a field away from their land. Bella had slowed down her walking since she had picked up the sheep but it wasn't long before they got back to their own turf and then arrived at one of the trees. "Right this will do, hold this," Bella handed the sickle to Ben. He watched and waited for instructions. She took the other end of rope to what the sheep was attached to and started looping it up, she still had hold of the animal. Once she had ten or so loops she looked up at the tree and after a couple of seconds threw the rope up. It sailed up and over a branch. The coils unravelled and fell to the floor on the other side of the large branch. Bella picked up the dangling rope and pulled it until the rope was tight. The sheep was still a few metres away from the tree so she tugged at it and reeled it in until the creature was right next to the tree trunk. Bella looked at Ben, "Are you ready for this boy?"

"I think so, what are you going to do?" Ben was nervous but steely in his determination to do everything he could to save his Mum.

"I am not sure, the rabbit and cat were killed right, this time we will do it right next to the tree so it can see and feel the freshness of the blood. I just hope this will be enough." Bella then held up the rope that was in her hands, "I am going to pull the rope until the sheep is in the air next to the tree, then you will cut it open with the sickle I have given you." Ben looked at the gardening tool he had in his hand and swallowed hard. Bella never waited for a response, she hauled on the rope and the sheep lifted off the floor. Only its front legs were up and it bleated a distressing noise. She hauled again and the distressed noise increased in panic but was cut short and kind of broken as the animal struggled for breath. It was right up on its hind legs now and struggling and spinning around. "Get ready boy," with great effort she pulled on the rope again and the sheep's distress noise was strangled further and it lifted fully off the ground, it hung there kicking nothing desperately trying to get its hooves to grip onto something. Bella pulled once more and it lifted to two feet from the floor. "Now boy, do it." Ben hesitated and looked at the instrument in his hand. "Come on boy now, do it before the creature dies of its own accord. Now, do it, think of your mum dying in her bed. SAVE HER, DO IT!" Bella was yelling the last part and that spurred Ben on, the thought of his mum in hospital and leaving him. He stepped forward and thrust the curved blade towards the poor helpless creature dangling in the tree. The metal pieced the skin of the sheep in the abdomen. Blood started to pump from the wound and the animal let out an awful scream and kicked with the energy of pain and instinct. Ben couldn't stand the noise. He pulled back his arm and the removal of the blade opened the animal a little further. Ben swung the sickle once again and this time did not pierce the skin he sliced, its belly open and its insides flowed to the floor. The cries of panic and pain were replaced with the splatting of organs onto the ground. "Well done lad, splash some blood on the bark and then I can let her down." Ben threw the instrument of death on the ground and placed his hand in the ooze on the floor and then rubbed it into the bark. He was not feeling guilty, he was out of breath and his heart was beating a lot louder than he thought it should be. All he was thinking was, *I need to do this to save mum.* "Good, now say the words," said Bella.

Ben looked over, he didn't know what she was talking about, "Pardon, what words?"

"Say I appease the trees with blood."

Ben looked back at the tree and dipped his hand once again in the red gunge, as he rubbed it on the bark he said, "I appease the trees with this fresh blood." Bella let go of the sheep and it fell and splashed into the ground, Ben was already spattered with blood so did not notice more covering him as the poor helpless animal hit the ground. "Well done lad, now let's hope it is enough."

CHAPTER 26

Thinking Time

Del drove Bos to his house and came in with him for a while. He was offered a coffee and said he would like one. They took their drinks and sat in the lounge. The lounge was rarely used now since Helen died. They used to hold dinner parties and barbeques and host parties but the place felt very much like Bos himself now, an empty shell without her around. "What do you think the Butcher is up to?" asked Del.

Bos looked on blankly, "I honestly don't know now, he has thrown curve balls out of nowhere and seems to be one step ahead all the time." He sipped his coffee and thought about his car. "I don't know what he is trying to pull using my car but the only thing I can hope is he has left some kind of trace inside. If it turns out Bernie has left DNA in my car we have nailed him for good because he had never set foot in it before hand."

Del drank a gulp of his drink, "That is what is worrying me, the Butcher has been so far ahead of us all the way through and seems to be taking great pleasure in rubbing our noses in the murders." He took another swig, "My thought would be, if we found something why would he want us to?!" It was an interesting idea that anything and everything they had found so far was planned.

"I am not sure about it, if he is smart enough to leave no evidence for us to follow, why leave it? Are you thinking that Bernie is not our man then?" Bos was feeling very old and extremely tired again.

"Well after so little evidence, to suddenly find such compelling DNA traces! Well I just think it strange," Del took another gulp. He was also pondering the link to Bos, why? On one hand he writes personal messages to him and then uses his car to try and either wind him up or somehow pin things on him. "Do you think this is all to discredit you for some reason?"

Bos raised an eyebrow, "It is something I have been thinking about and to be fair he is doing a bloody good job of it at the moment." Del asked if he could think of anyone that had the intelligence and motive for such an undertaking.

Bos thought about it for a little while. "To be honest, and this is not to try and sound up my own arse but I wouldn't have thought that any of the criminals I have encountered in the past could have got the better of me, however the state I am in mentally and physically at the moment I am thinking that the dipshit we came across in the prison would give me a run for my money!"

Del laughed, "You do yourself a disservice, you

will be able to run rings around him when you are dead, however I don't think you are running on all cylinders at the moment Bos."

Bos took the last gulp of his coffee, "All cylinders, I don't feel I am running on any, I feel like fucking clockwork at the moment! My emotions are on edge and my head seems full of cotton wool, we really need to catch the bastard."

Del now finished his drink, "Well we will see soon enough if I am right about Bernie because if he is not our man there will be another body soon, because I don't think he will stop until he is dead or in custody."

Bos nodded sagely, "I am going to take some tablets and go to bed early, hopefully I will wake up back to my old self."

Del stood up to go, "I hope you feel better tomorrow, see you later have a good rest, I will see myself out." He walked directly to the door. Bos shouted after him saying thanks for the lift. Once the door shut behind Del, Bos realised that that was the first time since Helen was alive that another person had set foot in the place.

He looked up at her picture, "What do you think babe, he's alright isn't he? Good bloke really." He went to his bathroom and turned on the taps in the bath, he wanted to have a bit of a soak before he slept, perhaps that would give him a restful sleep and rejuvenate him ready for tomorrow. Tomorrow was the 27th and he had an appointment with the doctor so one way or another he was hopeful that he would be feeling a lot better soon. He ran the water until it was just below the overflow grate and then turned them off. He had fetched a large fluffy towel from the cupboard. The clothes he had warn through the day came off and were thrown into the wicker basket that was in the corner of the bathroom. Bos put one foot tentatively into the water and then brought his left leg up too. He stood for a while getting used to the temperature and then eased himself down to sitting. He sat for a few moments, it was hot but he wanted it like that to try and relax his muscles. His muscles seemed to have been aching for weeks now, slowly he slunk back and laid fully into the water. The level rose up and he heard the gurgle of the excess water exiting through the overflow pipe. Laying on his back just staring at his own toes, he thought of his life.

He had wanted to join the police as far back as he could remember, he could remember telling his foster parent when he was little about his ambition to catch bad people. He couldn't remember his parents, they had died when he was young. He had been driven from a very young age to join the police and everything he had done since was geared to help him achieve it. His young days as a PC were littered with arrests due to his ingenuity and thinking outside of the box. He rose quickly in rank and then joined CID and climbed that structure fast too. He hated to think of his career ending with a meltdown of his intellectual ability. He could think of nothing worse than losing his mental functioning. During his police career he had seen numerous people with mental health issues, most of them seemed happy with their lot but it was the families that seemed to suffer the most. He would never want to be that person who lives his life in blissful ignorance of the suffering and misery he causes to others. Not that he had anyone left in his life, his mood had changed from being okay to melancholy to downright gloomy now. He felt down now but at least he was relaxed, the hot water and steamy bathroom had done the job. His muscled and limbs were feeling loose. His right foot dipped in the water and his big toe flicked at the plug chain and the water started to disappear. Bos lay there for a minute watching the tide go out and then once it had reached the top of his shins, he stood up. The towel was fluffy and warm too, he dabbed himself a little and then stood out of the bath. It was warm in the bathroom but as he stepped out into the main house the temperature dropped to normal. He strolled over into the kitchen and took a glass out of the dishwasher, he took it to the drinks cabinet and poured himself a generous glass of vodka. "Sorry babe," he said again looking at Helen's picture. Bos made his way to the bedroom still wrapped in the towel he used in the bathroom. One large glug and a third of the drink had disappeared. He sat down on the bed and took a second shot of it, it was then placed on the bedside table as he went to clean his teeth. A few moments later Bos came back in and climbed into bed. He lay there for a little while thinking of Helen and some of the times they had together. A smile came over his face as he remembered the holiday in Rome and the white dress she wore that took his breath away. He swiftly fell to sleep.

CHAPTER 27

Bail

Bernie had been left for a while after his interview had been cut short, he had been taken back to his cell with no explanation of what was happening. After the verbal assault from Bos he was left alone again. He expected at any moment to be taken away and interviewed again but it was a long time coming. Bernie didn't know if the time was dragging or not, it was difficult to keep track of time correctly stuck in a cell with nothing to do apart from stare at the ceiling and read the graffiti that had been scratched into the wall. According to the wall, "All pigs will die" and if you call a certain number you can get a good time. Bernie presumed you had to ether remember the number or ask the custody Sgt for a pen to write it down! There was a humorous tally chart with about fourteen marks on it. Someone at some point had got away with bringing a permanent marker in too. They had drawn an outline of a naked woman on the door and the face was where the hatch was that the officers opened to look in. So now when anyone opened it and nosed in they would be framed as a large breasted woman with dubious pubic hair topiary skills! He was wondering how long he had been stuck in the place when the door creaked open with no warning at all. He was walked to the Sgt's desk and given his shoes and belt back. Bernie took his belt and started threading it back through the loops in his jeans. "What is happening?"

The Sgt looked up from his paperwork, "You are being bailed to return in two weeks."

"Why, I haven't bloody done anything," said Bernie trying to get his belt in the awkward loop around the back.

"You are being bailed so we can gather evidence, your bail conditions are here, this leaflet tells you all you need to know." The sgt pushed a leaflet towards Bernie, under the leaflet was another piece of paper. This was his bail conditions sheet. It didn't contain a huge list and Bernie read them as he stood still struggling with his belt. To be indoors at 76 Tulip Close between the hour of 21:00-06:00. Not to come within 100 metres of Inspector Boston.

"What the fuck is this about? He is the cock that just nicked and verballed me not the other way round!" Bernie was pointing at the piece of paper on the desk, leaving his belt to swing loose and hang around at the back like some weird dog's tail.

"Just read the rest and I advise you to stick to them, we will be checking!" The sgt hadn't even looked up from his paperwork.

"Look I am not complaining but that arse seemed to think he had me dead to rights, how come I am going out on bail then? If it is that cut and dry you would be charging me and putting me on remand?"

This time the sgt did look up, "Take it as an act of good will, now fuck off." Bernie did just pick up his papers and walk out.

The young PC standing next to the Sgt leant over when Bernie had left, "Sgt why is he on bail, he was in here for murder for fuck sake?"

The Sgt didn't look at him he just continued tapping on his computer, "Don't ask me son I just work here, Inspectors orders so I do what I am told."

The Inspector in question was Del and he had just watched Bernie leave. He was sitting in his car keeping an eye on him. He was going to track every movement of him, if he was the Butcher he would catch him before he killed again. If he wasn't, well at least he will know it wasn't him because he was going to stick to him like a phone on a teenager! He watched as Bernie walked to the taxi rank opposite and climbed into a black Toyota Corolla. It pulled away and Del followed, unsurprisingly it went directly to 76 Tulip Close. Bernie climbed out of the cab and stood leaning in for a couple of seconds, he walked away but the cab stayed stationary. Del wondered what was going on but a minute later Bernie came back out, "What the fuck are you up to?" Del said to himself. Bernie didn't get back in the taxi he just leaned in for a few seconds and then left and headed straight back to his front door. Del let out a little bit of a laugh, "Oh I see Bernie, no cash in your pockets when you are tossing off at work, good job too, don't want the queen feeling sea sick as you jangle your jollies about." Del knew where Bernie's car was as the garage was at the front of the house. He had also positioned himself so he could see the front and the back door of the property. Bernie was not going anywhere without him knowing. Del altered his seat ready for a night's vigil and then opened a flask and poured himself a nice cup of coffee. He had done many of these things over the years, granted not one recently but he knew how they went. The start would be easy, after a few hours your brain would start to drift if you didn't concentrate. You would get a second wind but a while later you would hit the wall and need to fight hard to carry through. He knew this so was ready for it, of course being on your own was worse but still the same pattern.

He had brought a few things he knew he would need. He had the essential couple of flasks with coffee to keep him warm and awake. He had a blanket in case it got a little too cold. He had a few bottles of water to stave off dehydration. He had brought some sandwiches to keep from getting hungry and a lot of snacks to stop him getting bored. He had also made sure that the bottle of water he had brought were the wide neck type, this was essential to be able to accurately pee in them later. He had also brought a couple of self-sealing plastic bags and some baby wipes but hoped it wouldn't come to that. It was a fairly well-lit street, as a male he could quite easily pass water nonchalantly in a vehicle but anything else is a bit more of a challenge! For the first hour Del never saw or heard a thing apart from a dog walker going past with a boxer that pissed up his car. He really wanted to open his door and kick the little shit but resisted the temptation and sat there while the dog relieved itself on his aluminium rims. He undid one of the paper bags and took out a sandwich, he took a large bite through the thick cheese and pickle. He then saw Bernie's back door open.

Del threw down the sandwich and grabbed his binoculars. Watching intently, he picked up his note book ready to jot down some details. Unfortunately, all Bernie did was bring out a bin bag and put it next to his fence. Del placed the note book and his binoculars back on the passenger seat and grabbed his sandwich again. It was a few hours until he saw any more movement, a pissed couple walking home, they were all over each other and at one point Del thought he was going to be viewing a sex show for free. He was starting to feel a little sleazy and they then recovered their composure and continued on their way. At three o'clock in the morning, a traffic police car pulled up outside Bernie's house. Two large men got out and went to his front door. Del could hear the knock from where he was. It took another couple of loud whacks on the door before there was any movement from inside. The conversation didn't take long and Del could hear parts of it but not a lot, most of the words he heard came from Bernie as he was slightly ill tempered about being woken up at that time in the morning just to check he was obeying his bail conditions. The words 'fuck' and 'arseholes' were mentioned alongside 'fucking time' and 'arseholes' a few more times. Del smiled, it was the time we get our own back on the bastards who break the law or piss us off. We are awake at that time, their bail conditions say they need to be in so they are checked, not our fault we are working through the night and that is the only quiet time we get to check. Del smiled again as the two coppers wished him a good night and walked away. Knowing the way it had gone in the past they may be back in a few hours to make sure he was still abiding by his curfew. Half past four and he was right they were back again, the same situation went through again and this time a few more choice words were heard to leave the lips of Bernie. This event was the last of the night for Del to witness. The early hours started the normal early hour traffic, milkmen, early joggers, commuters and then paper boys. It was six o'clock when Del pulled away to go home. It had been a wasted night but on the plus side at least he hadn't had to use the caught short bags. When Del arrived home Janice was waiting for him with a cup of coffee. "Thanks hun, it's been a long night, fruitless too."

CHAPTER 28

Shocker

Bos went to bed early, he nodded off immediately and seemed to wake up just as quick! It was actually 08:25 when he awoke with the sound of his phone. He was shocked to see the time but more shocked to feel as tired as he was when he went to bed. His arms ached, his head throbbed, his eye stung, he ached all over, oddly enough even his hands hurt. He let out a sigh that held the weight of the world in it, he shook his head, sat up and answered his phone. "Bos," was all he could muster as he answered his ringing phone. He waited for a while and then said, "Where is Del?" a longer pause then as the voice on the other end told Bos that Del would not be in work for a few hours as he pulled an all nighter watching Bernie. He stood up out of bed, his back ached too. He walked across the room towards the bathroom. The next thing Bos did was stop still and he said, "Where?" Bos waited for a moment and then pressed the red button on his device. A second passed and Bos was motionless, another second or two and then he exploded with anger. He threw his phone in rage, it hurtled across the bedroom and hit the wall on the other side of the room. On impact the phone smashed into many different pieces and they all decided to head off into different directions, "FUCKING BASTARD!" Bos shouted this at the top of his voice and he thought his head was about to explode. He spun around and flung his hand out in rage and sent the lamp that he was standing next to flying too. The lamp travelled horizontally with the force of the blow only stopping when the electric flex had reached the end. It bounced back and fell to the floor spinning out of control, it smashed, the ceramic base burst and the bulb popped.

Bos was panting with anger and spun and shouted, this time there were no words it was just an expulsion of his inner turmoil. He thrust out a leg and booted the wall. He hit the wall directly on the arch of the top of his foot. It was only plaster board and a large dent appeared in the white wall and pain erupted in his foot. He screamed either in pain or further rage and grabbed the door to the bathroom that he was now next to. He slammed it shut as hard as he could. The force of this cracked the plaster to the top of the frame. To say Bos was not in a good frame of mind would be putting it mildly, it would be more accurate to say he was in no state of mind. He was going on pure adrenaline and impulse. He was starting to fight to gain control but his temples were throbbing along with his heart and right foot. He was angry that it had come to this, there had been another killing and he was extremely frustrated that Del may have been right in that everything they have found so far had been the design of the Butcher himself. It was not the case that they were in any way getting closer to him, it was more the case that he was looking and taking the piss out of their ineptitude. Now he was going to have to visit another murder scene and look at the body knowing that he is no nearer catching the Butcher who did it than he was when he saw the first body of Mathew Broard hanging naked. Little did he know at that time that this case was going to go so badly for him.

Bos was at the point now that he didn't know what to do next. It was not a position he had been in before. He had instinctively known all his career what the next step would be and in most cases it turned out the right call and he had always got his man. But now uncertainty was the Boss not Bos. Was it the Butcher that was getting the better of him or his illness whatever it was? He was not going to find that out until his doctor's appointment which was later today, before that he had to visit a new murder scene and this time will be without Del. He had started to realise he had been leaning on Del during the investigation a lot more than he should have been. He had no qualms about Del's abilities, that is why he had been leaning on him so heavily. He had calmed down now and realised he was in his bedroom naked while throwing a bit of a hissy fit. Throwing his teddy out of his pram would have been fine but his phone, lamp and door were a little less robust than a teddy would have been.

He was careful where he walked because of the smashed glass and ceramic shards, he unplugged the lamp and put it in his bedroom bin. He walked gingerly to the other side of his room still naked and collected the pieces of phone that he could see. He was hoping that it was just cosmetic damage and a couple of clicks and the back etc. would snap back into place. He was unfortunately very wrong. The glass screen had been obliterated on impact, the rear cover had cracked with the force and had flown across the room. The battery looked fine but had also been unattached and flew in a different direction. Bos stood looking at the pieces he had picked up, it was not a search and recover scenario, it was a search and recover the dead type. He could not really say a lot but did utter the word, "Bollocks," as he removed his sim card and placed it on his side table. The other bits joined the lamp in the bin, Bos wasn't as careful as he had hoped to have been and stood on something sharp. The pain shot through him and he did as most people do when they do something like that, he lifted his foot extremely quickly in the hope it had not caused as much damage as it should have because he lifted it fast. Kind of the accident equivalent of the three second food rule, where if you drop some food and pick it up quickly it is still fine to eat. In this case if you remove your foot fast enough it won't damage you. Wrong! He lifted his foot behind him to look and there was already blood dripping. Bos shut his eye and stood still for a moment, a bad start to the day got worse and now even more so. He limped into the bathroom and stood in the shower cubicle. He took hold of the shower hose and held it just above his foot that had increased in the quantity of bleeding. He turned on the shower and the shower came on powerfully and hit him full on the head with cold water. "Oh shit, bastard," was all he could muster. He reached up and flipped the switch to swap it to the hose. He leant against the shower wall and hosed the blood from his foot, as he held the hose in his left hand he lightly felt his foot with his right hand. Typical, why would he think anything else when a day starts like this, there was a piece of something protruding from his foot, it was only small but he could feel it, he could not only feel it with his hand he felt it in his foot as his hand tweaked it. Bos took hold of a flannel and placed it on his foot, he put the shower hose back and turned it off. With the way the morning had gone, Bos realised he had to be careful now, one wrong move and fate he was sure would have him on his arse in the shower the first opportunity it could.

Bos took the flannel off and even though he was wet he just walked carefully to the cabinet and picked out the tweezers. He walked to the bed and sat with his left foot up on his right thigh, he used the flannel to dab the blood so he could locate the object imbedded in his foot. Very gently he manoeuvred the tweezers into place and found the grip he needed. Bos pulled at the object, it felt like he was pulling something that was attached, the pain was excruciating. He continued to pull and eventually the object loosened its grip and started to slide out. Once removed Bos put the flannel back on his foot and inspected the tweezers. The thing he had pulled out of his foot was only about a centimetre in length but was jiggered and sharp. It was white and was obviously from the lamp, "Arse hole, act like a shit and shit happens." The blood had subsided slightly but was not going to stop with a flannel stuck on it. He walked into living room being extra careful not to imbed himself on anything else. Once in the living room he put the flannel on the floor and laid down with his injury turned up to the ceiling. He was still butt naked and just laid there waiting for his foot to dry up. He lay there for a few moments and looked around the room and saw his reflection in the window to the garden. "Oh for fuck sake, what the hell do I look like?" The view he had was of his rear looking up. "Jesus you look like some poncey new art bike rack." He cringed at the site of his own arse and faced front again. It took some time for the bleeding to stop sufficiently. Once that had happened, he was able to go to the medicine cabinet and apply a couple of layers of sticking plaster to the bottom of his foot in the hope it would hold the wound together as he walked through the day. His head was still pounding and his body ached but he needed to try and put this to one side and concentrate on the next crime scene. He walked as gently as he could to his wardrobe and collected some clothes, he washed and then cleaned his teeth and was then ready to leave the house. He skipped breakfast and his morning coffee, he had already been far too long dealing with his injury when he should be at work. He also now had no phone to be contacted on, he would have to pick up a new one later.

He left the house and went to the garage and then realised he had no car, "Oh for god sake what next? Today's a bloody disaster and I have only been up a couple of hours." Bos called on his neighbour and asked to use their phone. It was the first bit of good luck he had today, his neighbour Frank had a spare mobile with the same network unlocked so all Bos had to do was plug his sim card in and he would be good. He was very thankful for his fortune change. Bos called the station and asked for someone to drop a car off to him. It was only a matter of minutes until a squad car pulled up. It wasn't a car for him to drive, he was being collected and dropped off at the station so he could use an unmarked vehicle. The PC was one Bos had never met before, there was a minimum amount of small talk, he was trying to be amiable but his mood was not helping this come off. To the PC and to Bos's relief, the distance to the station was not a particularly long drive. Bos went into the station to collect the keys and in the key safe was a note, *'Bos this is your car, meet me in my office before you go.'* It was signed by the chief Inspector. Bos's response was brief, "Shit, that's all I need." Bos had always got on well with the chief, when all is said and done he had been the perfect employee, up until recently.

He took the keys and went into the lift to the top floor. It was a short but very sharp meeting containing questions like, "What the fuck is going on? What the fuck are you doing?" and, "You better catch this bastard quick." It also contained lines like, "The press is crawling up my arse", the boss is all over me on this," and the classic, "He's been using your car you fucking twat." Forthright as ever, the chief had a perfect public speaking voice and knew exactly how to handle that area of policing. He did also have a very sharp tongue that he frequently used to tear off a strip from his staff. When you left his office you were never in any doubt as to his thoughts on the matter in question, whatever it was. The summary of the meeting was basically, catch the Butcher or your career with be proverbially hanging next to the Butcher's victims! Not a fantastic situation to find himself in at the moment, feeling the way he does. But he thought to himself if you want your mollies coddling then the police force is not the place to be, especially under Chief Inspector Charleston. Bos left the station with his ears ringing, the meeting had not helped his headache or for that matter any other of his aches and pains but it had put into sharp perspective his mission, find the Butcher or find a new career.

Bos completed the vehicle checks and headed off for Poplar walk. Poplar walk was as the name suggests, it was a public footpath and it had a number of fully grown poplar trees along its length. Around a mile or so along its path was quite a healthy wood, it did not contain any Oak as far as Bos knew. However apparently that didn't matter as much as he thought to the Butcher! The other side of Fox wood was a farm. Bos drove up the farm and made his way to the far end of the property where he knew there was a large gate that led to the wood. Bos parked near the gate, there were two squad cars already there. He got out of the car and took in his surroundings. The drive from the main road through the farm to the gate was quiet and well set back from the farm house so any car coming up would not necessarily have been seen or heard, but the occupants of the farm would be spoken to later. A tall hedge line covered the access from view from the road and the wood was even more secluded. The Butcher had picked his site carefully again. There were no particular tracks visible, it was a farm and well pitted with vehicle tracks of different types. The gate was open so Bos took a slow walk through it. It was a dark area covered over with foliage from the tree canopy. He walked a little way and as usual there was no sign of anything untoward apart from in the distance he could now see a line of police tape blocking off any further access for the public. Bos continued and the first person he saw was a young male PC he did not recognise. "I am Inspector Bos, could you tape off the beginning of this access road please, I want no traffic through here what-so-ever be that foot or vehicle?"

The PC replied with, "Yes sir."

"Thank you, call me Bos." He walked closer to the barrier tape and his senses picked up on something. To the left of the track lay an imprint of a tyre, it stuck out to Bos because it was not in the same direction as was normal. This one was as if a vehicle had turned towards the edge and stopped. He walked over and had a closer look, someone had come down here recently and this track made it look like they had turned around and gone back. It was quite a small width of tyre, which suggested a family car not a farm vehicle. That said one of two things to Bos, they had either seen something they didn't like i.e. a body hanging in a tree or they had done something to get away from i.e. put a body in a tree. Either one made him want to know who it was. Bos stood up and whistled loudly. Another PC came over, this one Bos did recognise, "Hi Tom, are the crime scene investigators here yet?" The PC looked at Bos and told him no. "Okay, I am going to have a look at the scene can you keep an eye on this tyre track for me? If I have gone before they turn up can you make sure they take a cast of that for me please?" Bos walked away towards the barrier tape again, this time a little bit gingerly, his foot was feeling a little uncomfortable. It was feeling wet and a little slippery, he was 100% accurate in thinking his foot had started to bleed again. He couldn't let that stand in his way though.

He ducked under the tape and walked a few steps and was met with the full horror of the latest Butcher's exhibit. It was a gruesome site and on first glance you could see it had progressed again. There was the usual naked body hanging in the tree, however this one was peeled! To Bos it now resembled a large red cheese string. Bos presumed the victims stomach had been sliced as before due to the intestines roped around the near branches again and it was only a guess because the flesh had been stripped from the chest, sides and back and peeled down to hang down to the body's knees. "Fucking hell!" Bos held his temples, his head still hurt and this sickening site was not going to make him feel any better. The victim had his eyes and ears removed like the last one and they were nailed to the tree this time. The heart had been removed again but like the eyes and ears this was also nailed to the trunk along with what Bos thought were a liver and… he had to take a closer look but a tongue was also nailed in. The blood pattern suggested the same death as before so most of the mutilation thankfully for the victim would have taken place after death. The Butcher really had gone to town on this poor bastard. Bos looked around and did find the tell-tale imprint in the grass, it was only faint but he was looking for it now. He looked at the gunge and offal at the base of the tree. He tilted his head and bent down, he looked a little closer, "Now is this one you want us to find or not, you shit?" He could see a partial foot shape in the blood, he looked closely around to see if there was any transfer and he would see very faintly that there was. Just a little to the right as the killer had stepped away, he had transferred a print in blood to the mud. "Huh, just like your crime scenes Butcher man, you are getting sloppy!" There was no way that Bos had any inkling as to who this person was, this was one that was going to have to wait for an I.D. to be found via prints or DNA. Bos went over to Tom, "Do you any idea when CSI will arrive?"

Tom said, "Well Bos, I was told imminently but we have all heard that before ain't we?!"

Bos wanted to hang around to talk to the crime scene unit but his foot was becoming very uncomfortable. "I am going to wait in my car, if I am still here when they arrive I will be up here with them. If you don't see me with them can you point out a couple of things for them to pay particular attention to please?" Tom said he would and Bos went through the tyre track, footprint and transfer and the indentation in the grass. He also asked if they could contact him ASAP when they had an I.D. Bos walked off to take a seat in his car, he was going to wait for a few minutes and then go home and re-tape his foot. He would then come and speak to the occupants of the farm. He didn't really hold out much hope but if they did hear or see anything it would definitely be a help. If they say, "Yes we saw him and he was driving a so and so vehicle with this index..." Bos may just have to kiss them. After 5 minutes he could wait no longer, he started the car and headed back to his address.

CHAPTER 29

Farm

Bos arrived at home with the intention of patching himself up and leaving again within a couple of minutes. He sat in his favourite chair in the living room and removed his shoe. It was immediately apparent that all was not great. His sock was very wet and sticky; the cut on his foot had opened and had leaked quite profusely. The plasters he had placed on the cut had been disastrously inadequate. They were not stuck to his foot anymore; they were quivering with fright at the bottom of the sock he had just removed. They were sodden; he could have rung them out if he had any desire to. He hobbled to the bathroom again and took some toilet roll damped it and wiped his foot; It didn't seem to be bleeding now but was a mess. He cleaned his foot with more damp toilet roll until his foot was free of blood. He didn't have time for this rubbish. He took another couple of plasters, one medium size and one large and walked off carefully into the kitchen. Bos rummaged through the kitchen draw for a while, then came out, and sat in his chair holding a tube. It was a small tube of superglue, he lifted his damaged foot and lay it on his other leg and undid the lid of the glue. He made sure the cut was nipped together and he squeezed a small amount of the clear liquid over the cut. He waited for a few moments and lightly touched the area, "Oh for god sake," the area was still wet, he blew on it for a while but it was not drying very well. "Sod this," he took the medium plaster, peeled off the backing, and stuck it over the glue. So not only was this plaster being held on by its own sticky pads, it was also being held in place by the glue that covered his cut foot. Did the job in hand perfectly, he would deal with its removal later! The larger plaster was placed over the medium one for a little further protection and then he put on a new pair of socks. He was about to put his shoe back on but thought better of it, he moved his forefinger across the inside of the shoe and it came out sticky red. He spent another few minutes searching and putting on his other pair of shoes and eventually left the house again, some half an hour later than he anticipated. His foot felt more comfortable now, which was good because he still felt like shit.

He drove back to Fox Wood farm. He didn't head on to the scene, he parked up and walked to the front door of the farm. There were a good number of buildings around but the farm house itself was quite small. Bos knocked on the door and waited, a couple of dogs were barking now. They sounded quite large animals too. After a few seconds he heard a lady shout, "Hang on I will be with you in a minute." A moment later the door was opened a crack and a lady's red face popped an eye through the crack, "Yes dear?"

"Hello I am Inspector Bos, would I be able to have a quick chat with you please?" Bos showed her his warrant card through the crack in the door.

"Yes of course, you will have to wait a little while so I can put the dogs away." Bos looked down and also in the crack of the door were three dog's noses poking out as much as they could to try and get a sniff or indeed a bite of whoever was out there.

"Yes of course, no problem," said Bos, he had no desire to add to his blood loss today by being torn apart by the farm's three dogs. It was a couple of minutes before the lady opened the door again, this time it was opened fully.

"Hello dear, do come in. Come into the kitchen, do you want a cup of tea?" The lady was in her 50s Bos guessed. In the kitchen was a male sitting at the table. He had a grubby look about him, he looked like he was close to retirement age. He had a face with stubble on and looked like he was as tough as old boots.

"Hello, I am Inspector Bos."

The man took his pipe from his mouth. "Right you are," he said and put the pipe back in and tugged a couple of times.

"I am Harriet and this old bugger is John, take a seat, do you want that cuppa?" Bos did sit down at the old table and said that he would actually love a cup of tea. Harriet put an old style kettle on top of the range cooker and got a couple of cups which were hanging from the rack above her head.

"Can I ask you about last night, have you been informed about what has been discovered in the wood behind your farm?" Harriet said that she had been told that a body had been found but that was all. Bos took a deep breath, "What you need to know is there has been a murder in the wood behind your farm. It is a gruesome scene and it is one of a series that we are trying to solve."

Harriet looked over from the kettle, "Are we in danger Inspector?"

Bos was adamant in his response, "No, I can guarantee you are at no risk from this serial killer."

John took the pipe out, "How can you be that sure Mr Inspector?" It was explained that the killer targets criminals so will not be interested in the two hard working farmers.

"The murders usually take place in the early hours did you see or hear anything between say midnight and 03:00?"

John took out his pipe again, "Dogs barked at 01:38."

Bos looked over in shock, "That is very specific, how do you know that?"

"Clock near my bed." Bos asked what happened and he said that he was woken up with the dogs barking, he looked at the clock and it was 01:38. He said he got up and looked out of the front window to see if anyone was at the door, there wasn't anyone there. He did see a car near the gate but paid no attention to it he just went back to bed. Bos was chomping at the bit now and was trying to control his eagerness so he didn't just rattle off a hundred questions a second.

"When you say you paid no attention, did you

notice any details about it?" John pulled on his pipe and thought, Bos got the impression that John was the kind of man who sat and said very little but took everything in and was actually very intelligent.

"I only looked at it briefly but it had one of those number plates with little lights above them, the car was dark blue and had G906 at the start." Bos was overjoyed to be proved right about John.

"I thought you didn't see anything love?" said Harriet as the kettle started to whistle. John looked at her and just winked and pulled on his pipe again.

"That is fantastic thank you, is there anything else you could tell me?" Bos had written the details down and was hopeful for another nugget.

John again removed his pipe, "Nope."

"I didn't even know that much Inspector," said Harriet bringing his tea. Bos was inwardly ecstatic but kept his cool, he told them that they had been a great help and sipped his tea. They spoke about the farm for a little while and how long they had been here. When he had finished his drink he thanked them again for the tea and the information and left. He got into the car and hit the steering wheel, "Yes." He started the car and left the farm to go directly to the station. It was not a huge amount to go on but if the Butcher could not use Bos's car perhaps he is using his own now and if that is the case they have just taken a huge step closer to catching him. Bos arrived at the station in a hopeful mood and went straight up to the conference room with his and Del's timeline in. He added some details on the site of the new murder and the details about the vehicle. He then sat down and picked up the phone. The phone was pressed a few times to dial out and then he waited, "Hello Inspector Boston, collar number 341, I would like a partial check on an index please?" he waited again and then said, "Yes, North Hill police station and part of an investigation. The partial is Golf 906 and I am after vehicles which are dark blue." Bos held on for another short time, "76 could you send that basic printout of owners and address to my email address please?" There was another brief pause and he then said thank you for your help and hung up. There were 76 matches for that partial index and now he just had to wait for the email. There was a computer in the conference room so he logged on and waited, he didn't have to wait for long, a few minutes later came another ping of an email. The ping was a regular occurrence if you had your emails open but the tittle of this ping had PNC vehicle check as the heading. He clicked the email and then opened the attachment, the usual danger heading popped up about trusted sources that was instantly deleted. Up came a list of 76 vehicles, Bos didn't scan it he just hit print and left the room for the printer he had sent it to. Printer Conf1 was the one he had highlighted and was happy to find it merrily printing away as he turned the corner. It was the one printer that served all the conference rooms so it was good to see it not being used. He collected the three sheets and walked back to examine them in a little more detail.

Bos laid them out and looked, he could see immediately that he could rid quite a few from his enquiries so he went to the desk near the white board and opened the draw. Bingo he found a highlighter and started to cross off vehicles that he thought would be of no interest, first one was in Yorkshire, deleted. Next was in Somerset, deleted. This process continued until he had reached the end of the list. He looked at it after and realised that there were just two serious contenders for him to look at. He picked up the phone again and dialled. He went through the same process as before but this time he asked for full printouts of both vehicles and their registered owners. When the email pinged up Bos was in no doubt at all on his next move. He was going to pay a visit to 16 Orchard Drive, according to the PNC the registered owner is a Mr Gordon Brand and the check on him shows him to have an extensive criminal record. He had been convicted on three separate occasions and served time for each. One was assault ABH, where he had used a meat cleaver on someone. The second was Burglary this included the use of force. The last one and most recent was rape, he had accosted a male in some public toilets, at knifepoint. "A possible candidate for our Butcher then," he printed the pages and added them to the timeline on the table. He then picked up the phone again, this time was to see if Del was coming out to play yet! It was now 13:45 so he was hoping to have him back with him.

CHAPTER 30

Groomed

It was two months since Ben had slaughtered the sheep and since then his grooming had upped a level. For the last four weeks Bella had helped moulding and twisting Ben. Susie was staying with them. Bella had convinced Mike that it was a good idea to have some company around that was closer to his age. Susie was 17 she was a tall slender figure and she was stunningly beautiful, with long wavy dark hair full lips and eyelashes that you would swear were glued on but were as natural as her ample chest and rounded bottom. She was stunning which was a bit of a mystery considering she was Bella's daughter. The one thing nature had passed to her from her mother was her talent for cruelty and love of passing that talent on. She was a very scary prospect for anyone who didn't see what she was, dangerous! What lay at the heart of her danger was complicated. If a town was to be called Susie and running into that town were roads called beauty, intelligence, charm, confidence and nerve you could get an idea of what

Susie was like but add to that the fact she knew all those things about herself too, you had a recipe for someone very special indeed. However, if you now add the main train line into the city and call that evil you could see how any person with any instinct at all would keep as much distance between themselves and Susie as they could. Ben on the other hand was in a very dark place himself, due to the relentless pressure to 'help' from Bella over the time they had been living in the same house.

Ben was infatuated with his new friend; she was a goddess as far as he could see. Whenever he saw her, it was as if she was being lit up from behind by some ethereal essence. Ben was standing at the edge of a playing field, he was standing next to Susie. Susie was watching the people on the field partaking in all the usual activities you see at such a place, rounder's, cricket, football, kite flying, picnics and the numerous dog walkers. Ben on the other hand was watching Susie. He had some kind of pathetic faraway look as if he had just been given a lobotomy. He was staring at the way the breeze caught hold of her hair and floated one way, then when the wind dropped, it would flow back as smoothly as butter from a hot crumpet. He was just waiting for the moment her lips may get dry and she would pass her tongue over them to moisten them. Every time she did this he thought his heart was beating in his throat and his stomach would summersault. "Ben look at that one there," Susie pointed into the distance.

"Sorry what?" said Ben trying to drag his eyes from her face to where she was pointing.

"Come on Ben we need to appease them again

otherwise you may never get your mum back, there look." She pointed again, "See the brown dog over there, it seems very reluctant to keep up with its owner." They both watched as a brown Labrador was drifting away from its owner. The owner was a mother of three small children, one in a pushchair and two on foot. The children were running her ragged so she was more preoccupied with them than with her dog. "Come on," Susie made her way down the slope they were standing on and headed towards them. She had a lead in her left hand and some treats in her pocket. Ben watched as Susie ran down the slope, her hair flying in the breeze. His stomach fluttered again and he followed her towards the dog. They caught up quickly to it and followed behind. After a little while the owner turned left around the corner of the hedge that bordered the field. Susie took out a treat from her pocket and whistled once. The Labrador turned around from sniffing at a patch of grass, she outstretched her hand and it bounded towards her with its tongue flapping around. Susie immediately bent down to feed it and as it took the snack she clipped on the collar and walked in the opposite direction to the owner. She walked fast, her long slender legs moving at some speed. Ben had to jog to keep up, as they rounded the corner at the other end of the field Susie slowed her pace down to look more inconspicuous. It took them a few moments to meet up with Bella who was waiting on the main stretch of road in the car. Susie put the dog in the rear of the hatchback and both her and Ben climbed in the back. It took seconds and they were off for home.

It was a warm day and the dog was panting like

crazy in the back and slobbering all over the windows. 10 minutes later they were driving up the entrance to the house. Even though he was doing things to try and appease them, the trees still freaked Ben out. Bella parked at the main house and turned to face the pair in the back, "Ben, get your knife, Susie take the dog. I will meet you at the tree near the east side of the lake in a few minutes." The sentence was swift and her exit just the same. Ben got out of the car and went directly to his room. He pulled out his top draw to its maximum and felt underneath with his hand. He jolted slightly and came away holding a knife. The blade on the knife was about 16cm in length and looked like a hunting knife. It had been wedged in under the draw, so could not be found unexpectedly. He felt the blade and it was as sharp as he had left it from last time. He walked downstairs and headed off towards the east side of the lake. When he arrived, Susie was waiting. "Mum is not here yet we will have to wait."

"Can't we just use the lead?" asked Ben. Susie told him not to be so eager, "It needs doing right if we have any hope of changing the trees' minds to release your mum. If it doesn't work I may need the lead again." It was a couple of minutes before Bella came along, she had brought a rope and tape with her.

"Here you are, get to it," she threw the rope down next to Ben. He did not hesitate for a second, he picked it up and found one end. The end was grasped firmly and the rest was thrown up over one of the high branches. The rope travelled in a direct arc over and down to the floor on the other side. "We are doing this one differently today, because your mum is still in a coma we need to up the sacrifice. You are to do it all today Ben, you need to hoist, fasten and dispatch it." Bella picked up the tape and handed it to him.

This information didn't cause a flicker of emotion from Ben he just said, "Okay." The tape and rope were taken to the dog who was happily sitting watching them all. The rope was looped and tied around the dog's neck and the slack taken up. Ben silently held out his hand to Susie who without a word gave him a treat from her pocket. The treat was offered to the dog who immediately took it and Ben quickly took the tape and wound it around the dog's nose. It yelped and tried to pull away but the rope was taught. The dog was whining and trying to scratch the tape off with its paws. Ben stood away from the animal and pulled on the rope, the poor creature was dragged a little closer to the tree still attempting to remove the tape. Another heave and the animal was lifted up on to its hind legs, it cried with pain as the rope dug in. The noise was not good but nowhere near as bad as before they taped them. This was not the first or even the second dog, let's just say from the air of normality around the tree the awful sight and sound was scarily matter of fact. Ben pulled again and the dog went higher, then higher and higher until its belly was just about eye level to him. The rope Ben was holding was taken to the tree next to him and tied so the dog was still dangling. It was actually writhing around trying to escape. It was choking and frothing at the mouth. Ben lifted his knife and light pinged off the blade. His left hand shot out and grabbed the dogs rear legs, he pulled down hard and brought his right hand up and over and sliced through the belly of the dog. The blood spurted out over Ben's left arm and over the bark of the tree. Directly after the cut the legs were released, the dog was still writhing and Ben went straight to the rope and lifted the dog higher, the blood was marking more of the trunk now and the poor animal stopped writhing and just hung limply in the height of the tree. Ben didn't even let the rope go gently, he just let go.

The carcass came crashing down the three or four feet and its entrails spilled out onto the floor. Ben walked to the tree, "I appease the trees with blood." He took his blade and looked at it, it was covered with blood. He held it out to the carcass hanging next to the tree trunk and callously wiped it on its fur. He wiped one side then the other and then moved to a different part on the dog's coat and did it again. This continued until Ben was satisfied that his knife was clean. He looked around to Bella, "Well what do you reckon?"

Bella smiled and said, "If that doesn't wake her we will need to up it even more lad, come on let's get back for a drink." Susie undid the rope and took it from around the dog's neck. They then walked away leaving the body of someone's beloved pet on the floor next to the tree to rot.

CHAPTER 31

Brand

Bos had dialled for Del and Janice answered, "Hello Janice speaking."

"Hi Janice, it's Bos here, how are you?"

"Oh hi Bos, I am fine thanks, how are things with you? Del is up and just in the shower at the moment," her voice was happy and friendly as ever.

"I was calling with the hope he was up and about, if I head on over will he be ready do you think?"

"If you give him 15 minutes I think he may be yes, do you want me to get him to call you?" Bos told her that it wasn't necessary but he will be round in about half an hour to pick him up. While he was waiting he looked at the PNC details for Brand again and searched his image on the police database. The situation seemed familiar but he didn't know why. He racked his brains but couldn't think. Bos searched the local police intelligence system for Brand but nothing, until he stumbled upon a couple of reports from three years previously. The reports where regarding the address of 16 Orchard Drive and a possible Gordon Rand and a sex slavery ring being run from the address. Everything clicked into place then, it was a collar he was working on a few years ago but never got enough evidence to take it forward. He got snippets from a number of sources but nothing concrete to work on. He was sure at the time Rand was dirty. Now he wondered if he was right, was his name Rand or Brand.

"Well Mr whatever your fucking name is I am coming to see you now," Bos turned his computer off and left the station to pick up Del. It was 14:10 around half an hour after his call when he arrived at Del's house, Janice opened the door before he even had chance to knock.

"Hi Bos, come in he is just getting his shoes on."

"Thanks Janice, how is he after his all nighter?"

Janice smiled, "He is okay, it's his first time in a while so I think it hit him but he doesn't like to let on much." Del came around the corner of the hall.

"How did the stake out go?" asked Bos.

Del sneered a little and said, "Not great, I will fill you in on route to wherever it is we are off to." Del kissed Janice and told her he would see her later.

As they left the house Bos said, "We have a lot to catch up on, first major question is, did you find anything out from watching Bernie?" The two men entered the car. Bos didn't start the vehicle immediately, he needed to know the information on Bernie before he went anywhere else.

"I am afraid not a lot, he never left the house, well apart from putting some rubbish out."

Bos stroked his chin, "Are you 100% sure about that?"

Del nodded, "I am positive he never left the house but that is still not proof that he is not the Butcher, I wanted to follow where he would go if he left." Bos said that it was more key than he initially thought as there was another murder last night. Bos told him that the level of destruction on the body had escalated dramatically on the latest victim. He also explained about the set up of the farm and then told him about the information that John had told him. "Shit, that means unless Bernie is in on it with another person he is off our hook, do you think the sighting was something that was planned by the Butcher or our first real break?"

Bos sat pondering this for a few moments, "To be honest I don't know, this bastard has been running rings around us from the start so who are we to say it's any different now? But we do have more info." He then went through the Police National Computer checks on the partial index and the resulting flag on Gordon Brand. "I know Brand but I thought his name was Rand, I gathered intel on him a few years ago and he was not a nice bloke. If he has a blue *Mini Metro* with the index G906 9BT on his drive, we will have a prime suspect as our Butcher." Now they were both caught up on proceedings the vehicle was started and they set off to 16 Orchard Drive. As their vehicle pulled into Orchard Drive the two officers could see a small dark blue car a little way up. "What are the odds that the house there is number 16!" Bos slowed down to a crawl and edged closer 10, 12, 14 and bingo the dark blue car was indeed parked in the drive of 16 and it was a *Mini Metro* marked as G906 9BT. The plain police car parked on the road blocking the drive of number 16 and the two Inspectors climbed out. Bos went one way around the *Metro* and Del went the other. Both men instinctively looked down to the tyres and a dirty soil mark was visible on each one of them. Bos stopped and called the station for a CSI unit to seize the vehicle for analysis.

They joined up at the front of the vehicle and headed for the front door of the property. Bos smashed down on the letterbox. They waited for a few seconds and he lifted the metal and blasted it down another few times. Bos knelt down and slowly put his nose to the letterbox he then put his mouth to it and shouted, "Mr Brand it's the police could you open the door please?" He looked through the gap and he could see that the layout of the property meant he could see the rear door of the house. So the owner had not run out since he had been here, however a closer look and he spoke to Del, "I don't like this, the back door is open." The letterbox was closed and Del was told to stay and watch through it while Bos went around and entered via the back door. Bos walked around the back, he passed a line of brick built sheds down the right of the garden and continued to walk until he reached the back door. He opened it and stepped in. "Hello, it's the police," he walked slowly toward the front door while looking in the side rooms. He entered via the kitchen and then walked past a living room that had furniture in but no people. He continued to walk past a front office type room and that was also uninhabited. Just to the left were the stairs, Bos opened the door and let Del in. "Nothing downstairs let's go up." He led the way up a silent staircase and there were three rooms with open doors. To the left was a bedroom, to the right was a bedroom and in the middle was a bathroom. Bos walked to look in the bedroom on the left and as he walked in he came face to face with a message on the wall beside the bed. Del had walked into the second bedroom and he heard Bos shout, "Del in here." Del ran from the room he was in and found Bos sitting against the wall to the left of the door. He didn't look at the wall, his first sight as he rounded the corner was his colleague on the floor.

"What's up, you okay?"

Bos started to bang his head on the wall behind him, "No I fucking am not, Brand is not our man!"

Del looked in astonishment at the sight he was seeing, "How do you know that?" as Del said this Bos raised his right hand and pointed at the wall that was behind Del, he didn't say anything else, just pointed. Del spun around and saw the writing too. It said '*PLACARE ARBORES. Don't be silly boys did you really think taking my car away would stop me? Blood needs to be spilt and better theirs than ours. I pull the strings and you move, don't expect anything different. "Bos" man, when you see Mr Rand hanging around, thank him for the use of his car.* This message was chilling and the end was worse, this one he had signed off with '*THE BUTCHER*'. Del stared for a few seconds and then said, "Fucker, so it's Rand in the tree?" Del was trying to take in what was said on the message. He didn't say anything he was just thinking through it. His car, he really was twisting the knife into Bos, *he pulls the strings and we move, cocky shit and he knows we are calling him the Butcher, he thought.* "Let's get out of here," Del wanted to get Bos away from the house, it was an awful note to read and it was specifically meant for Bos which made it worse. Bos stood up and followed Del out of the house. He didn't say a thing, he seemed to be in a state of shock. They walked towards the police vehicle and Bos just leant against it.

"What the hell is happening here, why is this bastard trying to ruin me each time, the bastard pushes just that little bit further. What next?" The time was 16:26 and Bos's appointment was at 17:00. "Can you drop me off at the doctors on Meadow Lane please, I will walk home after. You can take the car then." Del said sure and that he would pick him up at 09:00 tomorrow morning. They waited for a while for CSI to arrive and then left.

CHAPTER 32

Doctors

The Doctors' waiting room was not full but did have around a dozen people waiting. Bos was hurting physically and mentally now. He was sitting wondering if the other people around him could see the edges of his life fraying and unwinding. He was trying to hold his life and career together but the Butcher was picking it apart piece by piece. His head still hurt, his aching arms and sore hands had improved as the day went past but he was still ridiculously tired. "Mr Codworth, room number 2 please," was announced over the announcement system. Bos saw what he presumed was Mr Codworth stand up to walk to his appointment, the man looked over to him as he walked past.

"What?" said Bos loudly. The man looked shocked at the remark and hastened his pace to the door leading to the Doctors' rooms. Other people looked across to see what the raised voice was about.

"Miss Jennings, room number 5 please." One of

the people who had looked over was a female and she stood up and started walking to the door too.

"That's it, keep fucking walking," said Bos, what the hell was going on! He put his head in his hands and concentrated.

"Mr Boston, room number 1 please," Bos stood up and headed for the door, no one was looking in his direction they all seemed to have found something fascinating to stare at elsewhere. He walked through the door and entered a corridor. The layout was a rectangular block of rooms and the corridor around them had windows down one side looking out to gardens. There were around 10 rooms in all. Four along the first hall numbered ten to seven, Bos walked to the end and turned right, two more rooms on the right were numbered six and five. He went to the end and turned right again and the doors were now marked four through to one. *It had to be the last bloody one didn't it?* Bos knocked on the door and a second later he heard, "Come in". He turned the handle and walked in. The room was quite small, it had a desk along the right with the Doctor sitting out facing the entrance. It had a bed on the wall of the door he had just walked in, filing system on the left and the wall opposite was a large window that faced an internal garden that all the Doctors' rooms faced. Bos looked out and could see a couple of the rooms had their curtains drawn.

"Good afternoon Mr Boston how can I help you today?" It was a question that Bos didn't know the answer to, couldn't she help him?!

"I don't know actually," said Bos meekly.

"Oh, okay let's start with why you are here then." The Doctor was a thin woman aged in her 50s or 60s, she was well tanned and wore glasses on some string around her neck. Bos had always found them amusing before, they reminded him of the idiot mittens he used to see when younger. The mittens that were attached to a piece of string leading from inside one sleeve to another. He usually found that the string was too short and if you stretched out one arm the other glove would instantly disappear up the other sleeve like some kind of awful magic trick. Obviously if you were wearing both mittens, you ran the risk of smacking yourself in the face. The Doctor looked over the top of her glasses as him and put her hand out to show him to the seat next to her.

"I don't know where to start really," said Bos.

"I know this will sound a bit daft but the beginning is usually best," and she smiled at him. He did feel a bit more comfortable than when he came in, he knew he needed to come but wasn't sure what he should say and even if there was anything that could be done.

"Okay, erm. I am an Inspector in the police, have very high standards and have made a name for myself at, well being good at what I do."

The Doctor clicked a few buttons on her computer. "A few months ago I lost my wife in a hit and run accident, I miss her so much it hurts but I was getting through," he paused and wiped his head he had started to sweat. "A few weeks ago I started to get very tired during the day, it had never happened before and I was getting enough sleep. I would sleep all night, still do." The Doctor asked if he had been taking sleeping tablets. "No nothing like that I am just so knackered I go to sleep right away and don't wake up again until the morning. The trouble is I feel awful like I haven't slept at all, I ache, my head is constantly pounding, my eyes look like sacks never mind bags and it is affecting my work." The Doctor took her glasses off and they hung around near her chest.

"How is that then Mr Boston?"

"Call me Bos everyone does, I am dealing with a very important case at the moment. A killer actually and I pride myself on being sharp and a step ahead of the criminals I go after, but this one… this one is making me look an idiot, he is not only one step ahead, he is showing me where to walk and placing my feet there for me! I am losing my patience easily, I have become accident prone and at times rude and verbally aggressive, that is honestly not me." The doctor sat back and said that first things first would be his blood pressure, temperature and pulse. His blood pressure was a little high but not drastically so.

"I will take some blood and sent it off for you. Have you had any physical trauma recently?" Bos told her that he hadn't.

"Okay Mr Boston, sorry Bos, I think you are still stressed about the loss of your wife and you are feeling the stress of your job too, the more stressed you become the worse you are feeling."

Bos raised his eyebrow in the reaction he usually gives when he thinks people are talking shit. "I know this sounds a bit hairy fairy but try and relax an hour or so before bed, do you drink?" Bos said that he did a little. "I suggest you stop for a while, try a quiet walk or some yoga it may help. I will get the blood results in around 8-10 days, please phone for the results then. If you find things are not getting any better come back and see me in a few weeks."

Bos didn't know what to say really, "Is that it?"

"Well yes, what did you expect Mr Boston?" said the Doctor putting her glasses back on

"I am not sure to be honest but I was hoping for some answers of some kind," Bos deflated.

"I am sorry Bos, we are not miracle workers and humans are a complicated creature, there is a lot more going on up there than you realise," she pointed to Bos's head. "Relax, take it easy and you will come together again, I am sure."

Bos stood up, shook her hand and walked to the door, "Thank you Doctor, I do hope you are right, I have a serial killer I need to catch. It is difficult to try and relax when you have a killer gutting and stringing people up!"

The Doctors mouth opened as if to say something but nothing came out. Bos walked out of the room and went back along the corridor he had recently walked through. He hadn't had high expectations of visiting the Doctors' and getting cured, he had hopes alright but not expectations. "Fucking good job too," he mumbled to himself as he left the building. Bos walked the couple of miles to his house. He arrived about 18:00, as he walked through the door he thought about what the Doctor had said. "Well there is your walk doctor, now I should be as right as rain," although he thought it was useless he did actually heed her advice and not drink any alcohol, even though it was very tempting. He cleared up the mess left from this morning, listened to some music for a couple of hours and then decided to go to bed.

CHAPTER 33

Re-visit

Bos woke at 07:30 with his alarm ringing, he stirred and switched the beeping off. He sat up and thought about things. He felt a little better than yesterday, he was still a bit fuzzy but his head was not thumping. His body ached but not like yesterday and his hands were not sore. "Perhaps the Doctor was right." He pulled the quilt off himself and spun his legs off the bed. He looked at his foot from yesterday and it still had the two plasters on. He pulled the larger one off and then tried the second one, it came off but then stopped as it became closer to the cut. As he pulled it he could feel his skin pulling. Bos collected some scissors from the kitchen and gently cut the plaster around the glued area. Now he had a centimetre of plaster glued to the bottom of his foot, not ideal but a lot better than having blood everywhere like yesterday. The shower was very relaxing this morning as he stood in the water, washed and thought about the day's plan of action. He wanted to visit the last scene again with a fresh mind and to take Del. He wanted to update the timeline with the new information. Bos walked out of the shower feeling a lot better and looking forward to the day. On went his robe and he walked into the living room, "Morning babe." After a nice cup of coffee and some toast Bos was ready for the day ahead. Come 09:00 he was shaved, dressed and waiting to be collected. It wasn't long before Del walked up to the house and was about to ring the bell as the door opened. "Morning Del, ready to visit the last site?"

Del was happy to see Bos looking a little fresher than he had for a while, "You look better this morning."

"I do actually feel a little better, do you know where Fox Wood farm is?" Del did and they both walked towards the car. Del walked towards the passenger door and his colleague followed, "What are you doing around here? You have the keys you muppet, you are driving!" it was an odd moment for Del as he felt it was a kind of graduation moment. He opened the car and the two men climbed in. He had a grin on his face as he started the engine and was a happy man as the car pulled of and headed towards the scene of the Butchers 5th victim. The car pulled into the farm and Bos told him to head past the farm buildings and park near the gate at the end. They parked and exited the vehicle. Just as the Inspectors had reached the front of the car, three large German Shepard dogs came flying around the corner and stopped with a skid in front of the them, the dogs were growling and showing enough teeth to kit out a great white with a spare set! Del moved to try to get to the car door but one darted forward in a warning not to move or risk losing something vital.

"What the fuck are we supposed to do with these?" said Del in a voice like a ventriloquist.

"They are Harriet and John's dogs I think, when I visited they put them away." At that moment Bos looked across the yard and saw Harriet walking over. She reached about 5 metres away and recognised Bos.

"Inspector, nice to see you again," she saw the face of Del and then said, "Heal." All three dog stopped their growling immediately and walked over and stood around her. One was to the left, one to the right and one was directly behind her.

"Morning Harriet how are you? This is my colleague, Inspector Martin," said Bos, pointing to a quite petrified Del.

"Hello Inspector. Excuse my puppies, since the incident in the wood they are out making sure we are safe." Del looked at them now and all three were sitting. Their tongues were flying about as they panted happily next to their owner.

"That I have to say is very impressive, I have seen police dogs at work and they always astonish me."

"Are you a dog lover then Inspector?" Del said that indeed he was and she should call him Del. With that, she said, "Greet," and all three ran towards him. "Well in that case say hello to Sheeba, Lightning and Kaine." The dogs were sat at Del's feet now waiting for a fuss, one of them lifted its great paw and smacked it on his leg. "Ha typical Sheeba, has to be first." Bos told Harriet that they have just arrived to look at the scene again as Del had not seen it yet. She told them that the others had all finished a few hours ago about 04:00 she thought. "Okay then, if you need anything you know where we are, my pups will be fine now they know we are okay with you being here, so don't worry about them." Harriet turned to leave and the dogs continued to be fussed by Del. She got about 15 metres away and then whistled once and they all belted away after her. They walked in the pattern they had adopted earlier. They looked wonderful, like a hairy red arrows formation. The gate was shut but unlocked and they opened it and walked through and up the track. Bos stopped at where he remembered the tyre print was. It was still there but it now had traces of plaster in it. "Here is the tyre print."

Del looked at it, "Mm, yes I can see why you picked that up, glad to see they have taken a cast of it." They walked a little further up the track and Bos then stopped and pointed to the tree the body was in up until recently.

"Okay that was the one," there were still some stains in the bark but the blood and organs had been removed from the floor. There was a lot of water around as they had drenched it to remove traces of blood. Bos then pointed to the grass and told Del that the grass imprint was there and was consistent with the same size and shape as the others.

"Okay that would mean he is swapping the carpet from vehicle to vehicle. Logically it would be when the body was wrapped inside."

Bos looked over and asked, "Why is that?"

"Well if the carpet is from the Butcher then he

would arrive with it in his vehicle. Then subdue his victim, wrap him and then place him in the victim's car to use."

Bos stroked his chin while in thought, "So why use my car and then the victim's car, why not use his own? It would be less hassle!" Del thought and then said that it would be less hassle but would have a lot less impact and be less impressive! Bos wondered about that answer, he supposed that it made sense but was not entirely happy with the explanation. Bos then explained about the brutal disfigurement of the victim. "This victim was hung up and cut to bleed out over the tree presumably the same way as the others."

Del butted in at that part, "Why presumably?"

Bos looked over and told him, "The other damage was so extensive, while he was hanging I couldn't actually see the gut incision. His heart, eyes and ears were removed. However, this time they were nailed to the tree along with his liver and tongue." Bos could see Del sneer at the idea, "That is not all, unfortunately he had also stripped the skin and tissue from around the torso and hung it down over his waist, therefore covering any earlier incision."

"Holly shit, he went to town on him then," Del was thinking that it was no surprise that there was so much water about and why the farm couple had put their dogs on guard. "So was anything else different about this one?"

Bos thought for a little while then said, "There was a partial footprint in the blood, obviously it's not here now but when we get the scene report we can see what that was about. Something is niggling at me about this one though and I don't know what." He started to pace to think, he picked up a stick and snapped a bit off it. He continued to pass up and down and snap the stick into small pieces. He then stopped, "Let me run this past you, over the last few kills the Butcher has been trying to embroil me into this. Come to think of it he linked me in from the start with knowledge of all the victims." He started to pace again and picked up another stick, he started again, "He dragged me into it further by the message and then by using my car! Why has it not progressed further? The murder scene has!"

Del shrugged, "To be honest we don't know you are not linked any further, we haven't got the scene reports beck yet!"

Bos threw down the stick he had, "You are right, I wonder if we have the report on my car yet, come on let's go." Bos marched away from the site towards the car they had arrived in. The three German Shepherds were still patrolling around the farm, but just as Harriet had said they paid the men no attention what so ever.

CHAPTER 34

Odd

Bos and Del pulled into the station still pondering the last scene. Even though Del had not seen the actual body it was still an awful image to think about. They both walked directly to the conference room they had been using. Bos pushed open the large heavy door and it was exactly as he had left it. "I have updated the timeline with the details of Brand or Rand or whatever the fuck his name was. I have also added his car and the site of the murder. I was hoping at the time he was the Butcher unfortunately that didn't pan out so well." He then told Del to wait and he would go and see if there was a report on his desk. Del was looking at the timeline. He was looking at the array of information but very few cut and dry leads. This has to be an expert of some kind, he has been running rings around us and Bos is one of the most respected Inspectors about. The knowledge the Butcher has shown to not only evade our capture but embroil Bos into it so well is masterly. All these things were going through his mind and the thought, "Why

Bos, what is that link. All the victims are well known as criminals to Bos but why would the Butcher go for them because of that?"

Bos walked in as Del was near the end of saying this aloud to himself, "What was that Del?"

"Oh not a lot just thinking out loud, what have you got there?" Bos told him that he had picked it up from his desk and that it had a stamp from the vehicle analysis team on the front. The brown A4 envelope was opened and the single piece of printed white paper was pulled out. Bos quickly scanned through it. He looked inside the envelope to see if he had left anything in it. "What's up?" asked Del.

Bos was stunned, "I don't understand this, it must be a fucking joke!" He thrust the single page towards Del. Del reached out and tentatively took it to read. He looked at the details, it gave the index, the make and model, colour, registered owner, job number and the incident number of the job it was linked to. Del continued to read. Then in a box at the bottom it said numerous fingerprints detected and recorded and a number of hair and DNA samples collected and analysed. All samples collected test positive as the registered owner, Inspector Jeff Boston. Carpet fibres found in the rear of the vehicle match those found at the site of the victims. This carpet is untraceable. NO other evidence found. Del turned the page over as if missing something too.

"Is that it, that is all they found?!" Bos didn't answer.

There was a knock at the door, "Excuse me sir I have this for you." It was a quite quietly spoken plane clothes young lady at the door, she had a name badge on as working in admin.

Bos walked over, "What is it?" he asked as he held his hand out.

"It is a CSI report by the label on it, I was just asked to bring it to you." Bos took the recognisable brown A4 envelope from her and turned away.

As he started to walk away he turned and shouted, "Thank you!"

Del looked over, "Do you think that will be Fox Farm or Orchard Close?" Bos said that he would prefer it to be Fox Farm so he has no doubt in the slightest it will be on Orchard Close. The crime scene investigation unit had been flat out for a while and were doing an excellent job to churn out the results so quickly. Bos just hoped that it didn't mean they were missing things. Bos opened the envelope and pulled out the paper, there were some photographs too. The information on the sheet said 15 Orchard Close, Bos smiled as if to say see bloody knew it. He looked at the pictures and they were of the message on the wall. It was still a chilling message to read, he put the picture down and read the report. The main message was that all evidence in the house belonged to the owner.

Del watched Bos read, suddenly he frowned, "What?!" he dropped his arms to his side and looked at the ceiling.

"What does it say?" asked Del.

Bos turned to look downwards, "You were at the house with me, you have seen me search places before, how did I open the back door?"

Del thought about it for a second, "I don't know, I can't recall. Why?"

He sighed, "You have seen me before, how do I open doors?" Del said that when he had seen him open doors he puts his hand in his sleeve and then opens them but then again asked why. "It says that my fucking prints are on the door, I don't get it I never grab bloody doors. I must be cracking up! I know I have been off recently but now I can't be trusted to look at a possible crime scene without leaving my fucking prints behind." Bos didn't even look at the rest of the sheet, he gave it to Del and sat down. Del took the form and looked over it, he was trying to remember watching through the letterbox at Bos entering the house but he just couldn't recall it.

"Bos, it says here the writing on the wall was done in toothpaste." Bos was sitting with his head in his hands and mumbled that it sounded about right as the Butcher has always used things that are at hand in the property. Del cringed a little, "Yes but that is not all, it says here that hair was found imbedded in the toothpaste." Bos looked up suddenly interested again. "It's your hair Bos."

He stood up fast enough to knock his chair over, "What?" he snatched the page back off Del and scanned it. He searched the page and then found the sentence. It said that the toothpaste was a chemical match for the tube in the bathroom. Imbedded in the paste on the 'u' of 'Butcher' was a hair. When analysed this was a human hair and it was a DNA match for a profile in the police staff list. This profile was that of Inspector Boston. Bos was now angry, "This is fucking farce," he crumpled up the sheet and threw it in rage. It hurtled across the room and went straight into the bin. It was an amazing shot if it was meant but unfortunately wasn't, it was a complete fluke but looked excellent.

"But as far as I could see you never went near the wall!"

"I know that and you know that, it's the bastard Butcher trying to fuck me about again."

Del was thinking, "If this is the Butcher again he really is doing a number on you. Have you ever been to the house before?"

Bos was angry already and that question hit him like a hammer, "Of course I fucking haven't, what are you saying? You think I have been there and used his toothpaste to gel my fucking hair?!" Del didn't really know what to say, he wasn't thinking that but he was thinking that the evidence that is in place is pointing towards Bos and if they didn't catch the Butcher soon questions will be asked. Of course he didn't say that he was still the shadow in this team and didn't want to step on Bos's toes and get removed. Del was starting to dread the next crime scene report for the fear of what may be found.

"Do you want a cup of coffee while we decide where to go from here?" Bos said yes and quite frankly Del was happy to get away for a few minutes while he fetched them. As Del brought them back in Bos was on the phone, "Okay sir, right you are. Thank you sir I will do that right away." The phone was placed back on its stand and Bos looked over to Del who was at the door, holding two coffees. "Sorry Del I have some bad news for you, you are not shadowing me as from now."

Del was stunned all he could manage to utter was, "What?"

"Sorry," said Bos, "but I don't think it is working out, things seemed to have gone really tits up since you came on board and now I want to concentrate on it on my own."

Del put one of the coffees down, "I thought we were getting on!"

Bos looked down at the ground, "We have and that is another reason I actually asked for you to be moved, I don't like the way this case has gone and if it continues to go tits up someone's career is going down the pan. I would hate to see a promising career like yours get shut down before it really began."

Del was speechless, well almost, "Fuck, well it was good working with you while it lasted," he then turned and walked out of the room with his coffee still in his hand.

Bos walked over picked up his drink and then sat down in front of the timeline. "Now you butchering bastard it's just you and me, I will hunt you down you shit." He looked at the time line again and decided to go back to speak with one of the only links he had, Tony's wife.

CHAPTER 35

Dom

After the brown Labrador had been dispatched Ben, Bella and Suzie went back to the house for a drink. Bella had made the drinks and put them on the table in front of where they were all sitting. "If this doesn't work we will have to up the action to something that will work."

Ben said thank you for his drink but then added, "But what would definitely work?" Bella told Ben that for years she had been sacrificing her own blood at the trees and that this held off the trees vindictiveness for a while but was never enough to keep accidents from happening permanently.

"So we know our blood kept it at bay for a little while but obviously you couldn't keep doing it because of the loss of your blood, the animals we are getting are not enough to stave off the vengeance of them, so what is there left?" Suzie had said this and then looked directly at Ben. "Ben you are an intelligent young man, what can we do about it?" Suzie was fluttering her eyelashes and leaning towards Ben.

He thought for a while, "Okay your blood worked Bella but there was not enough of it to keep them going, animals don't work so we need more human blood."

Bella looked shocked, "Ben the three of us can't give enough to keep them at bay," she surreptitiously looked and winked at Suzie.

"Ben you can't expect Mum to keep cutting herself again and I am too small and weak, so that would just leave you… unless you get help."

Ben thought again, "We need to get someone else then." The two females were very happy and excited about the way Ben was automatically taking the conversation as they steered it.

"But Ben, nobody is going to willingly give us blood, they won't believe us about the trees and the trees don't like innocent people getting hurt," Susie said this and put her hand on top of Ben's.

Ben's pulse quickened, "Well we need to get someone who isn't innocent and get their blood then." *Fantastic*, thought Bella, *the boy was like a donkey, stick a carrot in front of him and he will take you exactly where you want to go.*

"Are you saying we need to get a criminal and bleed them at the tree?" said Suzie. "That is fantastic Ben, you are brilliant! That helps in every part of this, not an innocent person getting hurt, a lot of blood and it will be human blood for the trees." She leant over and kissed Ben on the head.

He went scarlet but was floating on air, "When are

we going to do it?" Both Bella and Suzie beamed internally however externally they were quiet.

"Are you sure this is what you want to do to save your mum?" said Suzie.

Ben looked at her, "Would you do it for your mum?"

Suzie again put her hand on his, "Yes of course I would, my mum has done so much for me but I am older than you." This sentence had the desired effect. Ben loved his mum and also wanted to prove himself to Suzie.

"We should do it, I will do it," said Ben. Bella then explained that if they were going to do it they should do it soon. This way Ben's mum may recover quickly. She also told the other two that she knew a criminal in a near town that was a likely candidate.

Ben asked who it was, "He is a nasty man who just came out of prison for burglary, the prison had let him out early," said Bella. "Okay then shall we go with Ben's idea?" They all agreed and Bella told them that she would find a way to get him there. Bella was evil but she was clever, after just a couple of seconds thought she knew what she was going to do. It was that night she would put the plan into action.

Bella attended the Flute and Whistle pub at 8 o'clock that evening, she was well known and knew everything that was going on too. This was Dominic Hill's local and since being let out of prison he had made it a very regular hang out. When she arrived Dom was at his usual seat at the bar. Bella sat near him and ordered a gin, she ordered it with a slur as if she had drunk a few too many already. She struck up a conversation with the barman and downed her drink very quickly, she ordered another and made sure she spoke loudly. She made a point of mentioning where she worked, she also said that she was looking after the boy as his parent were not there. "I am taking him out for the evening tomorrow to keep him occupied, not that he deserves it, rich bastards." She went on to describe how wealthy the family were and how much expensive stuff was around the place. "Makes you sick how much some people have while others have nothing, but I will still take him out and be with him all evening at the theatre no less." She made sure to slur some more, after a few more hints and another gin she got to her feet, unsteadily and then left. Knowing Dom the way she did, that would be enough to tempt him into action. Now she just had to wait.

The next evening she got Suzie and Ben to get a taxi out to the cinema. Bella stayed in and turned all the lights out, she locked all the doors and windows but left just one above the conservatory unlocked and open. She then sat in the corridor outside the room that the window was open in. She was sat on a wooden seat and in her hands was a shotgun. If she was any judge of people, and she was, Dom would be arriving at about 8:30-9:00pm. It was 7:45 at the moment and she was as stationary as she was when she first sat down. Bella was an extraordinary woman, a psychotic one, but extraordinary none the less. At 08:12 she saw a beam of light flick past the window, she looked at her watch and smiled. The light flicked back and highlighted the open window. Bella stood up and pulled the door shut and sat back down. It was around three minutes later when the door was opened by Dom. "Stop right there before I blow your fucking head off," Dom very nearly spat his heart out of his mouth.

"But you-"

That was all that came out of his mouth before Bella butted in, "Shut up before you die, do exactly what I say otherwise I will be pulling this trigger and you can say goodbye to your face, don't say a word just nod if you understand me." Dom at this point was in no kind of state to do anything else, he was petrified so nodded quickly. "Good man, at the bottom of the door you will see some cable ties. Pick them up and strap your feet together." Dom was shaking but picked up the ties that were on the floor, he bent down to tie his feet. "Sit down while you do it," she said.

"Why do-"

He didn't finish the sentence because Bella cut him short again, "Shut up, that is your one and only chance. One, just one more word and you will have to be identified by your fingerprints because not even you mum will be able to recognise you with this shotgun removing your looks." Dom's arse was twitching now and his knees were shaking. He sat down and placed a tie around his ankles and pulled. "Tight," said Bella. Dom did exactly what he was told. "Lay on the floor on your belly with your hands together and outstretched towards me." Dom was on an automatic game of Simon Says now but without the complication of listening for the word Simon. He just did exactly what he was told. Bella turned on the lights, stepped towards him and cable tied his hands together, she pulled the ties very tight. Dom squealed in pain, "I will let you off with that noise, but not a lot else." She stepped back again. "Now sit up," he did so immediately. As he sat, tears were rolling down his face. "Get a grip scum bag, happy to break into someone's house but don't want to take the punishment for it?" Dom opened his mouth to say something but thought better of it very quickly. Bella noticed a rug to the right of the room. "Roll over there and lay on the edge of the rug." He did this, it took him a little while but got there. "Good," Bella put her hand in her pocket and brought out a lock knife. She opened it up making sure Dom was watching her. "Now I am coming over to you and I am going to roll you in the rug, keep your arms tucked in to your front and keep still, otherwise I will bleed you with my knife." Dom's eyes were as wide as saucers now.

Bella grabbed the rug that was directly under him and rolled him, she rolled him until the rug was all completely wound around his body. The cable ties were picked up again and the rug was tied together. It was an odd site, Dom's head was sticking out of the top and his feet were just visible sticking out from the bottom. Bella went to the side of the room and picked up a roll of tape that she had put there ready. She undid it and went towards the rug roll. Bella placed the tape over Dom's mouth. "Excellently done, now it won't be long until you die!" You couldn't actually see but he did urinate himself at that point, he tried to move but it was impossible, it was as if he was paralysed. Bella from that moment didn't say another word to Dom, it was as if he was just a piece of furniture she had to move around. To get him downstairs she tied a rope around the middle of one of the cable ties and she just pulled it across the floor and down the stairs. Dom's head took a bit of a battering but it was not a concern for Bella, as long as he wasn't bleeding or dead she was okay with it. She dragged him to the front door and then eventually out to the front and then just around the left of the house to the nearest tree. She had got him to the tree and then just left him there. Bella walked calmly back to the kitchen and made herself a drink, she was very pleased with a plan that was superbly executed, she chuckled and said out loud, "Superbly executed plan, ready for a superbly executed Dom."

It was an hour later when Suzie and Ben came home. They walked in and Bella grinned at them. "What's up mum?" Bella told them to follow her and she walked outside by the front door. The two followed and Bella made her way to the tree. When Ben and Suzie caught up Bella was standing with one foot on top of the rug.

"I want you to meet someone, this, my children, is Dominic Hill." She pointed down to the rug and particularly towards the head that was sticking out. "He is a burglar and actually turned up at our property tonight to rob us, so I think we have our voluntary sacrifice." Suzie squealed with excitement, Ben didn't say anything, he did however walk over and look at Dom wrapped up tightly in the rug. He looked into the panicked eyes which had tears running from them. "Guilty man, do you think your victims cried too?" Bella laughed heartily. Suzie asked her mum how they were going to do it. Bella explained as she went. "First we need to get the rope around his neck," this was done, "Now I need to throw this over here." Bella took the other end and threw it over a high branch. The situation continued slowly but to Bella's exact instructions. The rope around Dom was pulled until he was on his feet. The cable ties were cut and the rug was removed by Ben and Suzie pulling on the rope and lifting Dom in the air so the rug could come away from under him. Dom was choking while this was happening but it did go quickly. Once the rug was gone Dom was lowered until he was on his feet.

Suzie spoke next, "This is not going to work, his clothes are going to soak the blood, none of the animals were clothed." She took the knife that was being held by her mum and walked towards Dom, he kicked up and caught Suzie on the leg. Ben ran forward and kicked Dom hard in the thigh.

"I will hold his legs," Ben held his legs, it was difficult as he was wriggling. Suzie did however continue to slice at his clothing and eventually after 10 minutes Dom was naked.

"Now you are hanging free, kick me again Mr and I will use this knife so you dangle no more," as she said this she cupped her fingers under Dom's testicles and gently lifted them up a couple of times.

"Leave them alone my girl, I haven't had anything like that for a while so if anyone was to be grabbing that it would be me, unfortunately Mr Hill don't get your hopes up that is not what we are here for. Ben get your knife." Ben left at haste to his room to collect his large knife from under his draw. He collected it and made his way back to the tree. He wasn't nervous, he wasn't scared, but he did have some butterflies fluttering around his stomach. Ben arrived back at the tree and they were all in the same position as when he left. Dom was shaking, presumably with shock and fright, the other two were standing next to each other admiring the lock knife Suzie had with her. Ben walked over, "Are you ready Ben?" Ben nodded and walked towards Dom, the knife Ben had in his grasp was seen by Dom who immediately started to squirm and wriggle, his eyes were wide open and the tape on his mouth was billowing out as he tried to shout. Bella and Suzie grabbed the rope.

"Ready?" shouted Suzie. Ben nodded and the rope was pulled, it was hard going for the females but they were stronger than they looked and determined. Dom lifted from the ground and started choking and snorting snot out of his nose. They pulled some more and Dom was lifted to about three foot from the ground. Ben stepped forward and hesitated, he looked at Suzie and she smiled at him. His turn was swift and his blade was accurate, it sliced through Dom easier than it had with the dogs. The blood was immediate it rushed out at speed and gushed onto the bark of the tree and the arm of Ben. The girls lifted the body more, Dom was still writhing as more of his life giving liquid spilled. Ben stood back and watched, the trajectory of the blood had lessoned with the loss of pressure. Dom stopped writhing and just swung while the last of his precious blood spilled out onto the grass.

"Ben."

Bella had spoken and Ben knew why, *"Placare arbores,"* uttered Ben. Bella and Suzie let the rope go and what once was Dominic Hill dropped limply to the floor. Ben went over to him and removed the tape, his eyes were still open and watery and the tape was wet. That night Bella put the body in a canvas bag with some concrete and it was tied together and dumped in the lake. The bottom of the tree was watered to help remove traces of the blood.

CHAPTER 36

Tragedy

It was 10:00 o'clock on the Sunday morning and Bella, Suzie and Ben were at the dining room table eating breakfast when the phone rang. Bella put down her grapefruit and stood. She walked over to the phone and answered it. She listened intently for a little while and then beamed, "Really that is excellent I will get him," she held the phone away from her and looked across the room to Ben. "Ben come here please, phone for you."

Ben was surprised but happy, there was only one person that phoned and asked for him, "Dad," he shouted and ran across to the phone, "Hello."

"Hello Ben, how are you?" Ben waited for that, it was his dad's opening line every time.

Ben then followed with his answer which was the same every time too, "I am okay, how is mum, is she any better?" The conversation usually faltered at this point because Mike always had to disappoint him. However, this time it was different.

"Well Ben, actually she is a lot better your mum woke up last night, she is feeling well and wants to see you." Ben couldn't say anything he had a ball of lava in his throat or at least that is what it felt like, all he could do was cry. "I know how you are feeling Ben, I cried my eyes out too. I am leaving the hospital in a while and am going to come and get you okay?" Ben sobbed an indistinguishable okay, Mike then said that it would take him about an hour and a half to get back. "See you soon, hopefully about 11:30." Ben put the phone down.

"Bella it worked, mum woke up, thank you," he flung his arm around Bella and hugged her, he then ran across the room and hugged Suzie.

"You had better get yourself ready to go see your mum then," said Suzie smiling at him. Ben ran out and upstairs. He was so happy and excited he couldn't believe it finally happened, the phone call he had dreaming about for months had come. He showered and put fresh new clothes on, he brushed his teeth and ran downstairs, he still had 45 minutes until 11:30. He started to pace up and down, Bella saw him.

"Why don't you go into the flower garden and pick some nice flowers for your mum, that will pass a few minutes for you?" Ben thought that it would be really nice to pick some flowers for mum, she has been asleep for so long. He left the house and spent quite a while picking some blooms that he thought his mum would like and would go well together. When he got back into the house it was 11:10. Bella had set up some plastic to wrap the flowers in so by the time they had done that it was twenty past eleven. Ben took the flowers and waited outside the front of the house. Unfortunately, every minute seemed like ten and Mike didn't pull up until 11:40. Mike stopped the car and got out. Ben ran to him and flung himself at his Dad.

"Okay Ben I am just going to go in the house for a wee and then we can go okay?" Ben jumped in the passenger side of the car and said that he would wait here while he goes. Mike was not long he had said hello to Bella and Suzie on the way through the house but he was as eager to get back to Madison as Ben was. He ran out and shouted, "Come on then Ben lets go see your mum." Thankfully the weather was fine and the traffic was light.

Ben had been bursting for the toilet for the last 30 miles but didn't want his dad to pull over, "No I can hold it, let's just get there." Ben was so excited when the car pulled into the hospital he could have gone for a wee two minutes ago but would have still needed another. The car was parked and Mike had to walk fast to keep up with his son. "Come on dad come on!" he shouted as he ran towards the front of the hospital.

"Wait Ben, mind the road," Ben waited at the hospital road that crossed in front of the hospital doors, this was the road that was used to drop off and pick up patients. They walked across the zebra crossing together and as they entered the large double doors Mike pointed to the toilets on the right. "Go on then Ben, there are the toilets."

"I don't need to go now, come on," said Ben eager to go straight to his mum.

"No, you have been waiting for a while go now."

Ben complained in the universal 'oh dad' kind of way but walked towards the toilet. It was fortunate he listened because as he entered the room his bladder decided that it could not wait another second and pains started to shoot through his stomach. Ben was standing at the urinal panicking to get his trousers open. Luckily they opened right away and were not in the mood to cause any obstruction. The relief was immense and Ben let out an enormous sigh, he seemed to pee for ages and just wanted it to stop. He stopped, washed his hands and hurried out of the door. "Come on then," said Mike grinning. It wasn't long before Ben walked into his mum's room with his huge bunch of flowers and saw her sitting on the chair next to her bed.

He just dropped the flowers and ran to her, "Mum." The force of Ben hurtling into her nearly knocked the chair flying. Ben was crying, Madison was crying and Mike standing after he had picked up Ben's flowers was crying. The reunion was amazing Ben couldn't stop just looking at his mum's eyes, they were open for the first time in a long time and she was talking to him, he was so happy he thought he was going to explode with joy. All too quickly Mike said that they had to go. "Why?" said Ben. Mike said that the hospital had to keep an eye on his mum for a few days and then if everything was okay she could come home. Ben's happiness burst suddenly. "But I thought she was coming home now," tears were welling up in his eyes, Madison gave him a big hug.

"I want to come home too Ben but it won't be long now," she kissed him on the head. The walk back to the car felt like someone had put lead in his shoes, his feet were so heavy. His heart was feeling just as heavy. The trip back was silent apart from a few sentences.

"I know it is irritating Ben but we will have mum back soon now." That night Mike slept at home, he left again the next day but Ben was at school anyway. Monday and Tuesday seemed to take weeks but Tuesday night Ben was told that he was going to go to the hospital with Mike at 16:00 after school to bring his mum home. He was elated and the Wednesday seemed to go backwards. The energetic, excited and thrilled little boy travelling to hospital to collect his mum bore no resemblance to the child that had so cold bloodedly ending the lives of numerous animals. The ending of Dominic Hill was as cold as anyone could get. It was 8 o'clock by the time the appropriate forms had been completed and Madison was allowed out. The weather had taken a turn for the worse and rain was hammering down. This did not dampen the spirits of the family that had just exited the hospital and were walking in the belting rain back to their car. It was just a short journey to the car from the hospital door but they were all soaked to the skin. The car started and it was time they were on their way. The journey usually only took around 90 minutes but due to the weather they were running a long way behind that time. By the time they got close to the house it was dark and the rain was vicious. It was thundering too. The windscreen wipers were on full, zipping back and forth as if crazy.

Mike turned into the drive, "Home sweet home people!" Mike put his foot down a bit more now, the weather was the same but he knew he was off the main road and on their private land. He picked it up heading towards their house, still the rain hammered and the wipers belted back and forth. The car smashed into a large puddle and the water lifted up, suddenly there was a white creature in the road, Mike steered hard right to miss it and the car hit the grass verge. The grass was soaked right through and the breaks had no effect what so ever, the vehicle headed for a tree. No matter what Mike did with the steering wheel the car went straight, no matter what he did with the breaks it continued at speed. The impact was loud and abrupt. Ben heard the air bags deploy but he smashed his head on the tablet he was watching. The airbag to the right deflated as soon as it deployed, the reason being was that the tree the vehicle hit had a large low branch. This branch had pierced the windscreen burst the right airbag and then pinned Mike to his headrest by impaling him through his right eye socket. Ben was dazed but saw the branch sticking through the headrest it had brain and hair attached. He heard screaming as Madison had turned and seen the life ending injury of her husband. Just then thunder smashed and lightning forked down and hit nearby outside. Ben could hear a creaking amongst his mother's screams. Then an almighty crash and a tree landed on the top of the car. Ben looked on in horror as a branch came through the roof and skewered his mum who stopped screaming immediately. There was a creaking and the tree that had landed started to shift to the right, Madison's head was removed by the force of the tree falling to the side while being imbedded in her skull. The slam of the rest of the tree flattened the right side of the vehicle and Ben was crushed and all went dark and quiet.

CHAPTER 37

Suspicion

Del was devastated to be removed from shadowing Bos. He always thought of him as fantastic at what he does, and the best to learn on the job with too. It had not gone exactly the way he had thought it would. Bos had been erratic at times, on the ball at others and completely irrational at times too. He didn't like the way he was being lined up to be shot by the Butcher. He had decided the hours after his dismissal that he was still going to take an interest in the Butcher case and if he could, help Bos in the background. The first part of that was to get hold of a copy of the scene report from Fox wood. He contacted a friend of his who worked at the CSI unit. His friend had agreed to furnish him with a copy of the report. He got hold of it the next day. Just as Bos had told him, the damage was extensive and brutal. The report said that again there were carpet fibres in the flattened grass area and they were red and blue. It suggested that the tyre tracks were from a medium sized family car. It showed on a photograph the track itself and then a cast of it. The description would fit with Brand's car. It confirmed that the victim was Gordon Brand of 15 Orchard Close. It said that a number of his organs had been removed and nailed to the tree and then listed them. The nails used were domestic 6 inch steel that could be purchased at many hardware shops. The pictures were extremely gruesome. There were no fingerprints left but there was a partial footprint. It had a photograph of a pool of blood with a front half of a foot shape embedded in it. The write up stated that the print was not associated with any regular footwear but matched patterns made by people wearing protective paper shoes. The type used by crime scene staff. It went on to estimate the shoe size as being size 11. Del thought to himself, *what are the odds that Bos is size 11? I know how this bastard works.* Del decided to test his supposition. He picked up his phone and dialled, "Hello this is Inspector Martin, I am calling on behalf of Inspector Boston, he would like to know if he could have a replacement for his size 11 hard wearing wellingtons please?" The man on the other end said it was highly irregular ordering for others. "No I am not ordering them for him, he just wanted me to call and ask when he had them last because they are looking a little shabby."

After a minute or so the male came back, "Well they bloody well shouldn't be looking shabby, he only had them four months ago."

Del sounded shocked, "Oh perhaps I am wrong and the boots I saw were not his, what was the description of the boots he had in January?" Del heard the male move away mumbling to himself.

When he came back he sighed and said, "Size 11 hard wearing wellington boots in dark blue, signed for by Inspector Boston." Del thanked the man for his help and dismissed it as a miss communication.

Del put the phone down, "Fucking knew it." He was sitting with the report in front of him. Every piece of evidence that was found linked Bos, how was the Butcher getting this stuff? Del thought about the rug fibres. If the Butcher is planting evidence, he must be getting it from Bos's home. It was then that Del decided that he would go on another stake out, this one was to keep an eye on Bos's property. Del stood up and walked directly to the chief's office, he would not do anything without his boss's say so. It was a bit of a cold atmosphere to start with but the longer Del spoke about catching the Butcher off guard by watching the property of the man he was trying to frame the more interested he became.

"Does Bos know?" asked the chief Inspector.

"No sir he doesn't, he doesn't even know I am working on the case." Del felt a little bit sneaky at that.

"Good, keep it that way. Let him continuing with his investigation while you take up yours, perhaps that way we may catch this bastard." Del stood up and thanked him. "The Butcher in custody would be thanks enough," he winked and got back to the paper work he was doing before Del came in. Del left the station and immediately headed for Bos's home address. He parked around the corner as he knew Bos would recognise his vehicle. There was an alley that ran the length of the houses in the road. Del walked down until he came to the gate that lead to his garden. He tried and opened the gate, not of the house he was watching but the garden opposite. He had noticed they had quite a convenient shed at the bottom of the garden and the apex of its roof was such that he could lay on it and watch the garden he needed to. He shut the gate behind him and walked to the main house. He knocked and a female answered. He put the index finger of his right hand to his lips and held his warrant card in the other. The woman was about to shout and tell him to piss off out of her garden but did stop.

"What?" she whispered.

"I am Inspector Martin can I have a quick word please?" The lady flicked her head to one side and ushered him in. "Thank you Miss."

"I ain't no Miss, I am a Mrs and my husband will be back soon," said the woman trying to make sure Del knew that she wasn't alone for long.

"That is fine, as I said I am inspector Martin, I am keeping an eye on a property nearby. So I am asking your permission to use the shed at the bottom of your garden," asked Del still holding his warrant card high in the air.

"Err yeah I suppose so, what for?" The woman was more than a little intrigued now as to what they could use her shed for.

"I just want to lay on the roof so I can see what is going on."

The woman deflated her anticipation, "Oh bloody hell is that all? You can do that I thought it might be something exciting then. Could have climbed on it without coming in here." Del explained that he needed to ask because if he was using it he didn't want her or her husband coming out and shouting at him at a crucial time. She understood and told him, "Okay knock yourself out love, go lay on it all you like." Del thanked her and left by the back door he came in through. When he arrived back at the shed, he looked around for something to climb on. There was an old bench on the other side of the garden so he dragged that across. He stepped up on to the bench, and up on to the table he then used his new height to put his foot on to the small ledge of the shed window and hauled himself up. He felt quite secure, it was a large well-built 8 foot shed so he had plenty of room to lay full length down the slope. He could see Bos's garden from here and he could see into his living space via the large window. He really wanted to make sure first that Bos was out, if he was Del could have a quick nose on the setup in the garden. For the first half an hour he lay motionless on the roof with just his eyes poking up over the ridge. After an hour the shed seemed to be a rather hard surface, he had seen no movement in the house. He slid down from his resting place and exited the gate. He tried the handle of Bos's gate and it opened, well there was one red mark for him. Del walked in the garden and had a look about. There was nothing exceptional to look at but nothing that would stop an intruder just walking wherever he wanted, as Del was proving. Through the window nothing was out of place but Del noted the setup, he had stretched his legs so returned back to his roof perch. It was hours before he saw any movement in the house. 17:15 to be precise and Bos had returned home from work. Del watched around the gardens for anything suspicious however the only thing odd was some idiot laying on a shed feeling as stiff as a board!

Bos sat in his chairs facing out at his garden so Del had to be very careful not to stick his head up as he would be in the direct line of sight for Bos. He just sat there staring out at the garden drinking what Del presumed was alcohol. It was about an hour and a half Bos just sat, he had got through two glasses of whatever the beverage was he was sipping. He then stood and went to the kitchen to Del's left. The large window stopped as the kitchen came off at a right angle to the main building, however there was a smaller window that looked into the room above the sink. Del still had to be careful not to be seen himself, he could see Bos riffling through his fridge or freezer. He then crossed the room out of view. A few seconds later he re-entered the main area and sat in his chair. It didn't take him long before he was up again. He went back into the other room and another couple of minutes later came out with a plate of food. Del surmised correctly that a microwave meal had just been pinged up. The view of Bos eating made Del realise how hungry he was. His stomach churned with the thought of even a micro meal, but he still laid in his place watching the area for any trace of the Butcher. He was drifting thinking of food when suddenly with no warning at all someone grabbed his right foot. He lifted it with speed and spun around ready to smash his foot down into someone face. Below him stood a man in his 30s. He had brown hair tied up in a ponytail, soft facial features and was smiling. The male was also carrying a plate of chips with tomato sauce on. The male held his free hand up to his lips and shushed Del.

"My wife told me what you are up to, thought you may be hungry by now," he whispered all this just enough for Del to hear. "I am Chris, do you want these up there or will you come down for them?" Del was shocked, he had seen many sides of human nature. He had seen the very worst, just a few hours ago he saw photograph of the hideous side and now standing here he was seeing the best. He shuffled down to the edge of the roof and took the plate from Chris.

"Thank you so much, you really are a life saver. You have no idea how good this looks," he took a chip from the plate that had a decent helping of sauce and put it in his mouth. He let out an 'ooh' and then said, "There must be a God of food because they have just answered a prayer." Chris told him to leave the plate on the grass after and he will pick it up later and walked off back to the house. Del sat and chomped away on the very welcome food and they seemed to disappear all too quickly. He climbed back to the top of the shed and slowly edged his eyes above the roof line. Bos had left the main room and Del couldn't see where he had gone, it was from now on that he had to keep alert. It would be now until around midnight he would expect some action of some kind. Del knew it was going to be a long one and was ready, especially after his recent plate from heaven. At 9 o'clock a lady walked through the alley with a medium sized dog. Del watched like a hawk to see if she was up to something criminal however the dog sniffed at the gate and then the pair continued on their way. At 22:30 Bos went upstairs, he was up there for 15 minutes when the light went out. Del's senses heightened ready, he could feel that he was on the brink of something. There was nothing more until

23:40 when the lights came on in the house. Minutes later Del saw Bos come down the stairs. "Can't sleep Bos?" As he watched Bos came outside and went into his own shed, he picked up a bag and left the shed and walked directly towards Del at the back gate. "What the fuck are you doing Bos?" He continued through the gate and walked to Del's right and walked out of the alley into the main street. Del was torn now, he didn't quite know what to do. He wanted to keep an eye on the property but was shocked to see Bos leave his home at this time. "Screw it," said Del and he shuffled down from the roof.

He walked out of his hiding spot and edged out of the alley. Bos was walking at pace in the direction to the east of his house. Del kept pace with him but a little way behind so he wouldn't be seen. They walked for around 30 minutes and Del was knackered, he had been stuck on a roof for God knows how long, he wasn't expecting to do a half hour bloody jog. Bos disappeared into a property on the right, "Have you found a fuck buddy Bos?" Del was thinking good on him after the loss of his wife and wondered who it was. Del turned and started walking back to Bos's home so he could keep an eye again. He was very nearly back when a car came past him from behind, just as it passed Del looked and he could have sworn it looked like Bos driving. It was a silver colour but that was all he saw, he was extremely confused now and picked up the pace back. As he turned the last corner to the house, Bos had just shut the boot of the silver car and was heading back into the alleyway. Del knew what he had to do now and he ran to his own car that was a little further down the road. He arrived puffing at his car and got out his keys, in his haste he dropped them. "Come on you twat," he fumbled around the floor picking them up, he knew he didn't have long. Del flung the door open and jumped into the seat.

The car started right away, he didn't put his lights on he just moved the car round the corner to see if the other car had left. It hadn't. Just as he looked on Bos reappeared and got straight into the car. The silver car took off almost immediately. "What are you doing man, did you forget your condoms?" Del did put his lights on and followed from as far back as he possibly could, he had a feeling that Bos would be heading back to the property he had just left and he was right. The break light came on so Del pulled over a distance away, as he watched, Bos kind of three point turned and reversed into the drive of the house he dropped in on before. "Reverse, what's up need a quick exit from her?" It was around 20 minutes before the car pulled off the drive again. Del pulled away and followed, it was more difficult this time as he was at a complete loss as to where the vehicle was heading, after 20 minutes Del struggled to keep up at a distance that wouldn't be conspicuous. Then the silver car pulled off and went through a kind of dirt track. Del knew where they were, it was one of the 10/10 sites they had pinpointed early in the case. They were driving down Willow Walk. The lead car stopped about 3 minutes down the track so Del pulled over too, he turned his lights off right away. The lights went off and a beam of light lit up small patches of wood. As he watched Del saw the boot open, it was difficult for him to see properly as he could only really see what the torch was illuminating. The beam was very erratic and flicked from side to side as the person fiddled in the boot. The light was held still and the person walked off carrying something on his shoulder. Del walked forward so he could try and find where the person had gone. The other person had disappeared into the trees to the right. Del picked up his pace to a jog, he could just about see the torch flicking in the distance. He started to run, the torch light was static now so he ran towards it.

Thud the pain in Del's nose was blinding, as he had run, something had come from behind the tree and hit him directly on the bridge of the nose. He had heard the crack before the pain hit and he knew he had broken his nose. He had fallen to the ground in agony. He got up slowly and picked himself up onto all fours then a hand came around the front of him and covered the front of his face with a cloth. The pain in his nose was excruciating as the cloth was pressed hard against him, the sting on his nose and then darkness, he had passed out. As he drifted back into conciseness, he could see a white shape in front of him. He tried to move but was unable to. He moved his eyes down towards his chest, he couldn't see anything it was too dark. His arms were tight in at his waist and all he could move was his head. He could see the torch beam moving around in the distance and after a few seconds it started coming closer. The person with the torch was now only metres away and the beam of light flicked past Del's face. He was light blinded for a moment then slowly his night vision started to come back. The beam lit up the white area a couple of metres away. Del took a fierce intake of breath, it was a naked body standing on tiptoes, he was attached to a rope that was strung up over the tree.

Del yelled, or at least tried it. His mouth was taped shut. The beam of light shot back and forth for a little while before it was static. It was wedged in the bow of a branch in a position to light up the body that was struggling to keep his balance on his toes. His mouth was taped too, his cheeks were puffing out at speed due to pure panic. Del could not see the identity of the torch man but he knew Bos must be around somewhere. Every now and again the person would pass in front of the beam and highlight himself. He was wearing a paper scenes of crime suit, the hood of the suit was pulled tight with the draw string. The white paper man walked to the side and Del could hear a bag being rummaged in. The paper man then walked back to the naked man. A glint of light hit and reflected off a shiny surface in the paper man's hand. Del realised very quickly that it was a large knife, he looked on in abject horror as the paper man grabbed the rope that was holding the man and pulled it. The man on the end lifted effortlessly it seemed. He was knee height from the ground and the paper man pulled again, he was now at a height so his feet were level with the paper man's waist. The body was writhing and choking, his arms were not tied they were up at his neck trying in vain to get the rope off so he could breathe. Unfortunately, that was not the sum of his problems. The knife glinted in the beam again and slashed at the poor man's belly. Crimson liquid flew across the gap between the belly and tree.

The paper man had blood on his suit, it kind of shone in the dull light and stood out against the once pristine white. The paper man walked back to the rope that was being tugged with the force of the victim's struggling. He pulled again and the victim rose like some awful killer's flag. Up he went again, slowly his struggles became less violent until he just swung gently and hung there. The blood had slowed now and the paper man let him down so his abdomen was a little closer to him, Del watch transfixed as the intestines were pulled from the body and left to hang. The knife glinted again and sliced up through the belly and up to the chest, the site was like something seen daily in an abattoir. Organs were spilling on to the blood soaked ground. The actions of the paper man were very calm and matter of fact in everything he did. Once all the organs were on the floor, the victim's left ear was pulled out tight and then cut from his skull, the left had the same punishment. His eyes were next, gruesome as it was the paper man walked to the bag and when he came back in the light, had a spoon with him. The spoon was inserted under the left eye and popped out, the sound made Del feel positively sick. The right eye was popped in the same way and the both were cut from the tether that attached them to their once owner. The tape that covered the man's mouth was ripped off and his mouth opened, his tongue was pulled unceremoniously and then removed with one swipe of the blade. The last part of the ritual that Del knew of started next. The knife was delved deep into the flesh at the chest area and was dragged straight down, this happened again and again at intervals around the body of around six inches. Once all these incisions were made, the top of a slice was cut and then peeled down so it hung down past the victim's waist. This went on until the body had no resemblance to human being, it looked like some horrific science fiction alien.

The paper man stepped back at this point and seemed to be admiring his handiwork. He went back to the rope and hoisted the mess higher into the tree. The bag was riffled through again and Del watched as each organ was lifted individually and a nail driven through it with a large claw hammer. The same macabre action was undertaken with the ears, eyes and tongue. It was quite odd to watch but once the tree had all its new accessories, the paper man climbed elegantly and swiftly up the tree. He lent over time and time again and grabbed pieces of intestine and hooked it over branches. It was terrifying to watch the man that he had been hunting in action. The Butcher was in front of him now making a new crime scene, which will in a few hours be looked at by staff he knew. It was odd but before that moment he had been so preoccupied with the victim in front of him that he had not put much thought into what was happening to him. He realized that he was in the rug, the blue and red rug that was present at all the crime scenes. *I am next,* thought Del. He wriggled as furiously as he could but he was bound too tight, any movement was impossible. *Fuck I really am a pig in a blanket,* he laughed to himself, which in the circumstances even he found odd! Del tried to shout again but the tape was still attached firmly to his mouth. He dribbled and licked as much as he could to try to loosen its hold on him. The tape did give a little and he blew out to try and loosen it further, it was working but it was slow going. If only he had of attempted this earlier and not been so transfixed by the spectacle that was happening in front of him.

The Butcher agilely climbed down from the tree. He stood in front of the tree and spoke in a low monotone voice, *"Placare arbores."* He walked slowly to Del. He stopped just at the side, bent down and picked him up still fully bound in the carpet. Del redoubled his efforts to remove the tape from his mouth, he didn't really know why because even without the tape he was still cocooned in the rug. After only a few second travelling he was unceremoniously dumped on the ground. Del looked about as much as he could and he could see the beam of light. He had been put the other side of the tree. The torch was removed from its home in the angle of the branch and was moving away towards what was now the left. The Butcher looked through the bag and pulled something out. *Oh fuck,* the voice in Del's head was exceedingly loud and panicked now, *Rope, more rope, you are next.* He was still spitting and blowing at the tape as the Butcher approached him again. Del was looking directly at him, the torch flashing from one side to another as he tied a loop in the rope. The loop was tied and he stepped slowly forward towards Del. The Butcher was right in front of him now, be bent down and placed the rope around his neck. Feverishly Del was attempting to remove the tape but then suddenly froze as the rope passed and he saw the Butcher up close properly for the first time. It was Bos! Del couldn't move he was in shock, Bos didn't pay him any attention he looked right through him and continued to prepare the double murder. Del eventually snapped out of his trance and continued with trying to get the tape from his mouth.

Bos the Butcher had stepped back and was readying himself to throw the other end of the rope over a suitable branch. The rope hurtled through the air and sailed clean over the branch that was needed, he had had a lot of practice. Del was very close to getting the tape off but suddenly Bos pulled the rope that was around Del's neck. Del's throat closed with the rope tightening around it. He lifted off the ground head first. His body didn't bend, it was stuck in the rug which made him stiff as a board. He was lifted again and again until he was standing upright. It was becoming more difficult to remove the tape as the restriction on his throat was reducing the amount of saliva he could produce. Bos went and collected the knife he had used before after he had wedged the torch in a new spot. Del put his tongue up through the top of the tape and continued to try and widen the gap. Bos the Butcher came towards the rug and cut off the cable ties. Still there were no signs from him that he knew or recognised Del at all. He walked away and picked up the rope. Del removed the tape from one side of his mouth with his tongue, it was enough to use his voice at last. "Bos, Bos its m…" the word me was cut short and strangled as the Butcher lifted him off the ground. His throat stung and his head filled with blood, he felt dizzy. He juddered as he lifted higher, eventually the rug came free and he could move his arms and legs now. He hadn't realised before but his ankles had been strapped together. Now the rug fell he was lowered, as his feet hit the floor the air started to flow through his throat again. He gasped and then shouted, "Bos, Bos you fucking bastard, it's me Del."

Bos stepped forward once more and stealthily and accurately sliced through Del's trousers. They were removed before Del even noticed what was happening. Del had a bit of a brain wave at that moment, he knew Bos and this wasn't him. "Fuck, you are asleep you crazy twat." Bos continued to slice, next was his top. His top took a little more effort to remove but Del was not interested in it, he was now putting all his energy and effort into waking up Bos. "Bos, this is not you, you are not a Butcher. You are more than this." Bos, the Butcher or the paper man, whatever he was called, he continued his relentless mission to remove Del's clothes. He was down to his underwear now and still didn't worry about it. This time he yelled as loud as his rasped neck would allow, "BOS YOU BASTARD, I am not some fucking criminal!" The Butcher stuttered for a second but then cut and removed the underwear. Del was in total panic now, tears were streaming down his face and snot and dribble was flying everywhere as he shouted to try and snap Bos back into reality. "Bos, Bos wake up, its Del, come on Helen wouldn't want you like this." As Del was shouting this Bos had walked away and grabbed the rope. "BOS, N…" Del didn't quite get the 'no' out of his mouth before the rope was pulled and the word was cut short. The strangling pain hit again and the heavy feeling of blood filling his head returned. The thumping noise of the blood pumping through his skull was immense. He could hear very little apart from the thumping sound of his heart. He tried to shout again, he couldn't manage it, he couldn't utter a word.

The Butcher lifted Del again. Del knew what was coming, he had just seen the barbaric stages undertaken on another person so was now just waiting for the pain and then the death. He relaxed and hung there accepting his fate. Bos stepped forward with his knife glinting in the torch light. It was thrust forward but stopped as it touched skin. Bos was frozen, he didn't move. The hand that held the knife was shaking, the knuckles were turning white. The Butcher was in a fight, he was fighting with Bos. The Butcher wanted to slice another belly, but Bos wanted to stop another life being lost. *BOS YOU BASTARD, I am not some fucking criminal,* rang in the unconscious mind of the police Inspector. It was a hammer to his policeman's soul. The hand shook more, with the shaking of the blade, blood started to seep out of a small incision that was being made. Del sensed the struggle and spent the last of his strength and energy to try and shout again. "B-b-b-ooosss," he croaked. Bos woke at that moment. He was immediately confused at what was in front of him. Last thing he knew was climbing into bed, he noticed Del and the knife in his hand. He sized up that part of the situation, he immediately stepped to one side, he shot out his arm and cut through the rope. Del dropped to the floor and gasped for air, he lay there wheezing, he ripped the tape off his mouth and put his hand down to feel how bad his stomach was cut. It was bleeding but not profusely. "Bos you cock, you were asleep," was what Del tried to say but nothing came out of his mouth, it turned out to be just a bad goldfish impression as his mouth opened and closed.

Bos was in complete shock, he stood and stared at Del sitting naked in the dark. "What the fuck is going on?" he could see Del but fortunately could not see his most recent victim hanging on the other side of the tree. "Why in God's fucking name are you naked and strung up, and what the fucking hell am I doing here… with a knife?" Del shook his head but still couldn't speak. His throat was still recovering. Bos was becoming more angry as his confusion mounted, "Del come on snap out of it, what the fuck happened?" Bos had shouted this and he was red in the face now. Del rubbed his throat again and tried to speak but what came out was just an inaudible rasp. Bos looked around a little more. Del naked hanging from his neck in a tree, a large oak tree, blood seeping from a stomach wound! "Jesus Del, the Butcher where is he?" Bos suddenly took a defensive stance waiting to be attacked at any moment by some psycho serial killer. His head darted from side to side to try and spot any movement. "Come on Del just point to where the fucker went!"

Del shook his head and slowly raised it looked directly at Bos, "It's you." This didn't have the effect that Del thought.

"Yes it's me, you are fine now everything is going to be okay, just tell me where the fucker went."

Del was getting his voice back now, "Bos put the knife down, you tied me up and you started to cut my stomach," as if it was needed for effect Del wiped his hand across his belly and showed the blood on his hands to Bos. Bos was getting angry again now, he was knackered and sore and didn't have the time to waste listening to the gibbering of a colleague in shock.

"Del concentrate, you have had a nasty whack and are in shock but it's imperative I find out where the Butcher went," Bos said this in the best calm but angry voice he could muster.

Del was still rubbing his neck but did not feel worried about being killed now, "Sorry Bos I know this is difficult to grasp, but you are the Butcher, tonight you killed the person hanging on the other side of this tree and were about to do the same to me but something in you stopped." Bos just stood there for a few seconds, he looked at the knife in his hand that was still covered in blood. He looked at Del, then back to the knife.

"Fuck off," he said throwing the knife to the floor.

Del sighed, "Look on the other side of this tree, there is a body of another male that was just killed, do you know him by any chance?"

Bos walked around the tree and came back a little later, "I don't know, I can't tell, there is not much left to identify him is there?"

Del needed Bos to understand, "Look for fuck sake Bos, you killed him in front of me. You were asleep, that's why you are so knackered. You haven't been getting a restful night you have been up and about."

Bos stopped and thought, but all he could say was, "But that doesn't make sense, why? How?"

"Why, I don't know. How? Well that was bloody scary."

Bos sat down on the wood floor, "Are you saying I was going to kill you?"

Del was sombrely nodding, "Unfortunately yes you very nearly bloody did, you did however kill him as I watched from inside a fucking carpet," Del pointed to the tree that had the Butcher's last victim hanging in it.

"I killed those people... I did it!"

"Yes but it wasn't you, you were asleep." That did not help Bos, he was devastated to say the least. He was an honest man who had spent his life tracking down and convicting criminals. He had led a life dedicated to law enforcement.

"Fuck no wonder my hands hurt, pulling all those bodies up, but why?" He slumped down, "What am I going to do? I can't handle this, I have killed them… all of them?"

Del shook his head, "I know but we can prove you didn't mean to."

"Didn't mean to?" Bos shouted, "I fucking strung them up and peeled them and cut them up!" Bos stood up, "I don't understand, I can't understand, I, I can't." Bos was pacing around in circles. "How the fuck can I recover from this? I am the Butcher holy fucking shit Del, I am the Butcher," Bos threw up.

Del was more or less speechless, there was nothing he could say that he hadn't already said, "But you were asleep."

Bos looked up with tears in his eyes, "But it was me! I am a killer." He walked forward and bent down next to Del, "I am sorry, so sorry." He sharply picked up the knife he had dropped and thrust, it imbedded deep into the stomach tissue and blood oozed out at speed. The injury was more than life threatening it was life taking and it would not take long. Del's face was covered in blood and Bos gurgled and dropped to his knees. Del watched as Bos went from knees to floor in a fluid fall. It was shock but Del couldn't move, he had just seen the man he had admired for years butcher a man and then attempt to murder him.

He then watched helplessly as he apologised and split his own stomach in front of him. Del sat for a while not exactly sure what to do next, he didn't remember for a couple of minutes that he was naked. He stood up and walked to the pile of clothes that had been stripped off him. He picked up his top and wrapped it round his bottom half, it covered his rear. He picked up his cut trousers and wrapped himself in them too, at least this would protect his modesty. He searched the pockets and found what he was looking for, his phone. He dialled some numbers and waited.

"Hello sir this is Inspector Martin, I know it's late, or early but I am in the wood at the end of Willow Walk. You need to get here now."

The chief was very insightful and realised by the tone of Del's voice that it was not something that needed a discussion, "Okay, be with you in twenty."

"When you leave can you make sure CSI units, Sgts and a shit load of other units are sent to arrive here after you?" He didn't wait for any other response he just hung up the phone. Del was still in shock and numb, he just sat on the floor and waited for others to arrive. It was around twenty minutes later that a car pulled up. Chief inspector Charleston walked along the path in the wood and soon came face to face with Del.

"What's up Del, the others are all on the way? And what have you been involved in?" The chief pointed to Del's injury that had stopped bleeding, it had however left a lot of dried blood on his stomach.

"This is going to be a little difficult to comprehend sir but the bad news is that there has been another murder by the Butcher," Del pointed to the tree that held the Butcher's penultimate victim.

The Chief looked over and said, "And?!"

"The good news is that there won't be any more."

The chief butted in on that, "Right stop the riddles Del, cut to the chase." Del sighed and signalled for the chief to follow him. He walked him around the corner and pointed to the body curled up on the floor. It was lighter now and the chief realised right away the identity of the body.

"Fuck, so Bos was the Butcher's last victim, am I right in thinking you came in on them and as the Butcher killed Bos you got injured trying to stop him?" This statement jarred at Del's emotions, *if only that were true,* he thought. *Could he get away with telling the chief that it happened like that? It would save the reputation of an excellent copper!* "Del, Del snap out of it man, tell me what happened!" Del came flying back to reality and made his decision.

"Yes, erm, yes sir, Bos was the Butcher's last victim, but only in the way that he actually killed himself." Del would have done anything to save Bos's reputation but the evidence in front of them was too much to blag, after all Bos was lying in a paper suit covered in the blood of his victims.

"What?" the chief looked sideways at Del as if he had gone mad.

"Sorry sir I don't like this at all but Bos was the Butcher," he pointed to the body on the ground.

"How the fuck is that possible man, he was a fantastic copper for, well as long as I can bloody remember?"

Del hung his head, "I know, but… well I don't know how to explain it but he was actually asleep when doing the killings and didn't even know he was doing it himself." The chief just stood and looked at Del and then at Bos and back to Del, he was frowning and shaking his head. "Sir I know it's fucking crazy and it was difficult for me to take in but I followed Bos here tonight trying to catch the Butcher following him."

"That makes no fucking sense."

Del sighed, "I thought that because the Butcher knew everything about Bos and the case, he must be following and spying on Bos, so I wanted to catch the bastard doing that. Unfortunately, I followed Bos and got caught by him, for God sake sir I was knocked out by him and bound up in the fucking carpet!" Del was becoming very animated now, "I watched as the person I tried to emulate hung and cut up a man and then… then started to do the same to me." Chief Inspector Charleston hadn't moved, he continued to shake his head. Del pointed to his semi nakedness, "I don't usually investigate in the nude you know."

"Okay so if that is the case why are you still here?"

Del looked over at Bos, "I don't really know, he had hung me, stripped me and was coming at me with the knife when he suddenly stopped, I shouted the best I could to wake him and Bos obviously won some kind of internal struggle and woke up." Del went on to describe how Bos had reacted by immediately cutting him down and demanding to know where the Butcher was. "He couldn't deal with it sir, it was just too much for his morality to take." Del wiped a tear from his eye and winced at the pain from his broken nose. "He then apologised and stabbed himself, I couldn't do anything about it." It was just then when other vehicles pulled up.

"Come on," the chief ushered Del away and took him towards the vehicles so he could get his injuries seen to.

Del glanced back at the body on the floor, he hung his head again and whispered, "Sorry Bos."

It took a long time for Del to try to come to terms with what had happened. The thing that saw him through over the difficult times was the knowledge that he knew Bos was now alongside his beloved Helen.

CHAPTER 38

Past

Ben was the only one to survive the accident. Both his parents were killed in the car, Ben was in hospital in a coma for a while. He was put up for adoption while unconscious. When he awoke Ben had no idea who he was or what had happened to him. He was put in Foster care for a while before he could be found a secure permanent home. His social workers re-named him. They didn't want any link to the tragedy that had come to him, his social worker was an avid football fan and named the poor memory stuck child as Jeff Hurst. Weeks past and then months, Jeff had become stronger. It was a Sunday afternoon when he was told a visitor was coming to see him. The visit was from a prospective couple wanting to adopt a young boy. Jeff was dressed in his smart cloths and hair combed. He sat in the room on an oddly coloured floral settee and waited. He was told they would be there at 2 o'clock. Half past one, he sat watching the clock, the hands spun but not at the same speed they usually do. Eventually after what seemed like 2 hours the hand struck 2. He waited, waited and at 2:15 he began to panic, at 2:30 he had all but given up. The smile that was on his face turned to sadness. Bing bong came the ring of the door. After a few moments a young woman with a bright blue dress and golden hair came in. She was with a slightly older man who was in a dark brown suit with short brown hair slicked down to one side. Jeff looked down and he had very shiny black shoes on, they looked like you could see the world in them. "Hello Jeff, I am Sherry, this is my husband John. We are here to see if you would like to be our new son?" The young Jeff beamed, he thought he was being tested to see if he could convince someone to want him, he had been scared that he would not be able to act properly to make them want him. Now it turned out they wanted to see if he wanted them.

"Hello nice to meet you, why do you want me? I don't know what I am like so how do you know?" Sherry and John had been told all about Ben who was now Jeff, they had been told he had lost his memory in a horrific accident and was now called Jeff. It was a speech straight from his heart and hit their full on.

"Oh my dear boy, we want a child so much and if you give us a chance we will spend the rest of our lives making sure you know exactly who you are and become exactly what it is you want to be."

Jeff beamed even more brightly, "That's good, I want to be a police man can I be one?"

Sherry laughed, "Of course you can, you can be whatever you want." The meetings continued over the coming months and Sherry's and John's arduous journey was nearly at an end. The next meeting was known as crunch time for the couple. All the paperwork and checks had been completed and this visit was going to be the last, one way or the other. It was after an hour of talking and playing when the social worker came in again.

"How is everything? Is everything going well?"

Jeff was the one to answer this, he walked straight over to Sherry and held her hand, "Yes, can I go with my new mum today now?" Sherry burst into tears, she never dreamed that their meetings would go so well and naturally.

The social worker looked over and said, "That's not a problem we just need to do the very last bit of paper work." They all sat down and some forms were put on the coffee table. "Okay please could the new adoptive parents sign here and here?" The two ecstatic adults put pen to paper. "Thank you for that, may your lives continue to be as happy as you all are now, any problems you know how to get me. You will be visited regularly over the next couple of years to see if we can help. Thank you, lovely to see you both again Mr and Mrs Boston." With that the three members of the new family left to start the rest of their lives together.

Jeffrey Boston did indeed become a police man and a very good one, until circumstances brought back some demons from the pits of his past. A past that he had forgotten. A past that reminded him that he had to appease the trees.

Printed in Great Britain
by Amazon